Praise for *Becoming Indigo*

*"Indigo has left home and spread her wings, and
she's now developing her intuitive gifts. This wonderful
story is packed with twists and turns that will have you
tearing through the pages. It's one of those books you can't
stop reading—but that you don't want to end. A great
addition to the Indigo series. Can't wait for the next one!"*

— **David Michie**, author of *The Dalai Lama's Cat*

*"Captivating! An evocative glimpse into a very different
kind of coming-of-age story. **Becoming Indigo** is a compelling
page turner that will leave any reader wanting more."*

— **Jordan Dane**, critically acclaimed and
best-selling author of *Indigo Awakening*

*"**Becoming Indigo** is a delicious mix of gritty realism
and mystical elements guaranteed to keep readers flipping
pages to see what will happen next! This fast-paced novel will
appeal to a wide variety of readers. Both contemporary and
paranormal readers will have elements to love!"*

— **Janet Gurtler**, author of the
RITA Award finalist *I'm Not Her*

*"This fascinating sequel to **Through Indigo's Eyes** takes
us deeper into mysterious realms, leading us through the
dark maze of the unknown and into the light. Indie takes us
with her as she explores love, sex, the meaning of true friendship,
and a hidden destiny she must claim as her own. Page-turning
excitement that will leave you wanting more!"*

— **Jacqueline Guest**, international award-winning
author of 17 books for young people

becoming indigo

becoming
indigo

TARA TAYLOR &
LORNA SCHULTZ NICHOLSON

VISIONS

HAY HOUSE, INC.
Carlsbad, California • New York City
London • Sydney • Johannesburg
Vancouver • Hong Kong • New Delhi

Published and distributed in the United States by: Hay House, Inc.: www.hayhouse.com® • **Published and distributed in Australia by:** Hay House Australia Pty. Ltd.: www.hayhouse.com.au • **Published and distributed in the United Kingdom by:** Hay House UK, Ltd.: www .hayhouse.co.uk • **Published and distributed in the Republic of South Africa by:** Hay House SA (Pty), Ltd.: www.hayhouse.co.za • **Distributed in Canada by:** Raincoast: www.raincoast.com • **Published in India by:** Hay House Publishers India: www.hayhouse.co.in

Cover design: Charles McStravick • *Interior design:* Riann Bender

Library of Congress Cataloging-in-Publication Data

Taylor, Tara
  Becoming indigo / Tara Taylor & Lorna Schultz Nicholson. -- 1st edition.
     pages cm
  ISBN 978-1-4019-3530-6 (pbk. : alk. paper)
  I. Schultz Nicholson, Lorna. II. Title.
  PS3620.A97546B43 2013
  813'.6--dc23
                                        2013000664

Tradepaper ISBN: 978-1-4019-3530-6

16 15 14 13   4 3 2 1
1st edition, July 2013

Part One

Chapter One

July 1998

The sound of water running woke me up.

Tangled, sweaty hair was stuck to my face, so I pushed it away. Who'd left the tap running? This was crazy. I needed sleep—big time. Light from the outside streetlight shone through the open window, and I covered my eyes for a second. We definitely needed a curtain on that window, but more than that, we needed air-conditioning or a fan. I pulled my T-shirt away from my body, hoping that would cool me off a bit.

What time was it, anyway?

The red lights on my clock radio said 4:30 A.M. I groaned; I had to work at nine. I rolled out of bed and stepped over shirts and pants and high-heeled shoes to get to the kitchen. Water was flowing full blast from the tap, and it sounded like it was splashing against the metal sink and onto the kitchen counters. In the dark, I stumbled to the sink and quickly shut off the tap. Then I stood there for a second before I decided to turn the cold water back on because I was so parched that I needed a drink. I took the one clean glass from the cupboard, filled it up, and gulped the water down. Then I put the glass in the sink with the other, now wet, dirty dishes. Sarah was supposed to do them—it was her turn—but she must have forgotten or gotten too busy. Between the three of us, they did manage to get done at least a few times a week.

I would do them in the morning before I left for my crappy job. Just thinking of another day at work almost made me puke. I leaned my butt against the kitchen counter and stood for a few minutes listening to the white noise: the refrigerator humming, the kitchen clock ticking, the gentle buzzing of night life. The sounds all blended and made me feel as if I were listening to a soft ballad. White noise had a calming effect on me. Too bad an air conditioner couldn't be added to the band. It would fit right in. I pulled at my T-shirt again, to get it off my skin and cool me down.

Then I heard a door slam.

I jumped at the sound. My heart picked up its pace, and all my senses kicked into high gear. Was it the front door? Was someone coming into our apartment?

I had to stay quiet. I sucked in a deep breath, held the air in my lungs, and stood ramrod straight.

We had all gone to bed around midnight, so I knew Sarah and Natalie were asleep. Unless they had gone out for a smoke . . . but . . . in the middle of the night? Besides, they wouldn't slam the door coming back in, and there was certainly no wind to push it shut. I grabbed a frying pan from the sink and tuned my hearing toward where I thought the sound had come from, which was the front door.

But I heard only white noise. No creaking. No footsteps. No anything. Just white noise and my own breath, which was now coming out in staggered rasps because I had held it in for too long. I lowered the arm holding the pan, letting my shoulders sag and consciously slowing my breathing, allowing it to return to normal.

I stayed in the kitchen for a few more minutes, leaning against the counter, waiting, listening for another slam, and when I was absolutely positive that I had imagined the noise, I knew I had to go back to bed. With the frying pan still in my hand, I tiptoed across the linoleum floor.

No matter how much things had changed since high school, I still felt like I had some weird disorder. I really wasn't normal. Was I being told something? Was I being warned? Did we need to buy a deadbolt for our door? Was that what this was all about?

Or was I just imagining everything?

This is not your imagination. His voice spoke in my head; he always came to soothe me and reassure me that these abilities that I had to see and hear and feel were okay.

"Really?" I whispered. "Then why am I hearing noises?"

Once I had scanned the hallway and found it empty, I padded down the hall and back to my bedroom. "It was nothing. Nothing at all," I whispered to myself.

The noises had to be all in my head, because there was obviously no one in the apartment but the three of us. After placing the frying pan on the floor beside my bed, I quietly lay down on my back and stared wide-eyed into space. I tried to suck in some air, but it was so stagnant that I felt I was being suffocated with a pillow. Again, I pinched my T-shirt away from my body, flapping it back and forth. The sticky, humid air hung around the apartment like an unwanted guest. When a heat wave hit Ottawa in the summer months, the air seeped with moisture, air conditioners ran full tilt, and everyone across the entire city complained. Newspaper headlines shouted it out in big, bold, black letters: NO LETUP IN SIGHT.

The television news coverage talked nonstop about how hot it was and where the warm front was coming from and how the moisture was building. Then they would tell old people to stay inside and parents not to let their little ones out. Find indoor activities, they would recommend. Pools and recreation centers were jammed to capacity, as were the lake beaches in the Ottawa Valley, because people didn't listen to the news reporters when there was a beach in sight. Businesspeople literally ran from their cars to the shelter of their air-conditioned buildings.

As I lay on my sheet, I wished I could jump in a lake or a fountain, or take shelter in a deep freeze somewhere. Or at least be in an air-conditioned apartment. But no, I had to be in a hot, stuffy room, awake in the middle of the night, with too many thoughts blasting through my brain.

I would *have to* buy a deadbolt tomorrow.

With that thought solved, my mind started bouncing, thinking about other things, like my life. What the heck was I going to do? This thought seemed to appear all the time, and it made me uncomfortable. Sure, I'd moved out of my parents' house and was living in an old, run-down apartment in the Glebe, and it was fun because it was summer.

But . . . then what?

I couldn't—I wouldn't—stay at my job for any longer than I had to. I hated it more than I had hated anything in my life. For now, it paid the rent, but that was all it was good for. I needed to find another job, and I needed to figure out what I wanted to do. So many kids my age knew exactly what university or college to go to. After my split with John, that unrealistic dream of living in England (yes, it was *totally* unrealistic, I realized now) was gone, and I had nothing. Nothing. I hadn't applied to any universities, because I had no idea what courses to enroll in.

John. My chest still constricted when I thought of what we'd had and how close we'd been, or how close I thought we'd been. I hadn't dated anyone since him, and I figured it was better to live a carefree single summer life, or at least that's what Sarah had convinced me to do. Our apartment motto was "Girls Just Want to Have Fun."

You have unfinished business with him.

"I know," I whispered.

Yeah. And you never told him how his father died. And you know how it happened.

"Stop," I whispered to myself. I squeezed my eyes shut to block out the mean voice that spoke to me.

I had to forget about John. And what I saw. And I had to forget about the voices.

I needed sleep.

If a girl wanted to have fun, she had to have money, so she had to work, which meant she needed to sleep.

Slam!

My eyes popped open, and I stared at the stucco ceiling that was supposed to be white but was really stained yellow. I didn't move a muscle. I just lay there, arms by my sides, listening.

Through the white noise, I thought I could hear the faint sound of someone singing a mournful lullaby.

Sadness seeped through my veins. My head pounded, right at the temples. I wanted a pain reliever to make the throbbing stop. But I couldn't move. Not even to put my hand down to reach for the frying pan. But I did know it was there. I did.

The old brick apartment building we lived in was constructed in the early 1900s and was probably once some rich family's residence. The landlord had converted it into apartments, adding kitchens to a few rooms. We were up on the third floor, and there were three other tenants. I knew old places came with noises, but this sounded different, like nothing I had heard before. It wasn't footsteps from the middle-aged Southern woman who practiced her clogging in the morning because she worked at night as a nurse, or the screeching sound of the man playing his accordion during the week because he was a banker by day and in a polka band on the weekend, or the blaring television of the elderly man across the hall who wore a hearing aid. No, this was definitely different. The mournful sound made my throat catch, and I gasped.

A wash of cold air circled my body, and my skin erupted in goose bumps, which was totally nuts. You didn't shiver in a heat wave unless you were dehydrated and ill. I didn't cross my arms over my chest, because I didn't dare move.

The wailing stopped.

Slam, slam, slam, slam . . .

My entire body tensed. I felt as if I were being watched by someone. I touched the frying pan on the floor.

Was I being watched? I grabbed my top sheet, which I had thrown onto the floor, and wrapped it around me. The cotton stuck to my skin.

Then the slamming just stopped.

And I could hear insects buzzing outside.

Hot air once again bathed my skin, and I felt clammy and gooey and gross and disgusting. My hair stuck to my cheeks. My T-shirt stuck to my body. My skin stuck to the sheets.

Clutching my top sheet in my fists, I rolled over and closed my eyes.

❖ ❖ ❖

"Who left the tap on last night?" I asked when I entered the kitchen a few hours later, feeling like a bag of trash.

Natalie took one look at me and started laughing. Then she took a clean mug from the drying rack and filled it with coffee. "Lahrd Jesus, as my grandma would say. You need this 'ere cuppa."

I took the steaming mug of coffee and wrapped my hands around it. "Thanks."

Natalie was Sarah's friend from Newfoundland. Why I was surrounded by Newfoundlanders, I wasn't sure, but Natalie was nothing like John. Bright, bubbly, and caring, she took everything in stride, and never judged, and never talked like she knew everything. And she had the cutest accent, which made Sarah and me howl with laughter, especially when she mimicked her grandmother.

All in all, she had been a well-packaged gift, complete with a ribbon and bow. Natalie had arrived in Ottawa at the perfect time. When Sarah and I made the definite decision to move out from under our parents' roofs, we scoured newspapers daily and finally found an apartment in the Glebe, but we needed another roommate to help pay the bills. At first I was a bit unsure about the apartment, because it was an old building, and every time I walked into it, my body got hot and felt a bit weird. But it was cheap, and the utilities and cable were included. Plus, Sarah convinced me it was the best we could do and a "rocking good deal" if we had three people. Minimum-wage jobs sucked and created limitations on what kind of apartment we could afford.

Sarah and I felt we'd hit the lotto when Natalie showed up and jumped in headfirst, paying her first and last months' rent no problem. It took her all of one afternoon to find a job.

"What are you talking about the tap for?" Sarah looked worse than I did. Her red hair had turned into a mass of curls in the humidity, and the sweat glistening on her face just made her freckles blotch together. Of course, the beer she had drunk the night before probably didn't help how she looked and felt. And, really, with Sarah, a lot could be chalked up to the fact that she was *not* a morning person.

Unlike Natalie, who was an any-time-of-the-day person. Her dark, almost-black, short hair looked like she had styled it, when really she had just slept on it. I honestly would have cut my hair exactly the same way if it would have looked like that. But mine would be everywhere and a disaster, and hers just suited her high cheekbones and sculpted face. Built like a wafer, with a backbone like a ruler, Natalie stood at around five foot nine, which in my world was really tall. I think she might have been the most striking girl I'd ever met, with her round dark eyes, full lips, thin eyebrows, and pale skin. Childhood storybooks, the fairy-tale ones, always had a queen, and to me Natalie looked like some kind of stately queen—but one of the nice ones, not the mean one from *Snow White*. As thin and majestic as she was, she had this huge laugh that came from the bottom of her stomach, and generosity and kindness oozed from her pores.

"Someone left the tap on," I said. "I had to get up in the middle of the night and turn it off." I sipped my coffee.

"Wasn't me," barked Sarah. "Holy crap." She picked up a newspaper and waved it in front of her face.

"I'll pick up a fan at Zellers today after work," I said.

"Maybe I left it on," said Natalie, shrugging her bony shoulders. "I don't think so. But maybe." She paused. "But this 'ere building is so old there could be plumbing problems."

"It doesn't matter," I said. "It's off now." I paused but only for a second. "I was thinking of buying some sort of deadbolt, too."

"Why?" Sarah scrunched up her face when she looked at me. "The stairs are so creaky it's not like anyone could come upstairs without us hearing. And if we hear them, we call the cops, then bang them over the head with something."

"A frying pan," I said. I thought about the frying pan that was still in my room.

"That would work," replied Sarah. "I've got a baseball bat in my room just in case."

I mimicked whacking someone to lighten the conversation, even though my brain was bursting inside just thinking about Sarah's creaking comment. I had only heard slamming. Sarah was right—if someone came up the stairs, there would be creaking.

Natalie giggled at my antics, with her hand in front of her face.

Sarah laughed too, but suddenly she just stopped, eyed me, and pointed. "Are you nervous about something?"

"Nah," I replied, trying to sound flippant.

Sarah narrowed her eyes until they were slits. "Do you know something we don't?" Then she turned to Natalie. "You probably don't know this, but Indie has this weird thing going on. She can actually see things before they happen. It is *soooo cool* . . . but also kind of creepy."

"Wow," said Natalie. She looked at me with wide eyes. "I had no idea. That does sound . . . interesting." She stared at me, full of curiosity, like I was someone she had never met before, someone who had three heads or came from some distant planet. This was not a conversation I wanted to have right now because, really, I just wanted to crawl in a hole.

Sarah stood up and slung her arm around me. "She was going to find out sooner or later. Aren't you glad it's out?"

"I got to get ready for work," I said quickly.

"Are you like the gal on *Sabrina, the Teenage Witch?*" Natalie's eyes were bulging out of her head.

"Girl, you are too funny," Sarah said to Natalie. "If that's the case, we need a big fat black cat. Hey, let's go to the Royal Oak tonight. It's Saturday night—it will be hopping for sure."

"I'd be up for that," I answered. Thankfully, Sarah changed conversations like she changed clothes.

"Sounds good to me, too," said Natalie. "I'm finished with work at six."

"I hate my job!" Sarah tossed her coffee down the sink. "I don't want to go to work today. I want to go to Britannia Beach and float in cold water all day."

"Trade yah," I said.

Sarah and Natalie both looked at each other, then they looked at me, shook their heads, and in unison said, "No. Way."

❖ ❖ ❖

I caught the bus, and, although normally I hated the constant lurching, this morning I was grateful for the air-conditioning. The driver had it on full blast. I stared out the window at the sky, trying to find the sun, but the thick haze wasn't allowing it to shine to its fullest, at least not yet. It would have to rain soon. Soon, that's what the news kept saying, perhaps by the weekend. Suddenly, I saw in big letters, written in the sky, the word *Monday*.

Okay, I thought. *It is going to rain on Monday.* Of course, because Monday was a day off for me. At least I would have Sunday to go to the beach and lounge in the water to get out of the heat.

The bus lumbered to a stop, and as soon as I stepped off, I went from being cool to being zapped of energy by wet air. I trudged across the street to the Victoria Park Suites, a run-down motel that had kitchenettes in every room. It was two floors, and guests entered the rooms from the outside. Some guests stayed for a night, and then there were the ones who seemed to linger on and on, like the smell of rotting banana peels.

Or fish.

A bell on the front door rang and announced my arrival. Esther and Juanita were already in the front lobby and had their papers with the numbers of the rooms they were to clean in their hands. They both said hi, all smiles, and I immediately knew that I had drawn the crap duties. Standing in the office, I felt like a stinky fish out of water. In her early 40s, Esther had one tooth knocked out and wrinkles that looked like knife cuts. And she was bone thin; I swear, it looked like skin and nothing else covered her bones. Then there was Juanita, who had to be in her 60s and was probably overweight by 50 pounds. She always got the lower suites to clean because she couldn't climb the stairs. Just the three of us cleaned rooms, and we rotated our days off. This week I had Sunday and Monday off—not nearly enough days.

Miles Mason, the owner of the suites, and the nastiest man I think I'd ever known, leered at me over his reading glasses. The hairs on my arms and the back of my neck stood at attention. He stared me up and down, and I wished I had on long pants and a huge baggy hoodie—but who could wear that kind of clothing on such a hot day? My short shorts and T-shirt clung to my body, because I was already sweating profusely. Was my clothing too tight? Could he see through my shirt? I crossed my arms over my chest.

"Blondie, here's your list of rooms," he said.

I hated how he pronounced the nickname he'd given me. He always raised his eyebrows and made a big deal of pronouncing the *BL* in the word. It took every ounce of energy I had to walk forward and take the sheet from his grubby hands. They looked like meat hooks. Dirt festered under his nails. Sweat glistened on his forehead. His slicked-back black hair looked slimy and greasy and in desperate need of a shampoo. My stomach heaved. My skin tightened. Everything about him oozed evil. I took the list from his hands, barely holding it by the corners, and stared at it. Even the paper that he had just touched smelled of fried food, bacon in particular.

Of course, I had room 112.

On the bottom level, at the very back, 112 was a room occupied by "Mrs. Fish Face." We housekeepers had nicknamed her that. She'd been here for weeks—she didn't seem to want to leave—and cooked fish every single day. Without saying a word, I headed outside into the heat.

We all retrieved our cleaning carts from the storage room outside and filled them with towels, little soaps, and cleaning supplies.

"I'm not sure I'll make 'er today," said Juanita, wiping her face with one of the clean towels. I so hoped she wasn't going to fold it back up and put it in one of the rooms. Sweat dripped off her double chin like a pouring fountain. Or like the tap last night. My stomach lurched again. I had to forget about the tap. Natalie had left it on. End of story.

"You're a young thing." She squinted until her eyes were slits surrounded by puffy fat. "You should be a kind little girl and offer to do the rooms for an ole lady like me who needs money 'cause her husband left her high and dry without a red cent."

"Never yah mind," snapped Esther. "Get a move on." Esther waved her hand in my direction. "She got Mrs. Fish Face. That's like cleaning ten rooms in one."

"Ladies," sang Miles from the front door, "rooms need to be cleaned today, not tomorrow." Then he raised his eyebrows. "Blondie, I forgot to tell you, I like those shorts." He winked at me.

If there had been any food in my stomach I would have thrown it up. Both Esther and Juanita looked at me. Then Esther whispered, "You better watch your ass, pretty little girl. 'Cause he wants it. And he's been known to take what's not his."

I sucked in a deep breath and pushed my cart forward. I felt really, really sick. *I need the money. I need the money.* I repeated the words over and over in my head.

As I unlocked the door to my first room, the man's voice spoke to me. *Gut feelings are important. It's called following your intuition.* His voice was soft and gentle, and it calmed me down, but I still had no idea who he was. Lately, he hadn't been around much, because I'd been way too occupied. But now he'd come to me twice in less than 24 hours.

Sometimes I didn't understand what he wanted to tell me, but today I understood exactly what he was saying: Miles Mason made me sick, and I needed to never, ever be alone with him.

It's your own fault he leers at you. Look at what you're wearing.

I knocked on the door of the first room on my list. When no one answered or snapped at me to come back later or get lost, I opened it. When I walked in, I let out a good round

11

of expletives under my breath. Some people were such slobs. Chinese takeout containers, potato-chip bags, and cigarette-filled soda cans lay scattered all over the furniture and floor, and wet towels were draped over chairs and lying in clumps on the floor. No use procrastinating. I snapped on my rubber gloves and got to work stripping the bed, throwing out garbage, scrubbing the toilet, and vacuuming up chips and pretzels. As I yanked the vacuum across the carpet, I kept saying, "I need a new job. I need a new job."

When I was finished, I put the little soap in the bathroom and took a quick look around. Satisfied that Miles wouldn't scream at me for missing something, I stepped outside. The hot air blasted me, and I had a hard time even breathing. I picked up my paper and crossed off the room I was just in. I wiped the sweat off my face and started to push my cart.

Suddenly, everything started spinning. I held on hard to the handle of my cart and stared straight ahead. I knew enough to just let go and not fight it. Since I was little, I had had visions. Last year, I had finally figured out that if I stopped fighting them and really focused on what came to me, I could help people. My mind twirled and spun, then stopped, and I saw white. A blank piece of paper. I breathed in and out. In and out. I saw . . . the words *liver and onions.* Juanita's chubby face floated into the picture; she was talking to a little boy. Everything was pretty grainy, but the child looked to be around four, maybe five.

The picture dissolved, and I was once again standing in the oppressive heat, gripping the handle of my cart. That made no sense. Was I supposed to warn Juanita about eating liver and onions? So gross. Grandma Russell liked to order liver and onions at our favorite family restaurant, which was just outside Ottawa, near their home in Maynard. Every time it arrived at the table, I excused myself and went to the bathroom just for a little breather. When I returned, I just tried to ignore the smell by not looking at her plate. But Grandma loved it, just like a lot of old people did.

I wiped my face with my arm and started pushing my cart in the direction of the next room I had to clean—Mrs. Fish

Face's room. I groaned. Suddenly, I felt eyes boring into me. I turned, and Miles was staring at my backside.

"The woman in one-twelve says she needs her dishes done," he said. Then he gave me a smile that made me take a step back. I desperately wanted to run away, yelling, "I quit."

Money. I need money.

I knocked on the door to room 112. The smell of cooked fish seeped through it, and I put my hand to my face, covering my nose and mouth. When no one answered, I sucked in a deep breath, put my key in the lock, and flung the door open. If I was going to do this, I just had to do it.

I propped the door open to let in some air, albeit stiflingly hot air. I knew if I wanted to get this room clean without throwing up, I would have to work like a maniac, fast and furious. First, I scrubbed the dishes with so much soap that the bubbles spilled over the edge of the sink. I kept squirting the bottle to add more to get rid of the smell. Every few minutes, I would run to the door and stick my head out just to get any kind of fresh air.

Finally, I had the dishes done and kitchen cleaned, which made the entire room smell a little better, not so much like fried fish. I leaned against the refrigerator for a second. How could one person use so many dishes in just one day? Yesterday Esther had this room, so she'd probably pretended that she had forgotten about them.

When I was completely finished, I looked at my watch. This room alone had taken me an hour. Usually I could get a room done in 30 minutes, but this one had pushed my limits, so I was going to have to work later than usual. I exhaled, loudly, knowing that tomorrow the room would stink again, but then I smiled, because it was my day off.

I stepped outside and was blinded by the sun, which had by now, midmorning, burned off the haze. I was about to move to my next room when I saw Juanita and Esther across the courtyard standing by the big metal ashtray. Esther waved to me. Five minutes was all I could manage.

"So?" Esther raised her eyebrows up and down when I approached. "How was Mrs. Fish Face's room?"

"Gross," I replied. I shoved my hands in the back pockets of my shorts and tried not to watch them smoke. I was trying to quit, and it was so much harder than I'd thought it would be. Right now, I desperately wanted a cigarette.

"Mrs. Fish Face needs to move on," said Esther. "Who the hell can eat fish every fuckin' night?"

Juanita's breath was coming out in rasps, and she wiped the sweat off her face, over and over. Esther sucked on her cigarette. I didn't want to look like I was staring at Juanita, so I snuck a glance, immediately noticing how yellow the whites of her eyes looked and her skin, too. I felt a sharp jab to the side of my body. Something was wrong with her.

"Juanita, you feeling okay?" I asked.

"I'm old," she wheezed, stubbing out her cigarette. "I never feel okay. But my grandson is comin' today for a visit. He makes life worth living." She waved her hand in front of her face, then she coughed and spit something into her handkerchief.

I turned my head and tried not to gag.

"How many grandkids yah got again?" Esther blew out smoke rings, totally ignoring Juanita's gross coughing fit and her chatter about her health woes.

"Jerrod's my one and only. And his mama said she ain't having no more." Juanita coughed again.

I tapped my fingers on my thighs, shifted my stance, and tried to listen. I really didn't know much about either of these women. Was the little boy in my vision her grandson? Probably. Why had I seen liver and onions and her grandson?

After a few more minutes, I said, "I'm behind. I got to go."

"Yeah, break is over, I guess." Juanita coughed one more time, then waddled toward her cart. As I watched her, I again felt the sharp, knifelike jab to my side. This time I almost doubled over. Then, as soon as it had arrived, it left and I felt fine. I started to head back to my cart, but I couldn't help turning around to stare at Juanita. Her yellow skin shone in the powerful sun, which had fought through the haze and won.

Yes, I was behind in my work, but I knew I had to help her. She didn't look well at all.

I walked back to Juanita. "Let me do some of your rooms so you can spend more time with your grandson."

She pinched my cheeks. "I knew you was an angel."

Chapter Two

By the time I got back to the apartment, it was eight o'clock. Sarah and Natalie were both home from work. Sarah worked at Denny's as a server, and Natalie was a receptionist at a spa. Both worked day and evening shifts depending on the week. I only worked days, thank goodness. I couldn't imagine seeing Miles at night.

Sarah sat at the kitchen table and methodically brushed red polish on her nails. When she saw me, she put down the brush and blew on the fresh paint. The smell of enamel lingered in the kitchen. With one leg curled underneath her, Natalie strummed chords on her guitar. I plopped the box with the fan down on the kitchen floor.

Sarah waved her hands in the air. "Awesome! You are the best roommate ever. I'd hug you, but I don't want to smudge my nails. Plus it's too damn hot."

"How yah gettin' on, girl?" Natalie asked, using one of her favorite Newfoundland expressions. She drew her pick across the strings, playing another chord. Natalie had just started to learn how to play the guitar, but she played a mean fiddle. We often jammed on our guitars, and Sarah joined us with her new set of bongo drums. But when Natalie took out her fiddle to play toe-tapping East Coast music, I just listened, amazed at how her fingers danced on the strings. Sarah tried to get her to play some Aerosmith on her fiddle, but Natalie stuck to her Celtic roots. Sarah had met Natalie through a friend, and in my gut, I knew Natalie was in Ottawa for a reason, but I just didn't know what that reason was yet.

"I'm okay," I replied. "I got the fish lady's room again."

Natalie wrinkled her nose. "Gross."

"You have no idea," I replied. "I got to get a new job. If you hear of anything, let me know."

Natalie strummed another chord, then set her guitar in the corner and said, "For sure."

"Let's get this fan going." Sarah stood up, still waving her fingers. "My nails will never dry in this humidity anyway. Gawd, I wish it would rain."

"Monday," I replied without thinking as I ripped the tape off the box.

"I never heard that," Sarah shot back. "Those weather guys can't seem to . . ." Sarah let her words trail off, then she grinned and high-fived me and said, "But you, my friend, can."

I yanked the fan and directions out of the box. "Let's get this going so we can have it running while we get ready to go out. I need to shower and do my hair."

Sarah carefully took the fan from me, placed it on the floor, then pushed me toward the door. "Go." She did a little dance around the kitchen, still waving her hands. "'Cause we are gonna party tonight." She raised her arms in the air. "And there will be air-conditioning in the bar. And men!" She bumped me with her hip. "Get your fake ready, girl. Once we're in, we can get guys to buy us drinks."

Sarah and I had recently managed to get some great fake IDs. Natalie didn't need one, because she was one year older.

The hot water trickled down my back as I scrubbed and scrubbed and scrubbed. Although I worked with soap all day, when I left that dumb job, I never, ever felt clean. Tomorrow I was going to seriously start looking for another one.

As I was blow-drying my hair, both Natalie and Sarah came into my room. Sarah plugged in the fan, then flopped on the floor and sat right in front of it. "What are you wearing tonight?"

I turned off my blow-dryer, tossed it on the floor by my full-length mirror, went to my closet, and rifled through my clothes. I pulled a yellow cotton sundress off a hanger. "Maybe this? What do you think? What are you wearing?"

"I want to wear one of your dresses." Sarah jumped up and joined me by my closet. She started looking through all my clothes.

Hanger by hanger, we went through all the possibilities. Soon Sarah had an armful of clothes that she tossed on the bed. Not modest at all, she stripped down to her bra and underwear and started trying on one outfit after the other.

"That green halter looks awesome!" I squealed. "With your red hair, green is perfect."

"We need tunes," said Natalie. "If you guys are wearing dresses, maybe I will, too." She crawled over to my stereo and sifted through my CDs, finally picking out *The Kinks: Greatest Hits!*

Once the music was blaring, Natalie ran from my room to her room, returning in minutes with a pile of dresses. She threw them on my bed, which was now heaped with clothes.

"I love the blue one with the spaghetti straps," I said.

The three of us got busy, curling our hair, putting on our makeup, and trying on different outfits . . . and dancing around the room, of course. It didn't take long for the floor to be covered with clothes, belts, shoes, and hair stuff.

"I think we need a predrink," said Sarah. "How about a vodka cranberry?"

"I'm in," said Natalie.

"Me too," I said, giving Sarah the thumbs-up.

Sarah raced out of my bedroom and headed into the hallway.

"What the heck?" She screamed so loud I jumped up and ran to the door of my bedroom with Natalie on my heels.

Water was flowing down the hallway from the kitchen, and now I could hear the taps running. The loud music had obviously drowned out the noise in my room. All three of us ran to see the faucets on full and the sink overflowing, water cascading onto the floor. Because the building was old, the floors were a bit uneven, so the water flowed like a stream down the hall and toward my room and the front hall. Sarah slid across the tiles and shut the taps off.

"That's so weird," whispered Natalie.

Sarah ran out of the kitchen and down the hall and toward the front door. "My new Birkenstocks!" She picked up a pair of sandals from the pile of shoes heaped at the front door. Water dripped from the sandals to the floor. She groaned. "I just paid a fortune for these. They said not to get the suede wet!"

She turned and glared at both Natalie and me. "One of you must have left it on, 'cause I sure as hell didn't."

"I know I didn't," I muttered.

"Wasn't me either." Natalie's eyes grew huge.

"Well, someone had to leave them on," moaned Sarah.

"We were all in Indie's room," said Natalie. Her voice sounded small and quiet. "It doesn't make any sense."

Sarah scowled. "No," she said. "It doesn't make sense."

My face grew hot. "I don't get it either," I said quietly.

"None of us could have left 'em on." Natalie shook her head. "My grandma would say, ain't that shockin'?" I knew she was trying to ease the tension in the room.

"I'm calling the landlord *right now*." Sarah stalked to the phone. "We must have major plumbing issues if none of us left them on, and this is totally unacceptable."

"I'll get some towels," I said quietly.

I ran to the bathroom and grabbed all the towels lying on the floor and the one strewn in the tub. What was wrong with the taps? Goose bumps invaded my body, and the hair on the back of my neck stood up as, once again, I felt eyes on me, staring me down. Quickly, I glanced around. Was I being watched? I ran to the window and pushed it open. Then I exhaled the air I had been holding in. There was no way that anyone could stare at me through the bathroom window, because we were on the *third* floor.

Suddenly, I heard the faint sound of someone singing coming through the bathroom vent, the same song from last night. I ran to the kitchen.

As I mopped the floor, I listened for the lullaby, but I couldn't hear it. What was wrong with me? Sarah was right; the plumbing was old. I closed my eyes to make all my feelings and strange sensations go away. Deep down, I knew that this was something more, something bigger than a plumbing issue.

Natalie helped me mop up the water with the towels, and when they were soaked, we wrung them out in the sink. Sarah didn't help because she was too busy arguing with our landlord. Finally, we were almost finished. As I was down on my hands and knees, I glanced at Natalie, who bobbed her head toward Sarah and whispered, "Wouldn't want to meet 'er in a dark alley. She'd kick my butt to China."

The absurdity of the situation, and my nervousness with it, combined with Natalie's obvious effort to lighten the situation, suddenly made me giggle, and because my giggles turned into laughter, I toppled to the floor. My sudden outburst caused Natalie to start giggling as well. Sarah slammed the phone down without saying good-bye and looked at us. "What? This isn't really a laughing matter."

"Lard, girl, you need a wee drink." By now Natalie was rolling on the floor holding her stomach.

"You got that right," barked Sarah. "That guy was a jerk with a capital *J*." Then Sarah slid across the floor to the cupboard with the glasses. "One huge mother of a drink, then let's get out of this joint."

❖ ❖ ❖

Our bar of choice was the Royal Oak Pub, which was within walking distance. We lived in the cool, funky area of the Glebe, and I loved strolling on my days off to browse through all the stores. We locked our door and headed down the creaky stairs and outside into the oppressive heat. After what had happened with the taps, I wanted to be out of the apartment. Located across from the University of Ottawa, on the corner of King Edward Avenue and Laurier Avenue, the Royal Oak stood right beside a fire station that had wooden statues of all these different people.

Fifteen minutes later, we were almost there when Natalie rummaged through her purse and pulled out her camera. "Lookie what I brought."

Since Natalie had arrived, she'd never left the house without her camera.

"Photo time, girls!" Natalie put the camera up to her eye. "I told all my friends back home about our bar that we named 'The Bar with the Wooden People.'"

Once we arrived at the fire station, Sarah and I sidled up to one of the male statues and pretended to kiss it. Natalie snapped four photos as Sarah and I hammed it up for the camera.

"Your turn," I said. I ran over to her, took the camera, and allowed Sarah and Natalie to get posed, then I looked through the lens and said, "Work it, baby."

Sarah upped the ante and made sexy faces and wrapped her legs around the statues. Natalie tried to be funny, too, but ended up looking awkward as she contorted her body. I laughed and snapped.

After I'd taken around ten pictures, Sarah waved her arm in front of her face and said, "Enough. I'm soaked in sweat. Let's get out of this heat."

The cold air blasted us when we walked into the Royal Oak. The place had three floors and a huge deck outside where we could smoke, and it attracted an odd assortment of people, from students to professors to neighborhood locals like us.

The scent of pub food, like chicken pot pie and thick, homemade French fries, combined with the distinct smell of draft beer, greeted me. I scanned the big room, looking for a table, but the place was jammed to capacity; there didn't look to be anything free at the moment. I didn't care, because for now, I was just relieved to be in the cool air. We jostled our way to the bar, with Sarah leading the way, and then we budged in line to order some beer. Sarah yelled over the noise and raised her hand to show that we wanted three.

The busy bartender nodded his head, and Sarah moved in closer. Natalie and I followed and waited for the beer to arrive. Once I had mine in my hand, I again searched the room. "There's a table," I said, pointing to the other end of the bar. I quickly wove through the crowd and nabbed it just in time.

"Good moves," said Sarah. She plopped down on one of the chairs. "Okay, girls, that cost a wee fortune. We got to find us some guys to buy beer. They upped the price in this joint. Probably 'cause it's so flipping hot out."

"It's summer," I said. "Beer is always inflated in the summer."

Natalie laughed. "Yeah, right. They're not going to raise the price because of the heat." She sipped her beer and winked. "Worth every penny."

As Natalie took her next sip, she looked at me over the rim of her glass. "So tell me about what Sarah said this morning."

"This morning?" I thought back to the morning, and, honestly, it felt like it had been eons ago. So much had happened. "About what?"

Sarah snapped her fingers. "I get yah. You wanna know about her seeing and hearing things. Right?"

"Yeah. I do," said Natalie softly. "I think it's fascinating."

I sipped my beer before I said, "I don't know what to say. Sometimes I see something and then later it happens." I shrugged and slouched in my seat, wrapping my hands around my beer glass.

"How do you see, though? I don't get it." She furrowed her eyebrows.

All my life I'd confused people, from my parents to doctors to my older brother, Brian, who thought I was just downright crazy in the head. Now here was Natalie looking at me the same way.

Although I didn't want to talk about this in a bar, I had to answer Natalie, because she seemed so interested. Everything she did was for real. "Um, well," I started, "my mind kinda goes white, then something just comes into my vision. Sometimes it makes sense, and sometimes it doesn't." I paused for a moment, tapping my fingers on the table. "Sometimes I get what I've seen right away, and other times I have to wait and try to piece it together like a puzzle."

"You mean, like, you just get a picture of something? Like a camera snap?"

I tilted my head and thought about what she had said. "Yeah. A little. I guess. Although sometimes it's more like a movie. Things come to me both ways." I thought about Juanita. "Like today," I said. "I saw this woman I work with, she was with her grandson. Then I saw the words *liver and onions* appear."

Sarah guffawed. "Liver and onions? What would that be about? I mean, honestly, who eats liver and onions?"

"Lots of people," said Natalie. "My grandmother loves it. But, yuck, liver has such a horrible smell when it's cooking. I would walk in the back door, smell it, and walk right out again." Suddenly she snapped her fingers. "Maybe the woman will get food poisoning from it. Could that be it?"

"I'm . . . I'm not sure." Food poisoning wasn't something that had come to me, but maybe Natalie was on to something.

"You better call her and tell her not to eat liver and onions this weekend," urged Natalie.

"I don't have her phone number."

"Can you call work and get it?"

"Probably. I could call Miles."

"Is that the creepy guy?" Sarah asked, scrunching her face.

"Yeah. He's so disgusting." I shook like I was having a seizure just thinking of calling him and hearing his greasy voice on the phone.

"We have to do it." Natalie pounded the table with her fist. "We have to call her." She stood.

Oh, right, go ahead and call Slimeball. The mean voice broke into my thoughts. *You'll be leading him on.*

Earlier today, my kind man's voice had told me to listen to how I felt. And right now, I felt confused. I didn't think it was food poisoning. But what harm would it do to make sure that Juanita was okay?

I stood. "Okay," I said to Natalie. "We'll make the call."

24

"I'll wait here," said Sarah. "I'll save the table and drink my beer."

Natalie and I went to the pay phone, and I looked up the hotel's phone number in the tattered phone book. Miles answered.

"Miles," I said. "It's Indie."

"Blondie," he said. Immediately, my heart sank like a rock in water and I started to shake.

"Would you have Juanita's home number?" I asked. "I have a little gift for her grandson."

"Aren't you just a beautiful angel. But I bet you can be bad when you want to be."

"Miles, just give me the number."

"Ahh, I like when you're bossy."

I wanted to throw the phone and rip the cord right out of the wall, but Natalie was hovering over me. I had to see this through. Finally, I got the number and said it out loud while Natalie wrote it down. After I hung up, I grimaced. "That guy is a revolting pig."

"You got the number, though, right?"

I tried to forget about Miles as I dialed Juanita's number. She answered after the fourth ring, huffing and puffing, like she'd just run stairs. "Hello?"

"Hey, Juanita, it's Indie," I said. "How are you?"

"Why you calling me at home, girl?"

"I just wanted to say have fun with your grandson this weekend and . . . don't eat liver and onions."

Juanita laughed then started to hack. I pulled the phone away from my ear and stuck out my tongue as if I was going to barf.

Juanita stopped coughing and said, "I hate liver and onions. You're a strange girl."

"Have a good weekend," I said, feeling like an idiot.

Tell her to see a doctor.

I was so surprised the man's voice was with me that I blurted out, "See a doctor." Then, feeling stupid, I quickly added, "That cough sounds like it's getting worse."

"Aren't you a nice girl to be so concerned for an old lady. Wish my own kids would be like you. I will, angel. I will."

I hung up the phone and said to Natalie, "She hates liver and onions."

Natalie shrugged. "At least you found out."

We made our way back to the table, where Sarah was drinking her second beer. "Took you long enough," she said. "Any luck?"

"She said she hates liver and onions. I must have seen it for no good reason. I don't want to talk about it anymore."

"Okay. Done deal," said Sarah. "I had to order another. Breaking my bank account, I tell you." Then Sarah slapped the table as if she had just had a huge epiphany. "I've got a great idea!" She stared me right in the eyes. "Since you can see things before they happen, let's try to get drinks for free. There's, like, a ton of guys in here tonight. Indie, try to get a vision about which guy is a sucker and who will keep us in drinks all night."

"Sarah!" Natalie almost squealed. "That would be wrong. Just plain wrong."

"Why? Free drinks are never wrong." Sarah scanned the bar. "Okay." She lowered her voice. "What about that blond guy standing by the bar? He's alone. And he looks like someone who might part with a few bucks. Do your thing, Indie. Close your eyes so you can see white or whatever your mind does."

"No. Way." I shook my head. "I can't. That's not how it works. Anyway, even if it would work, I just couldn't. And"—I stared Sarah down—"you said we wouldn't talk about it anymore."

"You're no fun."

Natalie waved her hands in front of her face like she was a hummingbird flapping its wings and bounced in her chair. "I don't want no voodoo hex put on me."

"Man, oh, man," moaned Sarah. "It's just free drinks."

"I think I agree with Natalie," I said. "It would be wrong. Let's just do the drinks the old-fashioned way, with smiles and smart conversation. Talk is cheap."

"And safe," said Natalie.

"'Kay," said Sarah, standing. "Have it your way. I'm going to need another soon, so let's get a move on."

While Sarah chatted to some work friend, Natalie nudged me with her arm. "Let's go outside to the deck."

If I went outside, I would want a cigarette. I must have hesitated too long, because Natalie hip-checked me.

"*Pleeease,*" she begged. "I hate standing alone. Anyway, we need fresh air. Lots of people outside aren't smokers."

"Okay," I conceded.

The busy deck was crammed with people, and we found a spot over by the railing. Natalie had just lit up when I heard a familiar voice yell my name. I quickly turned to see Lacey waving like crazy and weaving through the bodies to get to me.

Finally, she was in front of me, and I hugged her hard. "How are you? How's your summer?" Of course she looked amazing in her pink tube top and white skirt, colors that showed off her wavy dark hair and perfect golden tan.

"I'm awesome," she said, smiling. "Really awesome. I've had a great summer. I'm so glad to be finished with high school."

"You lifeguarding again?"

"Yeah. It's a fun job. I'm teaching swim lessons too, and I love the little kids. How about you?"

"I've got a horrible crap job, but it's money. I've never seen you here before." I changed the subject, not wanting to talk for a second longer about my stupid job.

"I'm here with a few friends from my volleyball team," replied Lacey. "They're going to the U of Ottawa next semester. I guess this is the local campus pub. They wanted to try it out."

Suddenly, I remembered that Natalie and Lacey had never met before. "Lacey," I said, "this is my friend and roommate Natalie. We live just down the street." Then I turned to Natalie and said, "Lacey and I go way back to, like, kindergarten days."

"Cool," said Natalie. She smiled at Lacey. "I haven't been in Ottawa long, so it's great to meet some new people."

"I get you," said Lacey. "I'll be dealing with that soon enough." She turned back to me. "I heard you moved out. Good for you." She held her hand up, and I slapped it. "I can't wait to get out of my house. My mother is driving me nuts."

"When do you leave?"

27

"End of August. Not soon enough!"

I turned to Natalie. "Lacey is going to Queen's in the fall. She's going to be on the volleyball team."

"No way," said Natalie. "That's where I want to go next year."

Shocked that Natalie wanted to go to university, as she'd never mentioned it before, I glanced at her before looking back to Lacey. Queen's was the hardest school in Ontario to get into; it was the Harvard or Yale of Canada. Suddenly, I smiled. That was why Natalie looked like a queen to me. It had nothing to do with fair skin, dark hair, and the queens of fairy tales, and everything to do with where she was going to school. It was so crazy how my visions worked. I thought about the liver and onions. I had to get it out of my mind, so I steered myself back to the conversation.

"What are you majoring in?" Natalie asked Lacey.

"Business."

"Cool." Natalie nodded. "They have the best engineering school in Canada."

"Are you thinking about going into engineering?" I asked Natalie.

"Yeah. That's the plan. I need to make some money first, though. My grandmother just didn't have enough. I got accepted, but I deferred for a year. For now, I'm working reception and hoping to get a second job."

"I'm so excited to live in res," said Lacey. "Just to get away from everything and *everybody*."

"How's Burke?" I asked.

"He's okay. Still doing a ton of rehab, but he hopes to be skating by Christmas. He's still begging me to get back with him."

"Burke is her ex," I explained to Natalie.

"You ever see John?" Lacey asked me.

Sharp pains crashed through my chest just at the mention of his name. How could he still make me hurt? I didn't get it. I wanted to be over him already. And I'd worked so hard this summer to forget about him. Now just the mention of his name made me ache.

"Not very often," I quickly replied. I had to change the subject, and fast. "You'll have to come over to our apartment one day and hang out."

"That'd be fun," squealed Lacey. "And you guys will have to take a road trip to Kingston to come visit me at Queen's."

"Really?" Natalie grinned. "That would be so awesome. I could tour around."

"Yeah, that would be fun," I said. "Road trips are a blast." I hip-checked Natalie. "And you have wheels."

"Bring your guitar," said Lacey.

"Natalie plays, too." The thought of driving down a highway with guitars in the backseat had made my night.

"Indie rocks the guitar," said Natalie.

"Yeah, but you play a mean fiddle."

"Bring all your instruments. That'd be so cool. We can have a par-tee." Just then, Lacey waved at someone in the distance.

"Listen, I got to go," she said. "But let's get together. And make sure you come to the river party at the end of the summer. It's going to be huge." She hugged me again before she turned to Natalie and said, "See yah."

The rest of the night cruised by, and soon it was last call. "Come on," said Sarah. "Let's get out of here."

Outside, the air was still hot and humid. I took off my high heels and walked in my bare feet, swinging my shoes back and forth.

"That guy you were talking to was so cute," said Natalie to Sarah. Then she hiccupped. Putting her hand to her mouth, she mumbled, "I shouldn't have had that last beer." She hip-checked Sarah hard, sending her flying across the sidewalk. "So who was he?" she asked.

"A friend of a guy I work with at *greasy, gross* Denny's," slurred Sarah.

"I thought he was cute, too," I said. "And he bought you two beers." I held up my fingers and gave her the peace sign. "Two means you have to give your girlfriends the goods."

"His name is Tyler."

Sarah squished in between Natalie and me and flung her arms around us. The three of us, like little Musketeers, tried to get in step but couldn't. We ended up laughing hysterically.

"And he just moved here from Toronto." Sarah tilted her head back and screamed into the black sky. Then she looked at Natalie and me and said, "And get this. He's looking for a place to live, and I told him the downstairs apartment might be for rent soon." She squealed and raised her arms to the sky.

"Are you kidding me?" I said. "That would be great. We'll have friends downstairs. That would be so fun." And that also meant that someone, mainly a big, strong guy, was going to be living downstairs. Tyler looked as if he lifted weights. With all the freaky stuff that was going on in our apartment, that would make me feel a bit better.

When we got into our apartment, I wanted to stay up and talk but Sarah and Natalie were done, and they went to bed.

The apartment took on an eerie silence as I sat at the kitchen table, drinking a glass of cold water. Only white noise again. I sat back and put the glass against my face, enjoying how cold it was on my skin. Then I picked up Natalie's pack of cigarettes and tapped them against the table. One escaped, and I rolled it around in my fingers. Oh, boy, did I want it. No one would know if I stepped outside for one.

"*I don't need one,*" I whispered.

Go ahead and have one. You deserve one. Again, my own voice; it was like it was me but with this huge attitude or ego that wasn't really me. Made no sense. Sometimes it helped me do things I didn't think I could do. But then other times, it made me do things I shouldn't. Like now. Did I deserve a cigarette?

I knew I didn't need one. I put the cigarette back.

Slam. Slam. Slam.

I jumped up.

Before I could grab my frying pan, I saw the outline of a tall, stately woman in the door frame. Her hair was piled into a bun on the top of her head and held in place with a beautiful tortoiseshell comb. She wore an olive green ankle-length skirt with a starched high-necked blouse and a little bolero jacket with fabric-covered buttons. Her lace-up boots shone in the dark. She rubbed her hands, and I immediately noticed her long, thin fingers, hands that were made for writing in a journal, smoking cigarettes from a long holder, and holding a wineglass by the stem. Her age was a bit uncertain, but from the lines around her eyes and mouth, I guessed 50 or 60. Her lips looked so severe, as if they had been drawn in a straight line with a marker. There was no curl to show any happiness, and she emitted so much anger and sadness through her mouth that I started to tremble. I couldn't move. Not even an inch. I wanted to pick up my trusty frying pan, but it just seemed so wrong to hit someone in such obvious pain.

"Who are you?" I whispered softly.

"This is my house," she stated in a stuffy British accent. Then she lifted her chin, straightened her backbone, and said, "I demand that you leave."

Chapter Three

"Let's go to the beach," I said to Natalie and Sarah the next morning. After seeing the ghost, I had to get out of the apartment.

Sarah nodded. "Good plan. This fan ain't cutting the heat. There's water and trees there."

"We could take our guitars," said Natalie. "And play in the park. I think that would be fun. Give us something to do when we need to get out of the sun. This lily-white body can't handle too many rays. The sun don't shine all that much in Newfoundland."

"I'm game," I said, rushing my words. "I can be ready in ten."

Sarah raised her eyebrow at me. "You? Ready in ten? What's that all about?"

I fanned myself. "I just want to get to some water."

❖ ❖ ❖

I *was* ready in ten. Record speed for sure. As soon as I stepped outside, I exhaled. My shoulders relaxed as well, and just the relief of pressure made me realize how much weight I had been carrying since I'd seen the lady the night before. She had really affected me.

I hopped in the backseat of Natalie's old clunker car and put my head back to stare at the frayed fabric on the ceiling. I had hardly slept. How long had that woman been stuck in the apartment? Fortunately, Natalie and Sarah were oblivious to my mood and how tired I was; they chatted about random stuff the entire way to the beach.

The parking at Britannia was scarce, but Sarah managed to find a spot on a side road.

Bodies of all shapes and sizes packed Britannia Beach, but fortunately there were tons of trees, and we found a table under a big maple situated a little bit away from the beach area. We were all fine with that, as it gave us some privacy to play our music. I put my guitar on top of the picnic table and sat down on the bench.

"Should we swim first?" Natalie whipped her T-shirt over her head to reveal her pale yet perfectly fit bikini-clad body.

"You guys go," I said. "I'll watch our stuff. We can take turns."

Sarah held up her hands. "No argument here." She threw a bottle of suntan lotion to Natalie. "You better lather up."

"I already did," replied Natalie.

"Race you, then."

"I'll take the lotion," I said.

Sarah tossed me the bottle, then they took off, laughing and running toward the water. I just sat at the rickety wooden table, staring into space.

And thinking.

Of the ghost. The woman in the green skirt.

She had been unhappy that we were living in the apartment. Well, really, her house, I guess. I wanted to tell the girls about her, but I didn't want them worrying or getting freaked out. Sarah would go ballistic, and Natalie would cower under her messy bedcovers. Anyway, there was a chance that they wouldn't believe me. I scratched at the peeling paint on the picnic table. Maybe she would just go away eventually. I flicked the little piece of peeled paint, then I tapped my fingers on the table. I shook my head when I realized how agitated I was, and I decided I needed to do something productive.

I picked up my guitar and strummed, random chords that had no tune. The sun peeked through the leaves, and I remembered I hadn't put on sunscreen yet. I set my guitar aside and squeezed the last of the cream out of the bottle. After rubbing it in, I glanced around for a trash can and spotted one on the other side of the trees. For fun, I decided to throw it and pretend I was a basketball player. Why not? I had never been good at sports, but what the heck? I tossed it so hard that it flew through the air and bonked someone on the back of the head.

"I'm so sorry!" I put my hands up to cover my mouth. How embarrassing.

He turned around and gave me a quirky smile. "No big deal." Then he picked up the bottle, jumped, and tossed it in the trash can.

"I guess you get a point," I said, my cheeks turning red.

"Helps that I was only a foot away," he said, grinning. "But, hey, I'll take any point I can." He glanced at my guitar, sitting on the picnic table. "I thought I heard someone playing."

"Yeah, that was me. I'm better at music than sports."

He squinted at me as if trying to place me. He looked to be about my age, maybe a year or two younger. Clean-cut, with sandy blond hair and a bit of a baby face. He wore blue-and-yellow baggy swimming shorts that hung to his knees and accentuated his scrawny body, his white legs looking like birch branches. A T-shirt covered his torso, unlike so many of the guys who walked around with no shirts on to show their dark tans and bulging muscles. I figured he was a guy who wore his T-shirt all summer long to hide his skinny, hairless chest.

After a couple of seconds, he shook his finger at me. "You, uh, go to Ridgemont, right?"

"Not anymore." I held up my thumb and smiled. "Graduate." Then I squinted and looked a little closer at him. "Do you . . . go to Ridgemont?" Perhaps he was a year younger than me.

"Louis Riel."

"Are you still there?"

"Yeah, I'm going into grade nine." He flexed his muscles, and I laughed.

"Kidding," he winked. "I'm on the small size for my age. I graduated last year, too. I think I saw you at a party once last year. You might . . . have been with a guy who used to go to my school?"

"John Smith?" Just saying his name made my heart pick up its pace.

The guy nodded. "That's the guy. He got kicked out of our school." He paused and shrugged. "We weren't really friends."

That didn't surprise me. John wasn't the kind of guy who had a ton of friends.

Suddenly I heard band music in my head, but it ended after about a bar with the blast of a trumpet. I quickly looked around. There was no band. When I turned back, I tilted my head and blurted out, "Were you in the jazz band?"

"How did you know? I played sax." He laughed. "I didn't think we had fans. We were a *bad* high-school band."

I shrugged. "I don't know. You look like you might be in the band."

"Ah. Yes. I am often mistaken for a geek."

"I didn't mean it that way."

Again he laughed. "It's okay. I've been called worse." He stepped toward me and held out his hand. "My name's Paul Thompson, by the way."

I took his hand in mine and shook it. "I'm Indie," I said. "Indie Russell."

"Nice to meet you, Indigo."

"How . . . do you know my real name?"

"Deductive reasoning." He tried to sound cool, but then this impish grin appeared on his face. "I remember someone talking about Smith and how he had this girlfriend named Indigo. I just put two and two together." He held up his hands and made peace signs. "Math's my best subject. Get it? Two plus two."

Just the mention of John's name quieted me down and made me speechless. Here was a guy I didn't even know, but yet he kind of knew me because I was John's ex. John's notoriety was bigger than I thought. For the next few seconds, we didn't say anything, and it was weird, because he just stood there, with his arms hanging like strings from the side of his body. The awkwardness made me mumble, "I should go swimming soon."

His shoulders slumped, and his smile left his face, but he said, "Gotcha," in this fake-cool voice. He gave me a finger salute as he started walking backward, pretending to be casual.

"Paul!" I said. "Watch out for the trash can."

But I was too late, because he smacked right into it, almost falling bum first into the piled-up fast food wrappers that heaped over the edges of the can.

"Are you okay?" I asked.

"Oh, yeah," he said, giving me a feeble thumbs-up. He quickly turned and walked away without looking back.

After he was gone, I heard the man's voice in my head.

There are no coincidences.

"Who are you?" I whispered.

My name is Isaiah.

Shocked that he had answered me, I said out loud, "You have a name?"

Yes. I have a name.

Just at that moment, Sarah came bounding up to the table. I wondered if she'd heard me talking to myself—well to Isaiah, really. She snatched a towel from her bag and wrapped it around her shoulders.

"Who was that guy you were talking to? He looked kind of cute." She shook her wet hair, and droplets landed all over me.

I laughed and backed away from her. How had she seen me with Paul? "I don't know. He went to Louis Riel and saw John and me at a party once. John went to Louis Riel before coming to Ridgemont."

"Yeah, I remember that. This guy remembered you?" She raised one eyebrow and made one of her funny faces. She had a million of them.

I laughed at her. "I guess. But only because of John."

"Stalker."

I continued laughing. "Hardly. He seemed nice. His name is Paul Thompson. It was just a . . . coincidence." Then I proceeded to tell her about how I'd hit him on the head with the sunscreen bottle.

Sarah laughed hysterically. "Only you could meet a guy *that* way," she said when I had finished embellishing the story. "But, hey, maybe he's a nice guy. Be a good one for you."

"I'll probably never see him again."

Sarah toweled her hair. "Nat is waiting for you. She's treading water by the orange buoy."

I stripped off my beach cover-up and grabbed a towel from my bag, slinging it over my shoulders. As I approached the beach, I saw Natalie in the water, frantically waving. I dropped my towel on the sand, ran to the water, and stopped as soon as it swirled around my toes.

"It's not cold," she yelled. Only her head bobbed out of the water.

"It is to me!"

"Just dive in."

I lifted my feet a few more times, waded a bit deeper, and when the water slapped my stomach, I dove. Coming up for air, I gasped to catch my breath, then I swam toward her.

"The water feels good," said Natalie. "Our ocean at home is so cold. I mean freezing. This is refreshing."

I treaded water and tilted my head to the sun. "Amazing."

"Hey," she said, "we saw you talking to a guy."

"How could you guys see me from here? We were at the back of the park."

"Sarah has hawk vision."

I liked swimming but only for short bursts, and I wanted to change the topic of conversation. "Come on, let's go in and get something to eat. I'm starving."

We waded out of the water, dodging the little bodies that were swimming like fishes along the shoreline and the bigger bodies stretched out on towels, catching rays. We strolled across the grass and headed back to the table.

When we arrived at the table, Natalie and I got some money out of our beach bags and headed over to the burger shack. I looked around, trying to see Paul, but he didn't seem to be anywhere.

The lazy summer afternoon crawled by, and we lounged on towels laid out on the grass and swam and slept. By late afternoon, parents started throwing sandy toys into beach bags and wrapping towels around their children. They herded them to the parking lot, and the beach became quieter.

"Your guy never came back," said Sarah to me, looking up from her issue of *Rolling Stone*. Madonna graced the cover, posing like an Indian goddess. I knew Sarah was more interested in the articles on Jewel and Steven Tyler.

"He's not my guy," I retorted. "We talked for all of five minutes."

"Did you get his number?" Natalie checked out her tan lines before putting on a cover-up.

"No." I flipped onto my back. "And I didn't give him mine either."

Sarah sat up and stared toward the water. Then she looked at Natalie and me. "Beach is almost empty. Guess we should head out soon."

I didn't want to go back to the apartment yet, so I said, "Let's get something to eat on the way home."

Natalie jumped up. "Ice cream cone! Let's stop by Licks."

That prompted immediate movement. With our beach bags and guitars, we started to walk across the grass and toward the street where the car was parked. We were almost at the sidewalk when I heard a soft crying sound coming from behind a cluster of shrubs. I froze. Had the spirit followed me?

I slowed my step and tuned my ears to the sound. I heard it again, but this time it was a mewling sound and not at all like the sad singing of the ghost.

"Did you hear that?" I asked.

We all stopped walking. "Sounds like a kitten," said Sarah.

I put my guitar down and walked to the shrubs. The mewling got louder and louder. I squatted down, parted the branches and peered inside the shrub. Stuck under a branch sat a scrawny black kitty. It looked at me with its big green eyes, opened its mouth, and let out a loud screech.

"It's okay," I said. "I'll get you out."

By now Natalie and Sarah had squatted down beside me and were pulling the prickly branches of the shrub apart to help me reach the kitty. I slowly reached in and let it sniff my hand for a few seconds before I gently pulled it out.

"She's really matted," I said, cradling the kitten close to my body.

"There's no collar," said Sarah. "Maybe it's a stray."

"She doesn't look like she belongs to anyone." Natalie scratched the top of the kitten's head.

"You look like Cedar," I whispered. "Cedar's my cat—she lives with my mom." I looked at Sarah and Natalie. "Should we take her home?"

"How do you know it's a she?" Natalie asked.

I shrugged and nuzzled my nose to the cat's. "I don't. But our motto is girls just wanna have fun."

"Let's check," said Sarah. "We need to know the sex. That's important."

I carefully turned the little kitten over, and I almost cried when I realized that *he* was just skin over bones.

"A boy," said Sarah.

"Yup," I said. "Doesn't matter." I eyed both Sarah and Natalie. "He's starving. Please. Let's just take him home for now and give him some food. We'll put up photos in case his owners are looking for him. If we don't take him, he will die."

"He would have to be a black cat." Sarah laughed. Then she lowered her voice and mimicked the opening from *The Twilight Zone*. "Do-doo-do-doo."

"That show freaks me out," said Natalie, waving her hands at Sarah. Then she turned to me. "I'll take your guitar so you can hold the kitty."

With the kitty wrapped in a beach towel like a baby and nestled in my arms, I made my way to the car, petting his little head to give him a feeling of security. When he looked up at me and meowed, I stroked his back. "It's okay. We'll get you food." Then I looked at the car clock. "Let's stop at the grocery store on the way to Licks. They'll have cat food."

At the store, I ran in and quickly bought litter, the cheapest litter box I could find, a small bag of dried cat food, one can of wet food, and some special little cat treats, ones that my Cedar loved. Sarah and Natalie waited for me in the car, watching the kitty.

"We'll have to think of a name for him," Natalie said when I was back in the car.

I ripped open the treat bag, put one in the palm of my hand, and held it out for the little guy to eat. He wobbled on skinny legs and sniffed before he took the treat and started to crunch.

Natalie turned around to face me and was watching every move he made. "He likes it," she squealed. "Okay, let's all think of three names, then we'll decide which one is best."

"Or we could put them in a hat and pick," said Sarah. She sped off, and within five minutes, she cranked the car wheel and drove into the Licks parking lot, lurching to a stop inches before the meridian.

"I wonder if your brother is working today," Sarah pondered, getting out of the car.

We made sure we unrolled the windows a little so the kitten could get air while we went inside to get our ice cream cones. Brian was there, hovering over a girl dressed in a Licks apron who was standing in front of the counter that bridged the actual restaurant to the kitchen. She was probably waiting for burgers for her customers. I hoped he wasn't harassing her to get her order out. He loved bossing everyone around. I was sure he was making the girl a nervous wreck.

As soon as he heard the door, he turned, smiled, and waved. Much to my shock, the second he saw us, he left the girl's side and strutted over to us. He never acknowledged my presence like this.

"Hey, little sis," he said. He was dressed in nice gray dress pants and a classic navy golf shirt.

"Hey, Bri."

Sarah nudged me, then whispered, "Think he'll give them to us for free?"

"I heard that," said Brian. "And not a chance. We're running a business here."

I rolled my eyes. One day he would own some great restaurant or bar and be the world's best businessman.

"How's the apartment?" he asked me. Then without waiting for me to answer, he turned to Natalie, winked, and grinned. "She got you seeing ghosts yet?"

"Brian!" I glared at him.

He put his arm around my shoulder. "Don't worry, little sis, it's okay. We all know that bed in the psych ward is saved for you."

I jabbed his stomach to get him to shut up. Then I stepped forward and ordered a chocolate ice cream cone from the girl behind the counter. As she made my cone, dipping her arm in the barrel of cold ice cream, I thought about asking Brian for a job. Why not?

Once I had my cone, I pulled him aside. "Do you have any job openings?"

"I thought you had a job."

"I hate it."

He shrugged. "Maybe in a couple of weeks. I've got a few people leaving to go back to school. It could work. But it would only be part time." Then he grinned.

"What?" I asked. He wanted something in return for his generosity.

He leaned over and whispered in my ear. "I get you a job, you get me a date. With your hot roommate." He glanced at Natalie.

I punched his arm. "That's not fair."

"Life's not fair, little sis. Get used to it."

We ate our ice cream cones in the car, which became a total disaster because the heat caused them to melt on the spot. By the time we arrived back at the apartment, my hands were sticky and gooey with chocolate ice cream.

"Dibs on the shower," said Sarah.

A shower wasn't my priority, so I didn't argue.

Right away, I made a bed for the kitty in my room out of an old blanket. Then I set out two little chipped bowls—which

I had bought for ten cents each at a garage sale before moving into the apartment—and filled one with water and one with wet food. As soon as he smelled the wet food, he went crazy and gobbled it down.

"He's an eating machine," said Sarah, toweling her hair.

"He's shoveling that in like my great-aunt Henrietta used to do," said Natalie. "Only he weighs a pound, and good ol' Aunt Henrietta tipped 'em scales at around three hundred big ones."

"That's his name," I said without thinking. "Henrietta!"

"Hel-lo. He's a boy!" Sarah squawked.

"I like it," said Natalie.

I bent down and touched the top of his head. "We'll fatten you up, *Henry.*"

"Okay," replied Sarah. "I can do Henry."

I placed a handful of dry cat food crunchies on the floor beside his bowl and sat cross-legged to watch him eat.

Suddenly, there was a knock at the door, and we all looked at one another. My heart started racing. Could it be the woman? Would she knock? Or just slam?

"I'm not expecting anyone," I mumbled.

"Me either," said Natalie. "Unless my great-aunt has arrived from Newfoundland."

The corners of Sarah's mouth lifted into an impish grin, and I immediately relaxed as she jumped up and ran to the door. Natalie and I burst out laughing when we heard a guy's low voice.

"I bet it's the guy from the bar," Natalie whispered to me.

"I bet you're right," I said.

Natalie glanced at me. Then she said, "What your brother said about ghosts . . . do you really see them?"

I opened my mouth to speak when Sarah and her friend walked in the kitchen.

"Ladies, this is Tyler," she said. "He just signed a lease for the downstairs apartment."

❖ ❖ ❖

It was three o'clock before I went to bed. I didn't have to work in the morning, so I could sleep until noon if I wanted. Even though I had made a bed for Henry, he crawled into bed with me, just like Cedar used to.

The damp air just hung in the sky, and the night was still so humid. I had opened my window as wide as I could to try and get some air circulating in my room.

Shadows danced on my walls as I petted Henry. He purred and cuddled in beside me. When I told my mother about him, she freaked and said we needed to get him to the vet to get shots, and she'd instructed me on how to check for fleas.

"You don't have fleas," I whispered. "Protect me, okay?"

Slam. Slam. Slam.

I hugged Henry to my chest.

My door flew open. I immediately sat up.

The stately woman stood in the doorway, glaring at me. "Have you no respect? The doctor is paying a visit. There is a sick child in the house!" She took a few steps toward me, and I jerked back until my body was pressed against the wall. She stared at me for a few seconds then she turned, swished her green skirt, and walked out of my room, slamming my door behind her.

I stuck my face in Henry's fur. "I don't care if you have fleas or bugs or if you pee in my room. Stay with me. Green Lady scares me."

❖ ❖ ❖

Raindrops hitting glass woke me up at 11 the next morning. I glanced at the window. Who had closed it? I was positive I had left it open last night. Had Natalie or Sarah come into my room when they saw the rain and shut it for me?

My bedroom door was shut, though. Suddenly, I remembered the kitten. I jumped out of bed and began searching my room. "Here, kitty, kitty. Here, Henry."

I got down on my hands and knees and looked under my bed. I smiled when I saw him curled up inside one of my big, pink, fuzzy slippers. I had bought each of us girls a pair at Zellers for our slumber parties. Recently, it had been too hot to wear them, but I figured come winter, we'd all be strutting around the house with gigantic furry feet. Henry must have sensed me looking at him, because he opened his eyes, yawned, and stretched. I pulled him out from under my bed to take him to the litter box.

The apartment seemed quiet and eerily still as I padded down the hall to the bathroom with Henry in my arms. Natalie and Sarah had both left for work, and I had the rainy day to myself. After Henry did his business and I praised him for it over and over, I put him on the floor and sat down on the toilet myself. I was unraveling toilet paper when the bathroom door flung open and there she was, standing at the door, staring at me.

"Go away!" I tried to shut the door. "Have *you* no respect?"

My natural instincts were to cover up, but then when I realized what I was doing, trying to stop a ghost from staring at me on the toilet, I started to shake. The woman was following me everywhere. She scowled at me and swished down the hall. I quickly finished, washed my hands, and stared at myself in the mirror. Blue bags hung under my eyes, and my face was the color of paste. She was draining my energy.

As I walked to the kitchen, I kept peering over my shoulder to see if she was trailing behind me, her long skirt sweeping the floor, her eyes boring into my back. The taps were off in the kitchen, which was good. I sighed and listened to beating rain for a few moments, waiting for her to show up.

With my steaming tea, I plopped down on the sofa in our little living room with Henry in my lap. On rainy days I loved curling up and reading a good book, but I had just finished my last novel, so I flipped through the collection of videos we had in our cardboard box. I smiled when I pulled out *Labyrinth.* I'd watched it dozens of times, but on a rainy day, it was like comfort food. Sarah had brought a small television from her house that had a built-in video player, so I stuck the VHS in and settled back on the sofa.

I lifted Henry up to my face. "You are perfect."

His loud meow made me rub noses with him. Then I nestled him on my lap so I could watch the movie. The music started. And so did the noises.

Slam. Slam. Slam.

Then a horrible wailing.

Heavy footsteps stomped down the hall, and I grabbed Henry and held him tightly. The woman swept into the living room, glaring at me, and I trembled, almost as if I was having a convulsion. I watched as she fell to her knees and tilted her face upward. "I won't let you do this to me." I knew she wasn't yelling at me this time.

And just like that, she disappeared again. I put my hand on my chest to try to slow my heart. Then I leaned forward and rocked back and forth, rubbing my temples. Silence took over the apartment, and I breathed in and out. I couldn't let her beat me, so I tried to watch the movie again. But I sat shaking on the sofa. What was she so upset about? It had to be more than us living in the apartment.

Everything was fine for ten minutes. Then the mournful sound of her singing what sounded like a church hymn echoed through the heating vents. I couldn't understand the words, but the tune caused my heart to ache. I put my hands to my ears and shook my head. No more! The pain was too great. I got up and shut off the television.

I was dressed and running down the stairs in mere minutes. Henry was safely locked in my room, or at least I hoped so.

As soon as I stepped outside, the rain hit my face, and I inhaled, bringing fresh air into my lungs. The humidity was gone, and the air was clean, and I just kept breathing. Relief washed over me—it felt good to be out of the apartment. I walked fast, going to the heart of the Glebe. I could browse through shops and hit my favorite used bookstore. That might take my mind off the woman in the apartment.

The little bell rang when I entered the store, a musty little hole-in-the-wall, and I shook my head and wiped my face to get rid of the excess raindrops. Paperbacks lined the shelves and were crammed in every nook and cranny of the store.

I walked down the aisles, not sure what kind of book I wanted to read next. As I passed the travel section, my feet stopped and I felt as if were stuck in the mud. A book on Scotland started pulsing in front of me, and I reached over to touch it. It felt hot.

Could I travel on my own? Without John? Maybe not to England; that was *our* plan. But I could go to Scotland and visit the castles. That would be *my* plan. Lately, I'd been dreaming about ruins and castles and the word *Scotland* kept popping up in my head, almost as if it were calling to me. Was I supposed to go there? Could I go overseas without John?

I picked up the book and flipped it open. It was only two dollars. Should I buy it? Was that why it had pulsed in front of me? Why not? It wasn't like it was going to break my bank account.

As I was walking toward the cashier with the book under my arm, another book stopped me short. This time it was a book on ghosts. My breathing became shallow. I had come to this store to buy a novel, so I could forget about Green Lady. For the second time since I entered the store, my feet just refused to move. I stood in front of the book and stared at it. There was a 50-cent sticker on the front. I didn't give it time to start pulsing in front of me. I just picked it up and almost ran to the cashier.

After paying for the books, I stepped outside into the rain. I had two hours to kill before Natalie came home from work, so I wandered through different stores in the Glebe, asking to see managers about jobs. Two asked me to fill out applications, which I did on the spot. I figured I could work days and get a part-time job at night too to save money. Once I had something in my savings account, I would start planning my trip. *Trip.* The word sounded exotic.

Back at the apartment, I stood outside with my hand on the door of the building. I didn't want to see her again. I glanced at the antique store, The Past Is Here, that was attached to our building, and when I saw the CLOSED sign, I sighed. I would have loved to have stalled for time and visited the owner, George, but he had gone out of town for a few days. Every time I went in the store, I was there for at least 30 minutes just chatting with George and sometimes his wife, Claire.

If only I still smoked, then I could stand outside and have a cigarette and wait for either Sarah or Natalie to walk down the street so we could hike up the stairs together. At least the rain had subsided, so I wasn't getting soaked as I stood on the street trying to figure out what to do.

Finally I decided I had to go inside.

As I plodded up our stairs, I could hear Natalie's melodic voice singing a Celtic song, and I breathed a sigh of relief. She must have gotten off early. I stopped for a second just to listen, wishing that I could sing like her so I could go to a music school somewhere. I shook my head; every week I had a new idea about what I could do with my life.

I entered the apartment, and Natalie stopped singing. I slipped out of my sandals and walked into the kitchen. Henry lay at her feet. Sarah sat at the table reading a magazine. They must have both gotten off early.

"How was work?" I asked.

"Fine," replied Natalie.

"Stupid," said Sarah. "I work in a grease pit." She looked up. "How was your day?"

"Good." I held up my book on ghosts. "I got a new book." I paused. *Come on, Indie, you can do this. Talk to them. Tell them the apartment is haunted.*

"You bought a book on ghosts?" Natalie grimaced. "I don't want to believe in ghosts."

"You're such a wimp," said Sarah.

This was my chance. "Listen, you guys," I started slowly.

Suddenly, there was a sharp rap on the door. Sarah jumped up and bolted to the door. I'd never seen her move so fast.

"Tyler." Natalie gave me a quirky grin. "Again."

"In high school, she never ran for any guy," I said. "They ran for her."

"I'd say someone is in love. Lucky girl," said Natalie.

"Ahh. She deserves it if she is," I said. Cold air washed over me, and I wrapped my arms around my chest.

"I wanna be in love," moaned Natalie.

I stuffed my book in my bag, knowing now that the conversation on love wouldn't be changing anytime soon.

Chapter Four

"Where's Juanita?" I whispered to Esther.

Miles stood at the counter leering at me, and every muscle in my body tensed. The rain had ceased, the humidity was gone, and the sun shone in a clear cobalt sky, and I was trying to enjoy the weather. But with Miles staring at me, the day seemed dark and dreary. Again.

"She quit," lisped Esther.

"Do you know why?" I stared at my room list, noticing that I had twice as many rooms to clean today.

"Liver problems."

I immediately looked at her. Esther scratched her neck. "Liver's got too much damn booze in it."

Liver and onions. That's what I had heard in my head: liver and onions.

"Is she okay?"

"She's fine. Fat but fine. I guess her doctor said she could have been headed straight to the hospital if she hadn't gone to the walk-in." Esther paused and gave me a funny look. "She said you phoned her right out of the blue and told her to get her fat ass to the doctor."

"I'm not sure I said it that way." I had to laugh. My mood had lifted a little, knowing that I had helped Juanita. I couldn't wait to tell Natalie. Maybe I could tell her and Sarah about Green Lady at the same time.

"I love that laugh, Blondie." Miles said from behind the counter as he pulled a toothpick out of his yellow teeth. Vomit soured in my throat, and all my good feelings dissolved.

"I haven't hired a new girl yet," Miles barked, "so get moving, you two, or you'll be here until midnight." Then he licked his lips and winked at me. "I bet you're not such a good girl when the clock strikes midnight."

Esther followed me out of the office. "I told yah, girl, watch out for him."

I nodded. "I will. Believe me, I will."

Halfway through my list of rooms, I was listening to Pearl Jam on my Walkman and doing my final perusal of the room when my body stiffened. I shut my music off and listened. Footsteps. On the concrete outside.

I was alone in the room. I quickly grabbed all my cleaning supplies and glanced around. There was nothing to tell him that I was in the room. The footsteps drew closer. I knew it was him. Yes, my cart was outside, but it was in between two rooms. My heart sped up. I had to do something. If I made a run for it, would he meet me at the door, push me back in, shut the door?

Beat him at his own game! My ego voice gave me a jolt of energy.

Trust your intuition.

"Okay, Isaiah."

I heard the key scratching in the lock, and I dove under the bed. I held my breath.

"Blondie," he called. I could see his fat feet, which were shoved into leather sandals, walking across the carpet. My heart ticked uncontrollably, and I hoped he couldn't hear it. I held my breath. Sweat dripped from every pore in my body.

He checked the room, then the bathroom, and har-rumphed to himself as he left.

My body went slack in relief. A wash of air cooled me down. And I inhaled and exhaled. I waited for a few seconds, listening for his footsteps to get quieter and quieter. My heart still pounded through my skin but slowed with each breath.

I crawled out from under the bed, the carpet scratching the skin on my knees and elbows. Then I creaked open the door, and when I saw he had his back to me, I quickly snuck outside. He must have heard me, because he turned. But by then I was standing at my cart, trying to look as if nothing had just happened. A puzzled look punctuated his face.

"Blondie"—he walked toward me—"I was looking for you."

I know that.

"What's up?" I asked, trying desperately to appear nonchalant. I stared at my work sheet.

He stared me up and down. If I could have covered myself with a robe, I would have.

"Your *knees* are red," he said with a smirk.

"That's from scrubbing the tubs," I muttered. Why didn't he leave me alone? Heat spread from my neck to my cheeks, and I just knew they were as red as a ripe Ontario tomato. My hand shook as I tried to read the paper with my assigned rooms, but the numbers became one big blur.

"There's no need to blush, Blondie," he said. "I just wanted to ask you if you know anyone who needs a job. You got some cute little girly friends who could replace Juanita?"

I looked up and attempted to smile, but it was hard because all I wanted to do was shove my cart right into his fat stomach. "I'll check," I said. "Most of them have jobs already."

Although I had four rooms left to clean, I was done in the time it normally took to do three. I left my Walkman on my cart, because I needed all my senses firing. But Miles never came around again.

Was I reading too much into this? He might be all talk and no action.

Always trust your intuition.

Stand up to him. Have some guts.

❖ ❖ ❖

I finished work and caught the bus home. I got off a few stops before mine, however, as I wanted to walk in the sunshine and think. I *had* to get another job. If I quit working for Miles, I would have to move back home because, like it or not, the rent had to be paid every month. Right now this was the only job I had. And I desperately wanted to turn my small life into something bigger, something exciting, to see the world. I wanted my dream of going to England with John to become my own dream of going to Scotland without him.

When I was almost home, I glanced at my watch. I hoped The Past Is Here was still open. George and Claire were due back last night. He told me he would reopen today. I walked by the store and saw the red OPEN sign blinking. A thought flashed through my mind. I bet George could answer some questions about Green Lady.

I walked into the store, crowded with furniture and old stuff, and was immediately taken back in time. I loved thinking about the past. Sometimes all the old furniture and books and gadgets felt familiar; I almost felt as if I had lived long ago.

"Hello, Indie," said George.

"Hi, George," I said cheerfully. My mood always lightened when I saw him.

"Beautiful day out there."

"I love the sun."

"You just browsing today?"

"Yup. Just coming from work. Thought I'd stop in and see if you have anything new. And I want to pick your brain about something."

His eyes lit up, and he gave me a friendly wink. "I have some new jewelry that I purchased at an estate auction."

I clapped my hands and squealed. "Let me see!"

From under his glass counter, George brought out a silver tray full of old jewelry all neatly arranged and all incredibly different. "I haven't tagged most of it yet. It was from the estate of a rich Jewish woman who loved to travel." His face shone with passionate excitement.

"Oh, wow," I said, gazing at the tray.

On a velvet backdrop, and lined up perfectly, sat a pink quartz necklace; a full turquoise necklace; freshwater pearls; thick and thin gold and silver bracelets, some with engravings; thin gold chains; thick-linked gold chains; jade and amethyst pendants; large, gaudy brooches, all gold with different stones embedded in them; chunky stone rings; turquoise bangles that looked like they came from the Middle East; an ivory elephant on a long gold chain; and—

I stopped when I saw a ring that looked exactly like the one my mother had given me as a gift when I moved into the apartment.

"I have this ring," I said, pointing to it. Then I held out my right hand to show him.

He picked up the ring from the tray. He tenderly touched it before he peered at me over his glasses. "It's an Egyptian ankh ring."

"My mom gave me mine," I said. "She said it was some sort of family tradition. My grandfather gave one to my grandmother, then she gave one to my mother. That's all I know about it."

"The origins of the ankh are a bit unclear," said George, the passion rising in his voice, "but it does resemble the Christian cross." He lightly ran the tip of his finger over the top part of the ankh symbol before he continued talking. "The theory of the loop in the cross has ranged from being just the common sandal strap to having some sort of sexual meaning. But really, it could have been a knot from ancient times that had either religious or mythical meaning. One thing we do know about it is that the meaning of it is *life*."

"Cool," I said.

"More specifically, eternal life and life in the afterworld."

I tilted my head and looked at George. "Do you believe in the afterlife?"

He smiled, his warm eyes crinkling in the corners, and he shrugged. "I'm not sure what I believe, dear. I know I believe in beautiful jewelry, and I love finding out where it came from."

I smiled back at him. "And you know so much, too." I paused before I said, "Stones make me feel alive."

"Well, a lot of people feel that gems and semiprecious stones hold energy." He looked down at the jewelry. "I'm not sure I believe in any of that either. But they are pretty to look at."

"I can't afford any of this today," I said, "but I did come in to ask you a question."

"Sure. Ask away."

"When did you buy this store?"

"Twenty years ago," he said proudly. "I was fifty-five and had just retired from the government. I wanted something to do with my time. I'm lucky to still be in business, the way the economy is now." He glanced at me over his glasses. "Why are you interested? You want to buy me out?" He winked at me.

I laughed. "I don't have the money to buy jewelry, let alone a store. It's just such an old building. It has to have history. I love knowing old facts."

"You're an inquisitive young lady. I like that. So many kids today don't think of the past."

"Who owned it before you?" I asked.

"It was a family business that had been passed down." He picked up a silver ring and began polishing it. "I bought the store from the original owner's grandson. It was built in the early 1900s. I guess that could classify it as a heritage building." He looked up and smiled. "So, to you, being as young as you are, it's old. Just like me."

"You're not old." I nudged him on the arm.

"Claire wants me to retire in another year. Maybe next winter."

"What do you want to do?"

"The thought of getting away from winter does appeal to me."

"Do you . . . know anything about the original family?"

He laughed. "If it's old, my dear, I've done a bit of research. The original owner had the last name of Schmidt."

"What nationality is that?" I asked. Green Lady had a very distinct British accent.

"Schmidt is German. He came over on a boat when he was just a young man."

"Was he married to someone German, too? Did they come over together?"

He wagged his finger at me. "I should have known. You're interested in the love story. I don't know if he came over with a bride or married when he got here. I do know that over the years, he and his wife developed a flair for fashion. This wasn't originally an antique store but a fine cloth store. They imported fabric and sold it to the upper class in the city."

"Did that first family live here long?" Perhaps the woman I was seeing was someone else. Could there have been another owner?

"If my memory serves me, that grandson's name was Gerald. So it was in the family until I came along. Gerald turned the building into apartments and didn't live on the property. He just rented it out. But I think the original Schmidts built it so the store was attached to their family residence. Your apartment and all the other apartments were rooms in their house. I think Gerald made all the changes, adding extra kitchens and whatnot."

He put down the ring he was shining and smiled at me. "I forgot. I've got a nice kitchen clock that might work for you girls." He moved his step stool and climbed up to get an adorable, round, daisy kitchen clock.

"How much?" I asked.

"No cost. It's a 1960s clock, but suits a young girl like you who is always sunny and bright." He stepped down off his little stool and handed the clock to me.

I really wanted to ask more questions. But the doorbell tinkled and George turned his attention to the door. He waved at a man who had entered the store.

"I've got that table for you on my truck," said the man.

George moved from behind the counter and toward the door. "Enjoy your clock, Indie," he said.

"Thanks," I said. I left the store with it under my arm.

❖ ❖ ❖

Henry greeted me when I unlocked the apartment door. I slipped out of my sandals and picked him up. With him resting in my arms, I called out, "Hello."

No answer. Where was everybody? My chest constricted. I didn't want to be alone. I headed to the kitchen and immediately looked at the white message board we had tacked up on the kitchen wall. There were two notes written in black marker.

Have to work pm shift. Home at nine. Natalie.

GOING OUT WITH TYLER. SARAH.

I exhaled and looked around the small kitchen. I placed the clock on the table and sat down. Drumming my fingers on the table, I wondered how I would survive the night alone.

First, I called Lacey, but she wasn't home and her mother said she wouldn't be home all night. I thought about calling my friends Zoe and Carly, but they lived so far away now, and I didn't have a car. At first, when I got my job, I was going to save for a car, but the idea of traveling kept coming up. The thought of traveling made me think of John. Again.

I wanted to call him . . . but couldn't. How many times had I wanted to pick up the phone and call him? Hundreds. Thousands. Millions.

Slam.

I covered my face with my hands. She was back. Why wouldn't she leave me alone? My body started trembling, and my heart ticked like an out-of-control clock. The clock. I would ignore her and put up the clock.

The tool kit my dad gave me when I moved out was in my room. Walking across the hall, I heard the taps on in the bathroom. I sprinted down the hall. Sure enough, water was blasting in the sink and splashing onto the floor. I shut the taps off, grabbed my purple bath towel, and mopped the floor.

I did manage to get the nail hammered into the wall and the clock put up without her slamming a door or turning on any other taps. The clock looked pretty above the sink, and it read 7 P.M., the correct time. George wouldn't have it in his store if it didn't tell the right time.

I had to get more details. I would ask George to finish telling me about the family. Perhaps that would help me understand Green Lady, and I did want to, because she obviously had been through something horrible. I wrung my hands. The apartment was too quiet for my liking. Where was she hiding? When would she appear again? I needed music. That might stop me from hearing her. Natalie would be home by nine.

I needed a drink, too. Just one. Although I never drank alone, ever, I really wanted a drink to see if that would stop me from being able to see her—perhaps just a glass of wine would make her not come back. Wine was nothing. One glass wouldn't hurt.

I poured my glass and took it and Henry to the living room. Tonight I wanted to listen to Jim Morrison. I put on the Doors greatest hits CD and plopped down on the sofa.

The music, no matter how I cranked the volume, didn't drown out the pitiful singing, but thankfully she left the taps alone. I didn't move from the sofa except to refill my wineglass. When Natalie arrived home, I was still sitting. She called out, and I answered, "In here."

"How yah gettin' on, girl?" she asked when she saw me.

"Good," I answered.

"You drinking alone?"

I shrugged. "Just wine."

"Not like you." She eyed me.

"Is tonight." I petted Henry on the head.

Natalie frowned at me. "What's up with you?"

I shook my head.

She flopped down on the sofa beside me. "I don't believe you."

"Get a drink. We can have a party."

A few drinks later, and feeling a lot more tipsy, I looked at Natalie over the rim of my glass.

"I have something to tell you," I slurred. "Our apartment is . . . it's *haunted*."

"Haunted?" Natalie stared at me wide-eyed.

"Yeah. Haven't you heard her slamming the doors?"

"I, um, thought the sounds were because it was an old apartment." Natalie's voice trembled. "So . . . it's, this ghost or whatever it is, is a *she?*" She wrapped her arms around her body.

"Yeah," I slurred.

Natalie furiously shook her head, making her short hair stand on end. "I don't want to believe this. I—I can't believe this."

"She's the one who turned on the taps," I said. "She did. I know she did."

Natalie put her hands to her ears. "No more, please. This is too scary." She flapped her hands. "Let's not talk about it anymore."

"I had to tell you."

"I can't deal with a *ghost*. That is just, just crazy. And I thought weirded-out stuff only happened in Newfoundland. Wait until I tell my grandmother."

❖ ❖ ❖

By the time I went to bed at midnight, I was definitely bordering on being drunk. I liked the feeling because it dulled everything, helped me relax, and made the woman go away. I must have fallen asleep right away.

It was still dark outside when Natalie came crashing into my room and jumped on my bed. "I saw her!" she screamed.

Groggy, I sat up. "What?"

Natalie's entire body shook, her face was ashen, and her pupils were dilated.

"You were right! There is this woman from the past in our apartment. She has this stuffy British accent." Natalie gasped for air. "I saw her. I saw her."

I hugged her and tried to get her to stop shaking. I hadn't told Natalie about the woman being British. She really had seen her. Natalie's screaming and my trying to calm her down must have woken Sarah up, because suddenly she flew into my room.

"Holy fuck!" Sarah scurried onto my bed as well, clutching her baseball bat. "Did you guys know that we have a ghost in our apartment? She wears this long green skirt, and I just saw her, and she told me to leave."

"I saw her too," said Natalie, her voice quivering. "Indie told me about her."

"You saw her before tonight?" Sarah stared at me.

I nodded. "I wanted to tell you, but I kept thinking she might go away. I told Natalie tonight and would have told you, but you were at Tyler's."

"Who is she?" Sarah asked.

"I think she might have been the original owner of the house," I answered.

"What the hell is her problem? Why won't she leave? Isn't she dead?" Even Sarah trembled, and I mean *trembled*.

Natalie started crying. "She told me that I should be quiet because her children were trying to sleep. And she kept staring at me, and it made me feel as if she really thought I was intruding in her home. She didn't yell, though. She sounded really, really sad. Did something horrible happen in this place?"

"Something happened," I said. "I just don't know what."

"Oh, my gawd! What if it was, like, some mass murder or something?" said Sarah.

I shook my head. "It's not that," I said. "It's something to do with her. She told me a doctor was coming. I think she might have died too early and maybe left her family, her children."

"Maybe we should try to be nice to her," said Natalie softly. "Maybe that would make her stop crying."

I looked from Natalie to Sarah. "I think that's a good plan."

"No way!" Sarah barked. "We have to get rid of her. I don't want to make friends with some ghost."

"Okay," I said. "I'll find a way. I promise."

❖ ❖ ❖

The next morning, I left for work while Sarah and Natalie were still sleeping, the two of them in Sarah's double bed. The three of us had moved into Sarah's room, because she had a double bed and we all wanted to sleep together. The bus stopped in front of my work, and I swear I could hardly remember being on the bus I was so tired. I dragged my weary body across the street and entered the lobby.

"Well, Blondie," said Miles. "Are we a bit hungover this morning?"

I wanted to tell him to shut up, but I clamped my teeth together and took my room list. When I scanned it, I couldn't believe how many I had to clean.

"Why do I have so many rooms today?" I blurted out.

"I gotta leave early," lisped Esther as she picked at her teeth with her fingernail.

"And I ain't got no other girl yet. Blondie, you was supposed to get me someone."

"None of my friends want *this* job." Tired and cranky, I'd had it with Miles.

He laughed at me. "Getting feisty, eh?"

I stormed out of the lobby and went to get my cart, yanking it out of the storage room so hard it hit the side of the wall and almost toppled. My entire body shook, and I had a bad metallic taste in my mouth.

I worked hard with no breaks and didn't even stop for lunch. At around two, I saw Esther leaving and I cursed her under my breath. Brian had to come through. He had to. And I wasn't setting him up with Natalie either. I would tell Mom, and she would make him give me a job.

With sweat dripping down my back, soaking my shirt, I scrubbed and vacuumed and dusted. Finally, I had one room left. I stuck my key in the lock and entered, breathing a sigh of relief when it wasn't too disgusting—lots of newspapers, but no stinky, gooey garbage. I started to pick up all the newspapers when suddenly my hands tingled. I stared down at the newspaper, and the word *rape* shone like a red light, pulsing in my vision. It pulsed twice, then stopped, then pulsed twice again. I closed my eyes for a few seconds, and when I opened them and looked at the newspaper again, the word was just black and didn't stand out at all—it was just embedded in an article. This meant something. I knew it did.

My stomach soured, and my breakfast moved to my throat. Then I heard the key in the lock. I knew I didn't have time to dive under the bed like yesterday, but I knew exactly what Miles wanted.

"Blondie," he said, shutting the door behind him.

The sound of it latching made my pulse quicken; sweat started beading everywhere on my body.

"I have your paycheck." He waved an envelope in his hands. "I thought I would deliver it to you personally. I've put a bonus in it."

He approached me with a horrible leer on his face. "We're alone."

"Just give me the check, Miles," I said.

"Don't be a greedy little girl."

"Give me the check."

He licked his lips. "Did you hear me say I put a bonus in it?"

"Yes. I did."

"Don't you know how to say thank you?" He waived the check in the air.

My mind went blank, and I saw two walnuts.

Walnuts. Think, Indie, think.

He stepped closer, and as his stench hit my nostrils, I almost gagged. But I didn't. I needed my wits.

Closer and closer. "I've seen how much you want me, too," he said. He started to undo his belt.

Walnuts?

He stared at my breasts as he clicked his belt open. "I'm not asking for much from you." Leering at me, he unzipped his pants. Then he stretched his fat arms out and grabbed my arm, pulling it toward his open fly. "Just a hand job. That's all."

Nuts?

I yanked my arm away from him before I lifted my leg and kicked him as hard as I could in the groin. He doubled over. The check fell out of his hands.

"I QUIT!" I screamed.

I scooped the check off the floor and ran out.

❖ ❖ ❖

My lungs burned, and my legs screamed in pain, but I kept running farther and farther. I dodged by the people walking leisurely down the street. My vision blurred, and that's when I tripped, skidding on the concrete.

"Hey, are you okay?" A man helped me to stand.

My knee was bleeding, and my hand throbbed. "Thanks," I said. "I'll be okay."

There was no way Miles could have followed me; he was too overweight to run as fast as me. I started limping, and although my knee stung, it was my hand that was in the most pain. I kept walking, forcing myself to ignore the pain. Blocks away, I finally stopped and bent over at the waist. Dizziness took over, and I staggered to the wall and leaned against it. A horrible pressure in my chest made my breath come out in gasps. I hugged the wall until my heart stopped pounding. In front of me, on the other side of the street, was a bus shelter.

I crossed the street and sat down on the bench to wait for my bus to come.

Indie, I'm proud of you. You trusted what you saw.

Hey, I helped, too.

Tears loomed in my eyes. I looked down at my knee and tried to pull a few little pebbles out of it. Mom would know what I should do. Then I looked at my right hand and saw that my ring finger was starting to swell. Was it broken? I tried to pull my ring off, but it wouldn't budge. I tugged and tugged, but it was stuck on my finger and the swelling was getting worse by the second. The tears I was trying to hold in fell down my face, and I closed my eyes to the world around me.

Yes, I had used my intuition, and it had gotten me through something that could have been horrible. And that was a good thing.

But now . . . I didn't have a job. I needed money to pay my rent. And any of the other things I wanted to do. Miles had ruined everything.

I inhaled and exhaled, willing myself to stop and think of a plan. As soon as I got home, I'd phone Brian, tell him he needed to hire me *now*. I could scoop ice cream with a bad finger. I could, and I would. I would get another job, too.

I kept trying to twist the ring until the bus came. But it wouldn't come off.

When I got home, I almost crawled up the stairs. But worse than that, I walked into an empty apartment. I ran my hand under cold water, trying to loosen the ring.

Slam. Slam. Slam.

"Go away!" I yelled, sobbing. "Leave me alone."

Last night the wine had made her go away. I needed another glass. I pulled out the box, shook it, and figured there were a couple more glasses left. I poured one and sat at the kitchen table. One glass of wine on an empty stomach was more than I needed. Feeling tipsy, I picked up the phone and dialed home.

"Mom," I said.

"Indie. You don't sound good."

As soon as I heard my mom's voice, I started sobbing again. "I quit my job." I sniffled and grabbed a tissue to wipe my nose.

"What happened?"

"My boss was a total sleazebag."

I heard her breath catch. "Did he touch you?"

"No. I didn't let him. But he tried to."

I could hear her breathing and it wasn't coming out in soft rasps. "I'm coming over," she stated. "We have to press charges."

"We can't do that," I cried. "No one would believe me. No one saw anything. There would be no proof of anything. It would be my word against his, and you know how that works."

"It's not right, Indie."

"I didn't let him touch me. And I certainly didn't touch him like he wanted me to do." I paused momentarily before I said, "I kicked him in the nuts."

There was a pause on the line, then my mom suppressed a laugh. "Did you really?"

"Oh, yeah," I replied.

Just talking to my mom made everything seem better. "I fell running, though, and think I might have broken my finger."

After that comment, my mother proceeded to go through a bevy of questions asking about my finger, and in the end, she pretty much figured out it was sprained, but she told me to try and get my ring off.

"Should I come over?" she asked again.

I heard the door open and Natalie call out, "Hello?"

"I'll be okay. Natalie just came home."

"There's something else you're not telling me," said Mom.

Natalie ran down the hall. "I gotta pee so bad."

I paused until I heard Natalie shut the bathroom door. Nothing got past Mom. "There's a ghost in our apartment," I whispered. "She slams doors and turns on taps. She is freaking me out." My words came out in a rush. "The other girls have seen her, too, briefly, but she follows me everywhere."

"I think you need to come home, Indie."

"No, Mom. I can't. I promised the girls I'd figure this out. I'll deal with this." I heard the toilet flush. "Listen, I'll call you back in a bit."

"Indie, I can come over."

"Mom, no, please. Let me handle this on my own."

"Okay. I'm going to meet Martha for a quick bite to eat, but I will take my pager. And don't forget to clean up your knee with rubbing alcohol and ice that finger."

I twiddled with the telephone cord. "Thanks. Have fun with Martha. Say hi to her for me." Martha was an old high-school friend of my mom's.

I hung up the phone, and Natalie was staring at me. "What the heck happened to you?"

I put my elbows on the table and my head in my hands. "It's a long story."

"I have time."

After I had told Natalie everything, and she stared at me. Horrified, she looked at my finger. "Your mom is right. Ice it, and that will take the swelling down. And let's phone Sarah and get her to bring home pizza. Lard Jesus, you've had a day of sufferin' and need your friends with you."

I laughed for the first time all day. Pizza. That sounded good to me. But the friends sounded even better. "Thanks," I said.

✤ ✤ ✤

Later that night, my mom called me back. I knew she would. "I've made an appointment for you," she said.

"Mom, I don't want to go to a doctor. My finger is fine. I've been icing it, and the swelling is going down. And I'm not—I repeat, not—going to another psychologist."

"This has nothing to do with your finger or a psychologist," replied my mom. "I went to see this friend of Martha's at her angel store, and the woman wants to see you." She paused for a moment, then said, "She's a psychic."

"You're kidding, right?"

"Indie, just go to the appointment."

"When is it?"

"Tomorrow morning. Nine thirty."

"I have to job hunt tomorrow. Brian said he can't get me in for *two weeks*. As of today, I don't have a job, and I need money. I can't go two weeks without working. I need to pay my rent. I'm going to try to get another part-time job. What is this woman going to tell me anyway?"

"I don't know what she's going to tell you, but I just know you have to go see her. It is important for your future. And Dad and I can help with your rent this month."

Go see her.

I wanted to tell Isaiah to just shut up. But for some reason, I held back.

"Where is this *store?*"

―――

Chapter Five

My alarm went off at 8 A.M. I groaned. A horrible hangover hit every part of my body. Gross. I sat up and was pretty certain that I was still drunk. After Mom called to tell me about the appointment, Sarah came home with pizza and a case of beer. I wanted to chip in, but Natalie and Sarah insisted. They said I could pay them back when I got a job.

A job. I needed a job. And I needed to get it today.

I moaned again. I didn't want to go to this appointment. I wanted to scour the want ads. As I grabbed a pair of shorts and a T-shirt off the floor, my finger throbbed. It was still so swollen, and the ring looked as if it was cutting off my circulation. Perhaps George could get it off for me; he would have some sort of jewelry cutter in his store. Later. I would go to him later, once this dumb appointment was over. I got dressed, then I plodded down the hall to the kitchen and called a cab. Mom insisted I call one—she'd pay me back. While waiting for the cab to arrive, I lay on the living-room sofa until I heard a horn outside.

The cabdriver looked at me funny when I got in the car, probably because I smelled like alcohol and hadn't brushed my hair or my teeth. Who really cared? Not me. I would go to the appointment, come home and clean up, then hit the pavement. I leaned my head against the back of the seat and gave him the address. Then I closed my eyes until I felt the vehicle stop.

Upon opening my eyes, I realized I was somewhere in Ottawa I'd never been before. Whatever. My mom was being a bit weird, and I was just doing this for her benefit.

I paid the taxi driver, got out, and stared at the store's big window front. Crystals hung from what looked like wire attached to the ceiling and sparkled when the sun hit them. Books, massive chunks of rocks, and angel figurines lined the window ledges, along with what looked like white stuffing. Was it supposed to be clouds? Perhaps this was what heaven was supposed to look like?

Farther up the windows, near the top, in purple scrolling letters, was the store's name: Annabelle's Angels.

When I entered, the store was empty, which was strange, especially since I thought I had an appointment. I glanced around.

Although I was feeling unbelievably crappy, a mysterious peace surrounded me as I stared at the store's contents. Multicolored angel dolls and statues seemed to occupy every corner and crevice. They were so many shimmering shades: gold, yellow, white, pink, blue. They sat on counters and hung on all kinds of different racks.

But it was the walls that stunned me. Painted on the cream-colored walls were blue clouds, and embedded in these amazing clouds were golden flecks of angels. Had they been sponge painted to look like that? I looked up to the high ceilings. Golden angels looked down on me. A delightful warm air blanketed me.

Music played as well, and I recognized one of my new favorite singers: Jewel. Her distinct voice soothed me. At the far right of the store sat a big huge chest, and it was filled with stones like the ones I had seen at George's antique store, but they weren't in any form of jewelry. I walked toward the chest and picked up a stone. As I held it, I remembered that my dad had put all kinds of stones like this by our pool. The stone felt hot in my hand, like it had been sitting on a fire. I put it down.

Some of the stones in the chest were clear, but there were also many pink quartz and amethyst and topaz and turquoise. I knelt down and reached into the chest with one hand and let them sift through my fingers. I did this over and over. They felt so good to touch.

When my legs were numb from kneeling, I stood and glanced around the rest of the store. Books and decks of cards also lined a shelf on the left side of the store. But they weren't playing cards like for UNO and Rummy. They had angels on them and strange depictions of wands and swords and crashing towers. I stepped back and away from them.

I preferred to look at the angels, which wasn't hard to do because, seriously, they were everywhere. I craned my neck to look around the room, trying to absorb everything but knowing that wouldn't happen in just a few minutes. There was just too much to take in.

Then off to the side, I saw a door with a sign on it. I walked over and read it: *For readings with Annabelle call 1-613-555-1888.*

Readings? I shook my head. The woman did psychic readings? Of course I knew about this from John. He had been obsessed with Edgar Cayce. Sure, I was feeling some sort of comfort and warmth, but that still didn't take away the absurdity of the situation. I needed to go back to the apartment and get cleaned up and start looking for a job. I wondered about the places I had applied to a few days ago. I should go back and be persistent. Something would come up.

Open your mind, because you are meant to be here.

"Isaiah, why are you talking to me now?" I whispered.

I continued to look around the store for another minute, just gazing at everything and basking in the warmth of the surroundings. Then I figured that this Annabelle I was supposed to meet had obviously flaked. What a waste of cab fare.

I had just turned to leave when I heard violin music. I closed my eyes. Was someone playing tricks on me?

Then I heard a voice. "Indie. Come to the back."

"Okay. Let's play this out," I whispered to myself. "To the back I go."

I'd come this far, so I thought I might as well meet her.

The door to the back squeaked open, and I saw a hallway. Boxes lined the walls and were stacked up three high. Unbalanced from my hangover, I stepped around them, holding on to the walls. At the first door, I stopped and peered into the room.

Two fluffy, pearly pink chairs sat across from each other. An exotically beautiful woman was in one of them with a violin under her chin. I have to admit I was surprised by how attractive she was. She had to be in her 30s. She had dark curly hair and brown eyes, and she was slim and dressed in normal clothes: jeans and a pretty green-and-white shirt. Was I expecting someone old, gray, and frumpy—maybe a flower-printed muumuu, huge gemstone rings, a chunky necklace, and a scarf?

When she saw me standing at the door, she carefully placed her violin and bow in a black case on the floor. "I've been waiting for you," she said. "My name is Annabelle."

Okay. I have an appointment. Of course you're expecting me.

"It is nice to meet you," she continued. "And I enjoyed meeting your mom yesterday."

Then she stared at me and seemed to look right through me with these mysterious, beautiful, almond-shaped eyes that made me feel as if I was looking into a black lake with no bottom in sight.

"I knew you would come," she said. She didn't smile.

Yes, I had an appointment.

I didn't move to enter the room.

She got up and walked toward me, carrying a little brown leather journal-type book under her arm. Was she going to take notes on me? No way. I would not let her do that. Over the years, I had been to so many doctors, and they had all taken notes and diagnosed me with things like ADD and even ESP.

"Stay put for a moment. I have to lock the front door."

My throat went completely dry as I stood without moving until Annabelle returned. If she noticed my discomfort, she ignored it, because she passed by me. "Follow me to the other room," she said. "It's down the hallway."

A huge part of me wanted to go the other way and leave, but I followed her down a hall and made a sharp right. In the room, I saw a massage table and a couple of stiff-looking chairs. I wanted to be in the room with the comfy pink chairs. They had looked like chairs I could curl up in for a little nap.

As if reading my mind, Annabelle said, "I rent out this room. To a massage therapist, but I think it will be a better room for today." She looked at me and cracked a smile. "I don't want you to fall asleep on me."

She motioned for me to sit across from her. Once I was seated, she looked at me again, and although I wanted to turn my face away, I couldn't stop staring into her amazing eyes. They drew me in. She was a mystery, a piece of paper with writing in invisible ink.

"Who's John?" she asked point-blank.

I turned away from her. Pain crashed through me as it always did at the mention of his name. I had to hold myself together and pretend that nothing was wrong. This woman could not get the best of me. My defense mechanisms kicked in, and I rolled my eyes.

"My mom must have said something to you about him," I answered with a bit of cheekiness in my voice.

"You're heartbroken." She rested her hand on the brown book that now sat in her lap as if it were her cherished cat.

I refused to speak.

"His mother drinks a lot. That bothers him. And he doesn't have a father around to talk to. He can't commit, Indie, until he deals with the issues surrounding his father. Right now he is experimenting with drugs to try to forget. He will never find his father. At least not on earth."

"I know that."

She tilted her head and looked right into my eyes, which was unnerving.

I stared back at her, although I really didn't want to. I had never told Mom about Mrs. Smith's drinking problem. How could she have found out? And the only time she talked to her was on New Year's Eve. But more important, how could she have known about John's dad?

Without even a blink, Annabelle said, "You don't need to tell him what happened." Her words were matter-of-fact.

I sucked in a deep breath.

Annabelle continued talking about John, and as she did, I realized that so much of what she said my mother couldn't have possibly known. I wanted to get out of the room. Catch a cab and go home. But I couldn't move my body. I felt as if I were stuck to the chair with Krazy Glue.

After a while, she stopped. Then she stared me directly in the eyes again, and it was like sharp spears were piercing my soul. I pressed my back against the chair. The energy surrounding this tiny woman was massive. Even from across the room, she was invading my space.

"I know who you are," she said.

I needed water. Hot air washed over me, and I started to sweat, last night's alcohol seeping through my skin. I wanted to fan myself, but I couldn't move. I tried to ask for water, but I couldn't speak.

"You see and you hear things," she said. "You're like me."

Suddenly, the room started twirling, making me woozy. I blinked.

I have to get out of here. I have to run!

Run!

Get out! Go.

I tried to move again, but my arms hung at my sides like floppy bunny ears. My feet wouldn't lift, not even an inch. What had she done to me?

"It's okay," she said. She didn't move from her seat. Instead she sat still, with her fingers casually placed on that brown spiral-bound book that sat in her lap.

No, this was not okay. Not okay at all.

I wanted to thrash, fight so I could get out of this stuffy room. But chains seemed to encircle my entire body.

"It's time to face this," she said.

Face what? What did I have to face?

I didn't want to be here, in this closed little room, feeling as if I was going to pass out. Nothing about the room was okay. *Nothing.*

"Indie," said Annabelle. "You have to stop being selfish. You are here to help people, and you've been delaying too long. That's why you're here on earth."

Her direct, almost scolding tone burst a dam in me, and I started sobbing, my shoulders shaking uncontrollably. Was I being selfish? Was I here on earth to do something bigger than me? I had helped Juanita, and it had felt good, but I was scared. So scared. Scared of who I was. Who I was supposed to be. It was as if I were being forced to be someone I didn't want to be.

Tears streamed down my face like a released river.

"It's not okay." My body heaved up and down. I couldn't catch my breath. "Noth . . . nothing is okay. I have to . . . I have to . . . I have to get out of here. This is . . . all . . . wrong. Wrong."

My arms were still hanging limp, and my legs felt like bags of concrete. I couldn't get enough oxygen. I gasped, trying and trying to get air into my lungs.

"Relax," said Annabelle gently. "Breathe."

Oxygen. I need oxygen. I can't breathe.

I wondered if this was what it felt like to drown.

In, out. In, out. Breathe.

I knew I was hyperventilating, but I couldn't do anything to stop what was happening. The room closed in on me, the walls pushing toward me. Pushing. Pushing.

Darkness swam in front of my face.

I could still hear Annabelle talking, but she sounded tinny, far away. "Everything that is stopping you from following your path is being taken from you," she said. "All your negativity and doubt. Keep breathing." She didn't reach forward to touch me.

I inhaled and held the breath for as long as I could. Then suddenly the dark stopped swimming; it ceased moving and seemed to swallow me.

My world went completely black.

Crystal blue lights shone like little sapphire gems in a massive circle around me, shedding a light that warmed me with the most peaceful energy I had ever felt. Bathed in luminosity, I stood in front of my body, staring at the disheveled blonde girl slumped on the chair. I slowly turned to glance at Annabelle. She was staring at the body in the chair.

I turned back to stare at me, too.

I could see my body because I was standing outside of it. The world around me was 3-D, and everything had shape and form, lines and depth.

Then Annabelle started humming, what song I don't know, nothing I recognized, but she hummed. A loud chorus of high-pitched melodious singing or chanting, again I'm not sure what, joined Annabelle's humming, and the harmonious music was pitch-perfect. Peace overwhelmed me.

And then, like a sputtering halogen bulb, it all faded.

Thud.

Annabelle's hand was resting lightly on my shoulder. "It's okay," she said softly. "Everything is done now. Much has been pulled out of you. You should feel lighter. Your abilities to see and hear should be clearer and more focused. Your divine team will have better access to talk to you—and for you to talk to them as well, because you won't be so muddied inside."

Brought back to reality with a harsh jolt, I sat up in the chair. I glanced around the room. I was no longer standing. I was sitting in the chair, but instead of hyperventilating, I breathed easily, in and out.

"You were meant to meet me in order to move forward," said Annabelle.

I shook my head and looked at the clock sitting on a little shelf beside me. It read 10:47 A.M.

"Is that clock right?" I asked.

Annabelle nodded her head. "Yes. Should we go into the store now?"

"Okay," I replied, without hesitation. Again I looked at the clock. I had been out for exactly one hour. How was that possible? When I stood, I felt so weird, so light and free.

I followed Annabelle into the front of the store without question. Again, she carried the brown book under her arm. I wondered what was in that book. But I didn't ask. And I didn't even ask about how it was now almost 11 or where I had been for the last hour. I had so many questions for her, but I couldn't seem to talk.

Yes, I wanted to know about Isaiah. Who he was really? Had he chosen me? Or had I chosen him?

And what I was supposed to do with my visions?

What about my vision about John's mother? I hadn't told anyone yet about seeing John's mother kill his father. I was confused about so many things. It was as if this crazy world of mine that existed in my head and body had no rules to follow, no regulations. If I had a vision, I could tell or not tell, and I was supposed to be able to figure out what was right. It was a huge responsibility . . . that I had been avoiding. Was I really going to be clearer now? I wanted to know why I saw and heard things the way I did. I wanted to know how to figure out the visions that were like puzzles. If I had a responsibility, then they did, too. Even if I really didn't know who they were.

And I wanted to know how to talk to ghosts. I'd promised Natalie and Sarah I would find this out. Yes, that was my responsibility.

But I said nothing, because deep down I knew Annabelle was in my life to provide those answers. One day. Not today. And maybe I didn't want to talk because I was immensely enjoying the feeling of peace that surrounded me, and I didn't want to break the spell it had on me.

When I walked into the front of the store, the room again filled me with serenity—only the feeling was much stronger now. Once again, the angels seemed to swaddle me like a cozy blanket.

"Take care of your finger," Annabelle said to me, bringing me right back to reality.

"You noticed," I said.

"You did the right thing yesterday. You listened."

I thought back to my conversation with my mother. Had I told her about Miles before she went to see Martha? I couldn't remember.

Annabelle closed her eyes and pressed her fingers in the middle of her forehead. "I'm being told you saw something in the hotel room." She said this as if she had just read my mind. "There's more to whatever that is."

"What do you mean?" I asked.

She opened her eyes and shook her head, her forehead still creased from thinking. "I don't know. The messenger is gone. I guess you're to figure it out."

The warmth and peace I had been feeling suddenly vanished, and now I just felt stupid that I was still in her store. I had moved to the door to leave, because I really wasn't sure what to do next, when the light that had been streaming through the front windows disappeared and the sky outside went black. All shadows dissolved.

"Oh, isn't that strange," said Annabelle, unperturbed.

Really strange. Am I in some kind of sci-fi movie now?

Suddenly, the front door blew open and a woman rushed in and headed directly to Annabelle.

"I can't work here anymore." The woman handed Annabelle a set of keys.

"You didn't give me any notice." Annabelle said.

"I know. And I'm sorry. But I can't do it. I can't work anymore. My husband, he doesn't want me to work here anymore. He says it is changing me." Then she turned and left the store.

Annabelle tossed the keys in her hand for a second, then walked over to me and opened my hand. I didn't pull away from her.

A little stream of light filtered through the clouds and into the room at exactly the moment Annabelle said, "Guess you're working for me now."

There are no coincidences, Isaiah whispered in my head.

Chapter Six

I sat in the backseat of the cab and stared out the window at the trees and the people walking their dogs and shopping and going about their *normal* lives. Why couldn't I be one of them? I had just had an incredibly weird morning that had left me exhausted. When I got back to the apartment, I was going right back to bed.

My finger throbbed.

The cab pulled up in front of the apartment, and when I saw the red OPEN sign on George's store door, I wondered if he could help get my ring off. I entered the store, and George was busy shining a beautiful four-poster bed with some sort of brass polisher.

As soon as he saw me he stopped his polishing and smiled. "Indie. How are you?"

I wanted to lie and say "good," but I was anything but good right now. "Would you have some sort of metal cutter?" I held out my hand. "I need to get this ring off."

He took one look at my hand and said, "Yikes, that looks nasty. Although I'm no doctor, I did this exact same thing for Claire once. I'll see what I can do."

I stood on the other side of the counter as he rummaged through a drawer, pulling out something that resembled a nail clipper.

He held it up, "This little gadget cuts through metal. Let's see if we can get that ring off."

A few clips later, the ring snapped apart at the back, loosened from my finger, and I was able to slide it off. My finger throbbed, but I instantly felt relief from the pressure. George placed the ring on the counter and said, "You want to keep it?"

"Sure," I said. "It was a gift."

"I sold the one I had; otherwise, I would give it to you as a replacement."

"That's okay." I opened my palm and let him drop the ring in it. Then I tightened my fist. "I can just keep this one."

"If another one comes my way, I'll let you know." He put the little clipper away in the drawer. When he turned back to me, he suddenly waved his finger at me. "Oh, by the way, I found out more information about the owners of the building. Funnily enough, the next day after we talked, the grandson came in to say hello. Such a strange coincidence."

"Tell me, tell me," I replied quickly.

"It's a real *Anne of Green Gables* story," he said. "Mrs. Schmidt wasn't German. She came over from England as a child. Her parents died of influenza, and she ended up in an orphanage."

"I think it would be horrible to be an orphan," I said. My mother was like my best friend.

"I'm sure conditions were less than desirable." George kept on talking. "But when she got to Ottawa, she was adopted. I'm not sure if they treated her real well, though. Gerald, her grandson, said she wouldn't talk about her adopted family, and he couldn't remember meeting any of her relatives."

"How did she meet Mr. Schmidt?"

"She cleaned his house. Probably the only job she could do."

"I know all about that," I muttered. Then I said, "They must have had children."

"Three. They had a girl named Elizabeth. Then four years later, they had twins, a boy and a girl. They named them Henrietta and Henry. Not exactly creative."

Henry!

My body started shaking, but George obviously didn't notice because he continued talking.

"Little Henry had been quite sickly for most of his life, and he died of some sort of fever, probably scarlet fever at that time. I think, but don't quote me on this, he was around eight. He was the only boy, and I guess he was his mother's pride and joy."

I swallowed before I asked, "Did he die in the house?"

"I believe so." George glanced at me.

"He died of a sickness, though, right?" I asked quietly.

"Yes. And from what Gerald said, poor Mrs. Schmidt was never the same afterward. He said she scared the bejesus out of him when he was little. When they would visit, she'd sit in the rocking chair holding a doll, just rocking back and forth for hours. And his parents always warned him and his sister not to say anything about Uncle Henry. Looking back on it, they figure she probably had a nervous breakdown. She just couldn't accept that Henry was gone."

"Did she die in the house, too?" I asked.

"Yes. After she died, Gerald's mother turned it into a boarding house. And the parlor into a store." He waved his hand as he looked around his place. Then he turned back to me. "And eventually, they sold the building, and it was renovated into separate apartments."

"That's quite a story," I said. My mind was spinning with all this new information.

"That's why I'm into antiques. They tell a story." He tapped my hand, the one that held my ring. "I know that ring meant a lot to you."

"It's okay." I tried to sound cheerful.

He smiled and winked at me. "Just focus on where you got it from. And if you want to, focus on the historical meaning behind it."

It meant afterlife. What did that mean exactly? The woman in our house obviously hadn't gone to any kind of afterlife. She was really stuck.

I had to figure out how to help her. Maybe Annabelle would know.

❖ ❖ ❖

On Monday morning, the little bell on the door of Annabelle's Angels rang when I walked in, and it sounded like a gong being struck.

Annabelle cracked a tiny smile and said, "Good morning."

"Hi," I replied.

"You can put your purse in the back storeroom." She pointed. "Or you can put it under the counter, here. It's up to you." Then she glanced at her gold watch. "I have thirty minutes before my first reading, and I have to teach you how to work the cash register."

I opted to put my purse under the counter, because I really didn't want to go to the back. After finding a place for it on the bottom shelf, I stood up, pressed my hands down my skirt, and adjusted my blouse. Glancing around, I took in all the stuff again: the angels and feathery things and cards and books and stones. They all had price tags, so this job could end up being mindless, because all I would have to do was just sit at a counter and ring things in for people. Did anyone actually come in this store? Who bought this stuff? I wondered if Annabelle had any magazines hidden behind the counter. *Cosmopolitan. Elle.* I would even read *National Geographic* just to make the time go by.

Annabelle interrupted my thoughts. "Later this afternoon, we will get down to business."

Business? What business? What else do I have to learn but the cash register?

She opened the brown book, which was almost like an extension of her arm. "I have clients until noon." She tapped her forehead. "Oh, dear, I forgot to order the sandwiches for lunch." She picked up the phone and pressed numbers.

"You don't have to buy me lunch," I said, a wee bit shocked.

"Believe me, you will need it," she stated before talking into the phone receiver. "Andrew, it's Annabelle. I need to order some sandwiches."

She listened for a few seconds, then she put her hand over the receiver. "You like turkey?"

I nodded, still surprised that she would buy me lunch.

She ordered the sandwiches and hung up the phone. "After we eat, we'll start with cards."

"Cards?"

"Girl, I'm going to shock your system. I'm in your life to help you get on your path, and there's no time like the present. Don't worry, I will be gentle for the first little while. I'm going to start you on oracle cards. If you are going to follow your life's path, we might as well not waste time."

"Okay. . . ." Honestly, I did wonder what she did in her readings. And how she did them. So I had to admit that I was a bit intrigued.

After she showed me how to use the cash register, which was easy, she pointed to the appointment book. "I am going to the back room to get mentally prepared for my readings. When my clients get here, I want you to show them where I am. But knock. Don't just come in."

"Are you in that pink room?" I asked.

Her lips curled upward in a smile that lit her entire face. "Yes," she said, almost laughing, "in the pink room."

"I like those chairs." I smiled back, secretly thrilled that the woman did have a sense of humor. I thought about my slippers at home and how they would match. I had always liked pink fuzzy things.

"They were a gift from a client," she said. She turned and walked toward the back, but halfway there she turned around, faced me, and frowned, shaking her head. "I keep hearing the word *Paul*." She shrugged. "I'll leave that with you."

As soon as I heard the door to the pink room shut, I glanced around the store at all the angels and stones and cards. Paul? What was she talking about? Why would his name come up? I'd only met him once.

Although I was alone, in a weird kind of store, I felt comfortable, almost as if I'd arrived home. I went behind the counter and sat on a stool, waiting for someone to come in and buy something. I picked up a beautiful purple stone bracelet and twirled it around my finger, liking the feel of the smooth stones. It would make a good Christmas present for Natalie.

I put it back and stared out the windows. I wondered when my first customer would come in. When no one walked through the door, I jumped off the stool to walk around the room. I stopped in front of the shelf with the card decks. Something pulled me toward them. I shoved my hands in my back pockets and rocked back and forth.

Illustrations of angels, fairies, goddesses, pretty flowers, and even wild animals like bears were all over the decks. I was immediately drawn to a box with a purple angel on the front. I grinned. *Angelic Messenger Cards.* The angel on the front of the box was flying downward like a superhero, cutting through the air, heading toward something. I liked that she looked as if she were on a mission. I pulled my hands out of my pockets. Slowly, I reached out to touch the box, the heat drawing me in. My fingertips tingled, like they had been zapped by some sort of electricity.

I almost had the box in my hand when the bell on the door tinkled. I jumped back and dropped my arms to my side.

"Hi," I said in a chirpy, forced voice. I sounded as if I were five again and I'd been caught red-handed at the cookie jar.

"Hi," replied a blonde woman. She sported bangs and had her hair tied back in a ponytail. I tried to gauge her age—early 40s perhaps. Someone who definitely worked out and took care of herself but didn't go to extremes with makeup. A natural beauty.

She looked around the store, never really stopping to look at anything for any length of time. Even from where I was standing, many feet away from her, I could see that she looked almost scared.

"Can I help you?" I asked.

"Um," she said. "I'm here to see Annabelle."

"She's in the back." I quickly went behind the counter and opened the appointment book. I read the name, then looked up. "You must be Karen."

She nodded.

"Follow me."

"Thanks." Her voice trembled.

We went into the back, and I could hear Annabelle playing her violin. Did she always play before one of these readings? I gently knocked on the door.

"Karen, come on in," she said.

How she heard me knock over all that music was beyond me.

"Thanks," said Karen. She opened the door and disappeared, shutting the door in my face.

A huge part of me wanted to put my ear to the door and find out what Annabelle was going to say to this Karen woman, but . . . I made myself go back to the front.

Ten long minutes later, the bell tinkled and a man with salt-and-pepper hair and a runner's build walked in. I smiled. "Hello," I said.

He smiled back. "You're new."

"I just started today."

"I'm looking for a present for my wife," he said. "She loves angels."

My throat dried, and I swallowed. The guy wanted me to help him pick out a gift for his wife? I hopped off my stool and moved toward him. Annabelle had tons of books on angels.

"Angels, eh?"

He gave a big nod. "Yup."

Suddenly, I heard the word *purse*. *Purse?* I scanned the room. And then I saw it: a little black purse with beautiful purple angel wings hand beaded on the front.

I walked over and picked it up. "What about this?" I turned and smiled as I showed the purse to the man. It had a nice, long gold chain and a pretty clasp.

He took it and turned it over a few times, touching the beading. "I think this will work," he said. "I got her some clothes, but I wanted something small, too. I'll give this to her first and let her think I didn't get her anything else."

I laughed. "She'll open this and think it's the most perfect gift. She won't want anything else."

"You're quite the salesgirl." He grinned at me. "I never would have picked this."

Neither would I, if I hadn't heard the word purse *in my head.*

I rang the purse up, placing it and the receipt in a purple plastic bag that had *Annabelle's Angels* scrolled in white across the front.

The man picked up the bag, gave me a little wave, then left the store. I couldn't help smiling to myself. That had been fun.

Two ladies came in next, and for some reason, I said hello but didn't get off my seat because I could just tell, from all my years of clothes shopping, that they wanted to browse and touch. I lowered my head and tried to sneak glances at them, hoping they wouldn't think I was spying on them—I just wanted to be available if they needed my help. The tall woman with flaming red hair liked to touch everything, and the tiny, short-haired brunette kept her arms crossed and bobbed her head to say whether she liked the product or not.

Time ticked by, and the women chatted as they edged their way around the store. Finally, after a good ten minutes, they stopped in front of the cards.

They stood there eyeing the decks until the redheaded woman looked my way. "What can you tell us about the cards?" she asked.

"Um. What would you like to know?" I slipped off my stool but didn't move from around the counter. What did *I* know? Not a damn thing.

Help me.

"Well," said the brunette, "what are the differences between the cards? Some are called oracle and others are tarot." She picked up two different decks and showed them to me.

Suddenly, the bell tinkled and a heavyset woman with a head of gray curls limped in. A wave of relief flowed through my body. She had arrived at exactly the right time.

"Hello," I said.

She glanced at the two women, then back at me. "I have an appointment," she whispered. "For a reading. I'm just a little early."

"That's great," I said. Immediately, I went back to my safe spot behind the counter and looked at the schedule. "You must be Stella."

"Yes," she said.

Just then, Karen came out from the back, walking as if she was in a daze and wiping under her eyes as if she had been crying. What had happened in there? My heart suddenly ached, and I put my hand to my chest. I could feel it beating right through my blouse.

Shaking her head, Karen looked right at me and said, "That woman is amazing. Unbelievable." Her eyes welled with tears.

"That's good," I said. Again, my heart pained. If Annabelle was so amazing, why was Karen crying?

Annabelle told me she liked to have a ten-minute break between readings, so I turned to Stella and said, "Why don't you look around? Annabelle will be ready in ten minutes."

The two women who had asked questions about the cards had each chosen a book and a few other little items, and they came over to the counter. And here I thought the job would be boring and I just needed to learn the cash register. Happy for the distraction, I rang in their stuff and put it in bags. "Enjoy," I said.

They left, and Karen left, too, and now I was alone with Stella.

"I've never had a reading before," she said. "I'm excited. I've heard Annabelle is the best in the city."

"That's good to hear," I said.

We chatted for a few more minutes until I heard the violin playing. Guessing that was my cue, I took Stella back and knocked on the door. Once she was locked in the room with Annabelle, I went back to the front.

The steady stream of traffic in and out of the store for the next couple of hours surprised me, but I was happy for it because it made the time go by so much faster. Before I knew it, my watch said it was 11:45 and my stomach was growling.

Annabelle was on her last client. She had told me she would be done by noon and, if the sandwiches came, to pay for them from the cash register. Alone for the first time since Karen had shown up for her reading, I walked around the store, straightening things. I lined the books up and hung up fallen angels.

I had only covered half of the store when the bell tinkled.

When I looked at the customer, I stared wide-eyed.

Finally, I said, "Hi."

Chapter Seven

Paul was standing in front of me holding Styrofoam sandwich containers.

He gave me a big, lopsided grin and nodded. "Indie." He sounded as shocked as I felt. "Do you work here?"

"It's my first day." I pointed at him. "Paul. Right?"

"You remembered," he said.

I nodded. It looked as if I had just made his day.

"It's my first day at the deli, too," he said. "This is my first delivery."

I held out my hands to take the sandwiches from him.

Once he had given them to me, he glanced around the store. "Wow," he said. "There's some interesting stuff in here."

I shrugged. "I don't know much about it." I walked over to the counter with the sandwiches. "How much do we owe you?"

"I think it's on the bill stapled to the outside." In two strides, he was at the counter.

I reached for the bill at the same time as he did, and our fingers touched. Immediately, I withdrew my hand, surprised at the tingles that ran through my hand, into my arm, and to the rest of my body. They weren't the same tingles I had felt with John—his had been electrically charged, and these were, well, these were just pleasant.

He laughed awkwardly, then read the bill. "Looks like you owe $12.65."

With my head lowered, I rang in the bill, and the cash register popped open. I pulled out the money, looked up, and tried to smile as I handed it to him, unsure whether I should tip him or not.

He took the money, then I pulled out a toonie and gave it to him, thinking I would just replace it later and not let Annabelle know I'd given him money.

"What's that for?" he asked.

"A tip," I replied.

"Oh, okay," he said. "Thanks. Well, I better get going. I have a few more deliveries to do, and then it's back to the deli to clean up."

"A multitasker."

"I just do what the boss asks."

I nodded. "Me too."

"Well, see yah," he said.

"Yeah, see yah." I lifted my hand and gave him a little wave.

He was almost at the door before he turned and said, "You want to go for coffee sometime?"

For some reason, I didn't hesitate and just blurted out, "Sure."

"I'm off at four."

"Me too," I said.

"You want to go after work?"

"Tonight?"

He shrugged. "Any night that you're free. There's a Starbucks just a few blocks down."

I thought about my evening. I had zero plans. "Okay. Let's go tonight."

He grinned. "I'll pop by when I'm done."

The bell tinkled as he left. As soon as he was gone, I reached into my purse for my wallet, getting a toonie and putting it into the cash register. Not more than 30 seconds later, Annabelle and her last client entered the store from the back room.

"Oh, good, the sandwiches arrived," she said. "Did you pay the delivery guy?"

"Yep," I answered. I eyed her. She had to have known they had hired a teenager and his name was Paul. That's why she had said his name earlier this morning. Something jabbed me.

She can see and hear things too, yah know.

Annabelle said good-bye to her client, and when the door shut and we were alone, she sighed, her shoulders sagging. "Three is all I can handle in a day," she said. "I used to be able to do more, but recently, I'm just so tired. I don't know what's wrong with me."

I flipped open the sandwich containers. "You need to eat," I said. I patted the second stool behind the counter. "And sit."

"Aren't you a doll? It's rare that someone waits on me." Annabelle took her sandwich and sat beside me. She took a bite of turkey, lettuce, and tomato that was stuffed between slices of super-fresh multigrain bread. "They make the best sandwiches." She nodded her head in approval.

"Could I ask you something?"

"Of course."

I picked at my sandwich for a second. "When people die," I started, "and don't leave the earth, they become ghosts, right?"

"That's true."

"How does someone get rid of a ghost?"

"Ahh, so you have one hanging around. Man or woman?"

"Woman."

"Where?"

"She's in our apartment. It's such a sad story. I feel so sorry for her, even though she's kind of mean. Her son died, and she never recovered from that."

"She probably hasn't dealt with the fact that he died, or she would have been more than willing to walk through the light to be on the other side." She wiped her mouth with the napkin and put her sandwich down. "I can give you methods to rid her from your apartment. I'll put together something for you by the end of the week. Some of the things you need are on back order, and they won't arrive until Thursday. Plus, I don't want to overwhelm you today, on your first day at work, and we have other things to do. Just ignore her."

"Okay," I said slowly.

That would be hard to do. Annabelle was treating the ghost like nothing, and I knew that Sarah and Natalie were waiting for me to do something. "Um," I continued, "I'd appreciate any help you could give me. And so would my roommates."

"Sure. Ultimately, though," Annabelle said, "she has to make the decision to leave the earth. You can get her out of your apartment, but she will have to make the effort to walk through the light."

"Can I help her do that?"

"You can most certainly try."

We ate for a few seconds in silence before I got up the nerve to ask another question. I didn't want to keep bugging her, but I just had so many things that needed answering. "What's the difference between tarot cards and oracle cards? Two ladies asked me."

Annabelle put down her sandwich and closed her Styrofoam container, even though she'd only eaten half. "Tarot has a lot of structure. There are always 78 cards in the deck, and they're divided up into 22 major arcana and 56 minor arcana," she said.

To me, that information sounded like a foreign language.

She got up and threw her container in the trash. "Oracle cards don't have quite as much structure, and to me that makes the work harder in the beginning," she continued. "But it's easier in the long run if you learn by using them. So I will start you on oracle cards. Every deck is different, and there is no set pattern to the cards. But, sweetie, the cards are only for practice. When you start doing readings, you use your senses."

"Okay," I said.

She patted me on the back. "I know this is going to be a challenge for you, Indie, but I know you can do this. You are going to do wonderful things for people because of your generous soul."

I didn't know how to answer her, so I took the last bite of my sandwich and shut my sandwich container.

"Now, I need a smoke before we begin," said Annabelle.

"You smoke?" I would have *looooved* a cigarette.

"I hate to say it, but yes." She eyed me. "You just quit recently?"

I nodded.

She winked at me. "Okay, I won't tempt you. Watch the store for a few more minutes. I'll be right back."

She rushed to the back, and I heard a door slam. It took all my energy not to run after her and beg for a drag off her cigarette. But I didn't. I stayed put, and not much more than a minute later, I heard the door creak and footsteps and a horrible cough; a definite smoker's cough.

Annabelle's face was red and sweaty when she came back.

"Are you okay?" I asked.

"Oh, yeah. It is what it is." She attempted to smile. "Don't you go worrying about me. I'm here to worry about you. And since you're finished eating, we should get started."

Annabelle went to the front door, locked it, and turned her OPEN sign around to read CLOSED.

"You're closing up already?"

"Just for an hour." She went over to the cards, obviously with a mission, and pulled a box off the shelf, the same box I had reached for earlier, before the customers had arrived.

"We don't need distractions," she said. "Let's go to the back." She winked at me. "To the pink room."

I followed her and sat in one of the fluffy pink chairs, sinking low into it, wishing I could take a nap instead of learn about cards. I glanced around the small room, something I really hadn't done the last time I had come in, because we had been in the room for only moments, and I had been extremely hungover. Now I noticed the framed photo sitting on her small table. It was of Annabelle with a huge, fluffy white Persian cat. I couldn't help grinning, because even from a distance, I could tell the cat was trouble. He would give poor little Henry a scare.

"You have a cat?"

She rolled her eyes. "More like a monster." She shook her head. "I love him, but he is a nasty creature."

She turned back to me and opened up the box she had taken from the shelf. She pulled out a book—one that looked like a textbook—and another box, which had the same cover as the original box but was thinner. She placed the book on the small round table between the pink chairs and proceeded to open the slimmer box, pulling out a deck of cards. "This is the hardest deck to use," she stated without emotion.

"They are the Angelic Messenger Cards," she continued. "The angels will talk to you through the flowers that are on the cards."

I stared at the long, skinny turquoise cards. Each one had a drawing of a flying angel on it. I guessed the flowers were on the other side of the cards.

"Knock them three times," she said.

"Knock them?"

She made a fist with her hand. "Pound them hard. You need to get all the energy out of them if you want to make them yours. Always knock your cards when you start. Always. And when you begin readings with people, get them to knock the cards."

I made a fist with my hand and did what she said.

"Now shuffle them."

Again, I did what I was told, and, because I was so nervous and the cards were so long and skinny, so stiff and waxy—not at all like the cards my dad and I played with—I ended up sending a bunch of them flying to the floor. Embarrassed, I bent over and picked them up. That's when I saw that each card had a flower and one word on it; most had numbers, too. I hadn't been expecting actual photos of flowers. I guess I was thinking they would be just drawings.

"I like the photos," I said. "How many are in this deck?" I continued to awkwardly shuffle because the cards were almost too long for my hands.

"There are 42 numbered cards, plus four wild cards for divine guidance and two wild cards for abundance."

"Wild cards, eh? Those are the ones I want to pick." I said this and laughed, the echo ringing off the walls of the small room. My nerves were getting the best of me.

Annabelle cracked a smile, which made me calm down a little bit, anyway.

After three tries shuffling, I finally decided they were okay, and even though Annabelle didn't tell me to stop, I put them down on the table.

"That's good," she said. "You will always know when to stop shuffling. The cards are just messengers for you, and with this deck, it's the flowers and the words on the cards that will speak to you. When you read for someone, you want to open up your senses so you allow the messages to come through. For the first little while, I just want you to do readings on yourself. Fan the cards out in front of you."

I fanned the cards and sat back.

"Pick three cards. Any three, but allow your hands to move over the cards and let the cards speak to you. If you feel heat coming from a card or you just know you have to touch it, then pick that card. The three cards will represent your past, present, and future. This is a very basic way to learn how to read."

My hands drifted about an inch above the cards. Back and forth. I think I was waiting for something magical to happen, but it didn't.

"Close your eyes," said Annabelle in a soft voice.

I closed my eyes and kept moving my hands. Suddenly, I felt tingling. I placed my hand down and picked a card.

"What did you feel there?" she asked.

"My fingers tingled."

I flattened my hands again and, palms down, ran them over the cards. When I felt a surge of heat coming from the cards, I picked another one. Before Annabelle could ask, I said, "That one was hot."

"Good girl," she answered.

For the third card, I again felt the tingling in my fingers. I picked it and opened my eyes.

"The more you read, the more you will figure out the feelings. Now, I'm going to have you flip the cards over." She held up the book. "There are explanations for every card in this book. You will need to study it backward and forward to be able to read these cards properly. I want you to read the book at home because today I want you to really focus on your senses. The cards are a tool."

I carefully flipped the first card. It read *Emergence* and had the number 21. The second card was *Acknowledgment*, number 26, and the third card had *Divine Guidance* scrolled on it. I presumed it was a wild card, because it had no number.

"Indie," said Annabelle in a soothing voice, "look at the first card and give me the first image or sound or smell or feeling you experience. Firsts are so important. Don't ever edit your firsts."

I stared at the blurry photo of a flower as it opened. Suddenly, I felt cold, and I wrapped my arms around my body. I could feel the cold petals over my head covering me, and I was in the dark. I looked up and saw the hole above my head. I reached up, and the petals started to open and a waft of warm air rushed through me. The room lightened. I stared at Annabelle.

"What just happened?" she asked.

My throat dried. "I felt cold. Like I was stuck in the flower, and it hadn't opened. Suddenly it opened, and I was warmed."

"Good," she said. "Now, what do you think it means?"

"I'm opening to something." I tapped the card. "Emerging, I guess." That was pretty basic; anyone could have figured it out. I still wasn't sure that these cards had any value.

"What about the second card?" Annabelle asked.

The *Acknowledgment* card had these pretty sunny yellow flowers on it, and I smiled. They were light and fresh, and I saw them dancing and laughing. A string of them circled my head like a wreath. Instead of looking at Annabelle for reassurance this time, I continued staring at the card. Suddenly I saw an *O* and then I saw a *K*.

"I'm okay," I blurted out. "This is all okay."

"What is all okay?"

Electricity flowed through me, and my body felt alive. "What's happening to me. My meeting you. You helping me. It's all okay. It's sunny and bright, and I want to dance."

"What about the third card? Your future?"

I stared at the *Divine Guidance* wild card, at what looked like the fuzzy seed part on the inside of a flower. The photo got all blurry, and I wanted to take my eyes off it, but I couldn't. Suddenly, I saw angels flying, and I heard them singing. And I saw Papa's face, and I heard my friend Nathan, who had died recently, playing the violin.

I kept staring at the card. It swirled around and around. I saw Annabelle. And I saw my great-grandmother, the hat-maker. She smiled at me and winked.

Then I heard Isaiah's voice.

I'm in there, too, you know. There's a big divine team waiting to help you.

***

Chapter Eight

The hour with Annabelle passed by in a blur. Once I had done my reading, she made me pull card after card, and she explained each one to me, what they meant, how I was supposed to read them. The cards were fascinating, and I liked the pictures of flowers.

At the end of the session, she boxed up the cards and handed them to me. "This is your own set of cards to practice with."

"Practice?" I asked.

"I want you to go home and ask the cards questions. For each question, you can pull up to three cards to get an answer."

"How do I know if the answer is right?"

"Don't worry about that now."

"Okay. So in other words, I'm kind of doing homework, but I don't have to find the right answer. I like that." I laughed.

"I hated school, too." Annabelle laughed with me for a few seconds before she turned serious again. "All I want you to do is let your mind go and let your visions just come; allow sounds, feelings, tactile responses, and tastes on your tongues. Don't judge anything that comes to you; just let it flow. Like, how you felt with the warm and cold and tingles, that kind of thing should all be acknowledged. I think you know that you have the ability to see and hear, but now you need to develop your feeling and touch abilities. Oh, and make sure you read the book. It is important for you to know everything about the cards."

The back of my neck ached, and suddenly I was really tired. "Okay." I sighed.

"Indie, it is perfectly okay to feel tired. In the next few days, I'm going to teach you about protection. Make sure you get lots of rest. This takes energy."

She stood. "But you've had more than enough for today. Now, my sweetie, we have a store to open." She winked at me, and her brown almond eyes sparkled.

I walked back into the front of the store. Light from outside streamed through the windows, shining on the floor, creating a sparkle to the room. The air conditioner hummed in the background, so the sun didn't make it stifling hot.

Annabelle unlocked the door and switched the sign back to OPEN. "I have some paperwork to do in the back," she said. "You man the front."

Annabelle disappeared around the corner, and when I heard the door slam, I figured she was out for another smoke. I bit my nails. Customers came and went for the next few hours, and I rang up goods and set up readings for Annabelle. It amazed me how popular she was; I was booking appointments two months in advance.

At just after three, Annabelle gathered her purse and slipped on funky tortoiseshell sunglasses. "I have to go. I have an appointment," she said. "I want you to lock up. You have the keys I gave you the other day?"

My first day on the job, and this woman trusted me to lock up? "Yeah," I said.

She instructed me to just lock the front door, because she had already locked the back door. As she was leaving, she turned to me with a puzzled expression on her face.

"My divine team is telling me to tell you something."

"Okay," I said.

She closed her eyes and stood still for a few seconds. When she opened them, she shrugged and said, "Have fun with . . . Paul. I hope that makes sense to you."

❖ ❖ ❖

At exactly four o'clock, just when I was ready to call it a day, the bell chimed and Paul strolled in. He had changed from his deli uniform to board shorts, a royal blue T-shirt, and flip-flops.

"Perfect timing," I said.

"Cool," he said. "How was your first day on the job?"

"Good," I replied. My purse was heavier, but not because of money; my cards and book were stashed in it. Thankfully, I loved big purses that were like huge satchels. The one I had with me today was cloth, and I had bought it at a flea market.

As soon as I stepped outside, the hot summer sun beat down on my skin. I took a breath of fresh air and tilted my face to the sky.

"Feels good to be outside," said Paul.

"Amazing." I locked up the store and tucked the key in my purse. And it was amazing, after the day I'd had at my new job. My head was bursting with so much information. I needed to relax, come down almost, from the high of the reading. Is that what Annabelle meant when she said she could do only three a day now? Did it just take too much of her energy?

Lost in my own thoughts, I meandered down the sidewalk beside Paul, keeping at least a foot between us. Unlike John, I had no desire to touch Paul, reach out and hold his hand, have our shoulders rub together. Instead, we just fell into an easy pace, like brother and sister.

Neither of us said anything, and that was just as well. I breathed in and out, trying to take in as much air as I could to clean out my lungs. One block ran into two as we walked in silence, and I couldn't help but think that perhaps I had made a mistake agreeing to this coffee. What would we talk about? I didn't know him at all.

I lowered my head and let my hair fall in front of my face so I could try to steal little peeks at Paul. Since I'd last seen him at Britannia Beach, he looked to have a little more of a tan. Not much, but a little. More than mine, I guessed.

After another block, when we were almost at the coffee shop, I was feeling a little more relaxed, and I figured I should try to strike up some sort of conversation. "So how was *your* first day at work?"

"It's a job," he said, shrugging casually. "But the owner's nice, and that's a biggie."

"Oh, yeah, for sure," I said. Without even thinking or editing, I launched into a description of my last job, telling Paul about Miles. I left out the part about the almost assault.

"That sounds nasty," he said. "Good thing you got out of there. That store you're in now must be a huge difference. It seemed so calm when I was in there today."

"That's a good word to describe it." I smiled and nodded.

"If I worked there, I'd probably just want to sleep all day."

I laughed. And it felt good.

We reached the coffee shop, and he insisted on paying. "Someone gave me a tip," he said, giving me his lopsided grin. "I might as well spend it."

I ordered an herbal tea, and he ordered an iced coffee, and we took our drinks outside. We nabbed a table with an umbrella, which was great because the sun was still really hot. Our conversation veered to school and people we were mutual friends with and who was doing what this summer and next year.

"What about you?" he asked, sipping from his straw. "Any fall plans?"

I spun my paper cup around, staring at the logo. "I don't know," I said. "I didn't apply to any schools. What about you?"

"Carleton. I'm going into their journalism program."

I looked up at him. "Are you a writer?"

He shrugged. "I like writing, but I want to work in radio or television and be some kind of reporter or maybe even work behind the scenes as a producer." He rolled his shoulders again. "But it's all a crapshoot, really. I'll go to school and figure out which type of journalism turns my crank, I guess.

I worked for the high-school newspaper and really enjoyed it. So who knows."

I smiled. "Honestly, that sounds so interesting. Maybe I should look into something like that."

Here I go again, I thought, *coming up with yet another thing I could go to school for.* I really had no idea *what* to do.

We finished our drinks, finding lots to talk about, which surprised me, and when I looked at my watch, I was shocked to see that we had been at the coffee shop for more than an hour. "I should go," I said. "I've got to catch the bus home."

"I can drive you if you want," he said.

"That's okay," I said.

"I don't have anything to do tonight. Let me take you."

The thought of sitting on a bus for 30-plus minutes was enough to make my head ache. A ride would be so much easier. "Okay," I said. "Sure."

His car was a little, blue, crap-box Honda, and the seats were littered with fast food wrappers. He wiped the front seat off for me, throwing junk into the back.

"Sorry for the mess."

"Hey, no worries," I said.

I got in, and he started the engine. The car rumbled like a truck, and I burst out laughing.

"Gotta get the muffler fixed." He put the car into gear and backed out of his parking spot. "Where to?"

I gave him the address, then slapped my hand on the dashboard. "Does this car have a name?"

"No name."

"It needs a name. Let's think of one." I bounced in my seat.

He laughed, and when I glanced at him, I also started laughing. "Seriously," I said. "Let's name this baby."

For the entire ride home, we came up with names, and the sillier they were, the more we laughed. My sides were sore when Paul pulled up in front of the apartment.

"So," I said, "did we decide on Mable?"

"You decided on Mable," he answered.

"I like Mable." I opened the car door before I turned and smiled at him. "Thanks," I said. "This was fun."

"Let's do it again."

"Sure," I replied. "I'd like that."

I bounded up the stairs, full of some kind of weird energy, and when I heard Natalie playing her guitar from the hallway, I went even faster. I slipped out of my sandals and immediately headed to my bedroom to get my guitar.

I entered the living room where she was sitting on the sofa, legs curled up under her, strumming away, and plopped down beside her.

She stopped playing. "How yah gettin' on, girl?"

"Great," I replied. A part of me wanted to tell her everything about the store and the cards and my coffee with Paul, but for some reason I didn't say more.

"I'm so happy for you." She plucked her strings with her pick. "I'll have to drop by this store." She looked tired, and her voice sounded dull.

"What's wrong?" I asked.

"Nothing."

"You, uh, seen Green Lady today?" I asked quietly.

"Thank God, no." Natalie blew out air. "I tell you, I'm still freaked."

"I talked to my boss. She is going to help us. By the end of the week."

Natalie tried to smile. "A few more days, eh? I hope she stays away." She pointed to my guitar. "Let's jam. Our music might drown her out."

I picked up my guitar from the corner of the room and strummed a few chords. "What do you want to play?"

We played for another hour, and when Sarah came home, she joined us on her bongos. The louder we played, the better we all felt. Then Natalie pulled out her fiddle and we really made noise, clapping and tapping. The night cruised by at just the right speed, and around ten, my eyelids got really heavy and my shoulders felt droopy, and I couldn't stop yawning. I begged off and went to my room, closing the door tightly behind me. She hadn't come to see us tonight.

I flopped on my bed and stared at the ceiling. Although I was dog tired, I couldn't sleep. I was so hyped with everything that was happening around me. My cards. I was supposed to be doing my homework.

Homework in the summer? Now that was just plain stupid. Or was it? I wasn't getting graded.

I got my purse.

Shuffling the cards, I sat cross-legged on my bed with Henry curled up beside me. After I knocked them like Annabelle told me to, I played around again with how to shuffle them, but I kept fumbling. Honestly, I thought the cards were a bit weird. I mean, really, answers in cards?

Annabelle said to practice, but perhaps *I* should test *them* to see if they were helpful. Testing was good. If the answers came out wrong, then I would know the cards didn't work. I could ask questions I knew the answers to, just to see if the angels could come to me like they were supposed to.

I kept shuffling. She had also told me to call on my divine team and my angels to help me.

"Okay, team, and that means you, too, angels," I said, my voice laced with sarcasm, "I need you to show up and play cards."

The shuffling became easier, the cards swishing from one pile to the next. What question to ask? What if I just picked something stupid? I put the cards down on my bed.

"Is my mom going to get that new job at the hospital?"

My mom already had the new job, so what the heck. This was a good question.

I turned over a card. *Fulfillment.* With the number 26.

I could hear my mother's voice in my head: "I really want the job, because it will be so fulfilling."

"Okay," I said. "That was a fluke." I didn't even bother to read the book.

I shuffled and asked the question, "Will Brian be a businessman?" I giggled. That was all he ever wanted in life.

The cards slapped against one another as I continued to shuffle. Finally, I put them down and picked one. *Fulfillment* again. Brian has always said the only way he felt fulfilled was when he made money.

I shuffled again—like, really shuffled. No way could I get the same card three times, not after this shuffle job. "Does my dad like golf?" I said out loud, with a bit of cockiness. Dad loved golfing.

I almost threw the cards against the wall when I turned over the *Fulfillment* card again.

All right, I thought. I had to come up with better questions. That was bizarre, getting the same card three times.

I shuffled the cards for at least a minute, thinking of a question. Suddenly, I blurted out, "Why is Paul in my life?" If any kind of love or true relationship card came up, I would know the cards were wrong. Inwardly, I laughed. I so hoped the cards would be wrong.

I flipped over the top card. *Synchronicity.* The number 20 was on the bottom of the card. This was not at all what I had expected. This time, I opened the book to read the explanation.

I read down the page where it talked about how everything happened for a reason. I thought about meeting Paul twice. Then I read, "Some synchronicities are obvious: meeting the same person in unlikely places . . ."

It really was kind of weird how I'd met him on the beach and then he just so happened to come into the Annabelle's Angels store. I kept reading until I got to the last line: "Even if you don't want to move on, the events in your life show you that a greater purpose is being played out."

I wanted to move on. Didn't I? Thoughts of John flooded my brain. I snapped the book shut and picked up the cards. That answer was lucky, in its kind-of-right way. It wasn't really right. Or was it?

I bet I could stump them with another question. I shuffled again, then carefully placed the cards down. Henry meowed, and I stroked his back and talked to him. "They'll not get this one right, I bet." I lifted him and kissed his little face.

Then I asked the question. "Will I ever get back with John?" I knew the answer to that, and it was a definite no.

After I had said the words, the assuredness that I could outsmart the cards dissolved. I sucked in a deep breath and slowly turned over the top card. *Vulnerability.* And lucky number 13.

Immediately, I picked up the book, checked the index, and flipped to the pages explaining this card. The flower on the card had a golden center, but surrounding it were sharp, dark spears. Conflict. The card was about a relationship that was full of conflict. My heart picked up its pace when I read the part where I was supposed to take back my power and that I was to pick the relationship in my life that was important to me and in most need of change and make decisions about it.

"But I've already made the decision to not be with him," I said to the card. "So you are kind of wrong."

No, you haven't! You're still thinking of him all the time. You want him back.

You have unfinished business with him—that's all the card is saying. Isaiah spoke softly.

"You came when I called, didn't you?" I whispered to him, trying to ignore my harsh, mean voice.

Of course I'm here. I'm part of the team.

I picked up the cards again and started shuffling. They weren't right. They just couldn't be right. John was out of my life. I shuffled faster and faster. I had another really important question to ask, and it had to do with John.

Once again, I put the cards on my bed. This time, I fanned them out and placed my hands about an inch above the cards, just as Annabelle had shown me. I closed my eyes and moved my hands over the cards, letting myself be drawn into them. The question sat on the end of my tongue. I couldn't say it out loud. I just couldn't. Suddenly, I heard a buzzing and my hand started to tremble. I opened my eyes and stared at a card in the middle of the pile that seemed to be moving, vibrating, pulsing.

"Am I supposed to tell John about his mother?" The question was almost sucked out of me.

I flipped over the card. Number 24. *Trust.*

That made no sense. My body stilled, and I stared at the pretty purple flower on the card. I had seen that flower today in Annabelle's store, on the bracelet. I had picked it up, played with it.

The flower started to spin!

And spin.

And the purple became white. My mind went blank. I saw John's mother's face, and she was talking to me, but I couldn't hear her; it was as if she had no voice.

I tuned my ears, wanting to hear her, but nothing. Then . . . like a stab from a knife, a pain hit my lower abdomen, and I doubled over. I gasped for air. It was excruciating. I breathed in and out, willing it to stop.

And just like that, my vision snapped, and I was back in my room with the *Trust* card staring me in the face.

What had just happened?

I snatched the book up and, my hands still trembling, tried to find the *Trust* page. All the words blurred on the page except "Your own intuition about other people and circumstances is symbolically as brilliant and clear as the center of this flower."

"That's not an answer," I whispered.

❖ ❖ ❖

The next morning when my alarm went off, I groaned. My sleep had been so deep and dreamless—or at least I'd had none that I could remember. Thankfully, Green Lady hadn't come to visit last night. I don't think I could have handled her.

At the store, I didn't tell Annabelle about practicing with the cards or what questions I had asked or about the horrible stomach pains I felt when I saw images of John's mother.

The day started off with the same routine of Annabelle taking clients. After her first client left, I noticed the bags under Annabelle's eyes and her pupils that looked so dull and lifeless.

"Are you feeling okay?" I asked.

She nodded. "I'm fine. Some friends came over last night, and I forgot to protect myself."

"Oh," I said. I had no idea what she was talking about, although yesterday she had mentioned something about protection.

She shook her head. "I need to practice what I preach." As if reading my thoughts, she pointed her finger at me. "If we have time today, I will teach *you* about protection. That might help me remember to do it myself." She pinched her cheeks. Then, gesturing with her hands as she spoke, she said, "This is what happens when you don't. You wake up looking like a piece of shit."

I laughed because sometimes she was just so animated when she spoke. "You look great," I said.

This time she pinched my cheek. "Thanks, sweetie." She jerked her head toward the back door. "I'm off to meditate. Knock first, okay?"

"For sure."

The morning cruised by as people came in and out of the store, some buying, some looking, some booking appointments with Annabelle. Most of the customers were pleasant, but I did notice that some of the people coming to see Annabelle acted nervous, like they were scared of what she might tell them.

Noon arrived quickly, and Annabelle said good-bye to her last client at the front door. As soon as the door closed, she turned, and I immediately noticed again how tired she looked. To perk her up a bit, I went under the counter and pulled out a pair of pink furry slippers.

"These are for you," I said, giggling. "For winter. They match your chairs."

She burst out laughing, and I mean laughing. She had to hold her stomach. "No way." She almost gurgled her words, she was laughing so hard. "Where on earth did you get those?"

The fact that I had made her happy warmed me up inside. "Zellers," I replied. "They're so fun." I put them on and pretended to do Michael Jackson's moonwalk across the floor.

This made Annabelle laugh even more hysterically. "You're a crazy girl."

I was still sliding when the bell rang and the door opened and a man walked in.

Annabelle suddenly stopped laughing. A weird energy hovered through the entire store, making me shiver.

"Gary," said Annabelle with a real bite to her words. "What are *you* doing here?"

He furrowed his eyebrows. "I need to talk to you."

"No." She adamantly shook her head.

"As usual," he said, "you're messing me up."

"Me? Messing you up? Give me a break," Annabelle shot back.

I lowered my head and tried not to listen, but, of course, I heard every word.

I guess Annabelle must have noticed my discomfort, because she said, "Indie, I'm sorry. This is Gary. And, Gary, this is Indie. She is my new employee."

I lifted my head, and instead of stepping forward, I gave a little wave. "Nice to meet you," I said.

"Hi," he replied. He turned right back to Annabelle. "Why not?" He spoke softly. He stepped toward her and tried to stroke her cheek, but she backed away.

"You know why."

He looked at me. "See how *nice* I am to her?"

With that he left. Annabelle's shoulders sagged and she ran her hand through her hair before she said, "Sorry about that."

"No big deal," I said. I walked over to her and put my hand on her arm. "You want me to get us some lunch?"

When she put her hand on top of mine, I had to admit it stunned me. Her touch seemed to penetrate my skin and dive into my body, filling me with both pleasure and an immense sadness. Why the sadness? What was wrong?

And just like that, my mind went blank and I saw white, like a blank piece of paper, and I held my breath hoping it would go away before she noticed. And it did, but not before I saw a ribbon of blood flowing through a beautiful aqua-colored river.

She patted my hand, and I returned to the store. "Indie, I'll be fine," she whispered. "We've met each other for a reason that will benefit *both* of us."

Chapter Nine

The days working at Annabelle's store flew by, and when Thursday night rolled around, I could hardly believe it was almost the end of the week. My job was Monday to Friday because Annabelle didn't take clients on Saturday and she usually had a friend work for her, someone who had been with her for years, since the day she had opened the store.

I had hardly seen Sarah and Natalie all week, because both of them had worked a lot of evening shifts, and . . . I had the feeling they were avoiding the apartment. Now we were all in the kitchen, listening to music and chatting, but Natalie seemed unusually quiet.

"So, girls," said Sarah, "should we hit the Royal Oak? Thursday is the best night there for sure."

"I'm in," I said. "But first I want us to do something." I eyed Natalie.

"I ain't cooking," said Sarah.

"It has to do with Green Lady," I said.

Natalie wrapped her arms around her body and slouched in her chair. "She was in my room again last night." She lowered her head and tucked her hair behind her ear, and I could see the tears rolling down her face. "I don't know how much more I can handle," she whispered.

"Are you okay?" Sarah asked her quietly.

Natalie hugged her body harder and shook her head.

"I haven't seen her much." Sarah touched Natalie's arm. "But I haven't been around, and she doesn't seem to be in Tyler's apartment. Sometimes I hear a slam, but down there I feel safe because I'm with Tyler. Obviously she's been tormenting you."

Natalie looked up, and around her eyes was streaking black mascara. "This morning, honestly, she wailed and wailed. It was awful." Natalie wiped her eyes.

"She's grieving," I said. I still hadn't told them the full story of Mrs. Schmidt. I had been waiting for the right moment, when we were all together. "She lost a child, and she never recovered from the loss, from what I can gather from George. For all we know, she thinks he's still in the house."

I paused before I said, "The child's name was Henry."

"Henry!" exclaimed Sarah. "You've got to be joking. That is just too bizarre. Do you think he came back as a cat?"

"I doubt it."

"What a sad story," moaned Natalie. "But . . . how long will the woman live *here*? Will she ever leave? 'Cause if she won't, then I have to. I can't stand her crying."

I put my hand on Natalie's shoulder. "Before you make any big decisions, let's try something. My boss showed me things to do that can protect us from the woman."

"What kind of things?" Natalie asked.

I snatched my purse from the floor and pulled out an Annabelle's Angels bag and dumped the contents on the kitchen table.

"First we take this rose quartz." I picked up a pink stone. "And we put it in the four corners of the apartment. But since I only have four, let's put these in the living room. It will keep her out of there."

"I want her out of my room, too," whispered Natalie.

"This is just the beginning," I said. I picked up the four rose quartz stones that Annabelle had given me. "Let's do this first. If it works, I will get you four for your room."

We all walked into the living room, and the girls watched as I placed a stone in each corner.

"You honestly think that is going to help?" Sarah curled her lip upward.

"It's worth a try," I replied. "Okay, now for the little hematite stone."

I had memorized the stones at the store and was actually surprised that I could remember their names. I used to suck at memorizing stuff in high school, especially biology. And this was kind of the same thing. We walked back to the kitchen, and I picked up a silver-gray stone that was smooth and oval. "She said to put this one under the doormat or above the door."

We traipsed to the front entrance and all stood there, looking at the door. I pointed upward. "I guess we could set it on top of the door frame. It should stay put."

"I'll get a chair," said Natalie.

She was back in a flash. I stood on the chair and placed the hematite stone in the middle of the door frame.

Once I jumped down, Sarah asked, "So what's with the other stuff?"

I led us back to the kitchen and picked up the white Buffalo sage that Annabelle had given me and a half conch shell that must have come from some ocean somewhere. I would like to think Hawaii. "We have to light this in this little half shell," I said.

Then I pointed to an eagle feather. "Once this sage smokes, then we wave it clockwise around each door frame with the feather."

"Okay," said Sarah, not sounding convinced. "This is kind of weird. But, hell, I guess it's worth a try." She picked up the feather and brushed it over her fingers. "Nice feather, by the way."

"I want to do this," said Natalie. "If it makes *her* go away. Although I have to say, I feel kind of sorry for her if her baby died in this place."

"Annabelle told me it would be better for her if she moved on," I said. "We're doing her a favor." I broke off a chunk of the sage, which was just a funny-looking piece of plant, just like Annabelle had shown me, and I put it in the little half shell. Sarah handed me a lighter, and I lit the sage. The smoke swirled upward and had a very distinct smell.

"It smells like pot!" Sarah laughed.

Natalie's nose twitched as she sniffed the air. "It does!" She burst out laughing, too. "We're a bunch of crazies, believing this is going to stop our apartment from being haunted. This is like something out of a horror movie."

"Let's do the front door first," I said.

We gathered at the front entrance to our apartment, and as I went around the door frame, Sarah waved the smoke. It was black, and it kinked around and around.

"Annabelle told me to watch the color of the smoke," I said as I went around the door frame a second time.

Sarah kept waving the feather. "Okay, this is stupid," she said.

"If it is black and kinked, then it is not clear," I said, "and we have to keep doing every door until the smoke is white and goes straight upward."

But Sarah shook her head. "Like I believe that."

"I'm game to see," said Natalie.

I was, too. Annabelle had told me it worked, and I wanted to see for myself. And sure enough, after two times around the door, the smoke turned white and went straight upward.

"Lard Jesus," said Natalie. "That's amazing."

We all giggled and went down the hall to the next door. Within ten minutes, we had completed every door in the apartment.

After we were finished and I blew out the sage, I remembered something else that Annabelle had told me to do, even though I had laughed at her as she said it. "We have to go back to the living room," I said.

"We're not done yet?" Sarah groaned.

"I'm supposed to recite something to some angel, and we have to do this breathing thing. I laughed at her when she told me about it, but then she said it was 'no laughing matter.' So let's keep her happy."

"Okay, but this is it for me," said Sarah.

"I think we should open a window," said Natalie. "It reeks in here."

I pulled on their arms and dragged them into the living room. We all stood in the center, and I pulled out the piece of paper that Annabelle had given me.

"Okay, so let's breathe."

We all inhaled and exhaled three times.

Then I started to recite the words. "Archangel Michael, please remove any energies from our home that have not gone to the light and please help them find their way home. I ask you to now seal the four corners of our house with your protective energy.

"I like that," said Natalie softly. "I want her to find her way home to her little boy."

"Everyone in the building is going to think we were smoking pot," said Sarah. "And that we're nuts. And I sure hope she doesn't stay because she thinks Henry the cat is her kid. And who is this Michael?"

I shrugged. "I'm not sure. But there are a few archangels, and he is a protector. I think Annabelle said he is blue."

"Yeah, okay." Sarah rolled her eyes.

Once every window in the house was open, Sarah looked at both Natalie and me and said, "Let's get the hell out of here."

I nodded and grabbed my purse, and as I did, I heard a faint whooshing sound. I turned sharply to see the bottom of the green skirt leaving through the open window. Brilliant sunshine blinded me for a moment. Gone. She was gone. We'd driven her away and, with luck, into the light. I hoped she'd have the courage to see that light and walk through it, so she could be reunited with her family.

✤ ✤ ✤

As usual, the Royal Oak was packed. We looked around for a seat, but when we couldn't find one, we headed outside to the patio, as it was a beautiful, warm summer night. Natalie spotted an open railing, and we headed over to it. Sarah casually leaned against the railing and lit up a cigarette. I inhaled the smell and looked away; I wouldn't give in, although I wanted to. I shoved my hands into the back pockets of my shorts and kept them there until our first beer arrived.

I had finished half my beer when I knew it was time to brave the crowds and hit the bathroom. Fifteen minutes later (the line had been out the door), I was walking back to the patio to find Sarah and Natalie when I heard my name being called. Turning around, I saw Paul. Immediately, I smiled and waved.

"Hey," I said surprised, but pleasantly so.

He grinned. "Close watering hole for you."

Within walking distance," I answered.

"Who you here with?" Paul asked.

"A couple of friends. Hey, how did the rest of your week go?" He hadn't come by to see me at work, and I thought maybe he didn't want to see me again.

"Great," he said. "It's a job. Keeps me in spending money." He held up his beer.

I laughed. "A definite summer priority."

"Do you need one?" he asked, looking at my empty hands. I had finished mine while waiting in line.

"It's okay," I said. "I'll get one in a minute."

"No, I'll get you one." Before I could protest again, he had flagged a waiter and ordered me a beer.

"Thanks," I said, kind of shyly. "I owe you. You've bought me tea and now beer."

This time it was his turn to be shy. "No biggie." He rocked a little on his heels. "I, um, I stopped by your store today to see if you wanted to do coffee again. But it was just after four, so I guess you must have already left." He said his words in a hurry.

So he *had* stopped by. For some reason, that thought made my heart flutter. There were no electrical feelings that jolted through my body, like when I was with John. Instead I had light, butterflylike feelings. And they felt good. Really good. Easy.

"I did leave a bit early today," I said. "Annabelle said I could lock up fifteen minutes before closing."

The waiter arrived with my beer, and Paul immediately pulled his hand out of his pocket, bringing a $20 bill along with it. He gave the waiter a tip and shoved the rest of the money back into his pocket. I took the cold beer and had a little sip. "Thanks," I said.

There was a split second of silence, but then Paul asked, "So, how was your first week?" Before I could even answer that question, he asked another: "Is it a busy place to work?"

I nodded my head slowly. "Yeah, it is busy. I'm kind of surprised. But my week was great. I work tomorrow, then get the weekend off." Just thinking about my first four days and all that Annabelle had taught me in such a short time made my head spin. It was unbelievable, really.

"Hey, I wanted to ask you," he said. "What's the deal with your boss? How does she see into the future? That just seems so crazy."

For a brief second, I thought about lying to him and telling him I had no idea, but I remembered what had happened with John when I lied to him about my ability to see and hear things before they happened. I was tired of all my little white lies. And . . . Paul seemed so different and nonjudgmental—unlike John, who judged everyone and everything in the world. I just knew Paul was safe.

"Well," I started, "Annabelle holds on to a person's hand or takes some piece of their jewelry and then she closes her eyes, and she can hear and see things about the person. And she feels things, too. Or even smells. She's amazing, because she uses all her senses. And sometimes at the end of a session, she reads these oracle or tarot cards because they might help to answer a specific question the person has about some issue."

"Seriously?" Paul tilted his head in an innocent gesture. "She can do that? It sounds so . . . abstract, but—don't get me wrong—it also sounds kind of cool in a really freaky way."

I laughed. "I like that word. Abstract."

"How long does it take?"

"She books people for an hour, but she runs late all the time."

"So," Paul mused, "for example, if someone had applied for a new job and they went in to see her, she might be able to tell them if they were going to get it?"

I shrugged. "I guess so."

Suddenly, I heard the word *Starbucks* in my head.

"Did you just apply for a job at Starbucks?" I asked.

Paul's eyes opened to the size of baseballs. "You can do it, too?"

I blurted out, "In two weeks, I'll come in and buy a coffee from you." I laughed nervously. And took a long swig of beer.

Paul didn't seem to notice my nerves at all. "That's amazing!" He held up his hand, and I high-fived him back. "I need another job to help pay for school and put money in the bank."

I wanted to tell Paul not to tell anyone, but I didn't. And I was saved from any more questions from Paul when Sarah appeared with Tyler on her arm.

"What's shaking?" Sarah asked.

"Paul," I said, "this is Sarah and Tyler. Sarah's my roommate, and Tyler lives below us."

"Hi," said Paul. He gave a one-finger salute.

"Where's Natalie?" I looked around the patio.

"She went home," said Sarah. "She wasn't feeling well. I don't think she has slept all week."

"Oh, that's too bad," I said. I turned to Paul. "Natalie is our other roommate."

"And the ghost in our house is driving her nuts," said Sarah. Then she held up her glass. "But no more, 'cause Indie's got our backs."

I held up my hand. "Okay, enough."

"You have a ghost in your apartment?" Paul looked as shocked as he sounded.

"Well, we did. She might be gone now, though," said Sarah.

"I hope so," I said quietly.

"I thought you guys were smoking pot up there," said Tyler. "The smell was all the way down the stairwell."

I glanced at Paul. He had a curious look on his face. I bumped my shoulder against his. "I'll tell you all about it later."

The conversation, thankfully, veered to music and the upcoming local music festivals. We all decided the blues festival would be the best one to attend. Time ticked by as we sipped our beers. Paul's friends stopped by to chat but then disappeared again, making the rounds, trying to find cute girls. Darkness arrived, patio lights flickered, and Sarah laid her head on Tyler's shoulder and gazed up at him. "You want to get out of here?" she murmured. "I got to work in the morning."

He gazed back at her and kissed her forehead. "Love to," he whispered.

Feeling slightly uncomfortable at their obvious intimacy, I glanced away at the same time Paul did, and we ended up locking eyes, which was kind of funny, because I knew he was thinking the same thing I was. *Too. Much. PDA.*

"See yah later, Indie," murmured Sarah. "We're heading out."

And just like that, I was alone with Paul at the bar because all my roommates had ditched me. "I should go, too," I said. "I work at nine." I didn't really want to walk home alone, even though it wasn't midnight yet.

"Yeah, me too," said Paul. "I gotta work at seven."

"Where are your friends?" I glanced around the patio, which had filled up, but I couldn't see them anywhere.

Paul scanned the patio, too. "I wonder if they left." He craned his neck to look around the bodies. When he didn't see them, he said, "Darn it. I didn't drive."

"Did they ditch you?" I laughed.

"Possibly." He shrugged.

"How will you get home?"

"Buses are still running. You want me to walk you home? I don't think you should walk by yourself. I can catch the bus in front of your apartment. I remember seeing the stop there when I dropped you off."

I wanted to say no, I could walk on my own, but something pricked me inside me. All week, Annabelle had been teaching me about intuition, and she said that if everyone would listen to what their bodies were saying, the funny little twinges that appeared in certain situations, they would be a lot better off. Right now, the sickness I felt in the pit of my stomach was exactly how I had felt when Miles came into the room at the hotel. And it wasn't good.

"Sure," I said quickly. "You can walk me home."

As we took to the street, the fresh night air had a slight breeze, and it brushed across my skin, cooling and mellowing me. Bars and crowds often made me hyper. I liked the pleasant summer night. The humidity had disappeared with the last rainfall, and the weather was soothing. Neither of us talked as we strolled down the sidewalk. My high heels clicked on the cement and his flip-flops made squishing noises.

Finally, he said, "That bar was fun. I've never been there before."

"Yeah," I replied. "I like it there."

"Do you really have a ghost in your apartment?" he blurted out.

"Yup," I said without hesitation, which actually surprised me. Why could I talk so easily with this guy? "She wears a green skirt, so we call her Green Lady."

"That's nuts."

"I'm not the only one who has seen her. Both Natalie and Sarah have as well. But today, we did some protection work around the apartment. Hopefully, that will make her go away."

"Is she that mean, that you have to be protected?" Paul glanced at me, and I immediately noticed the innocent expression on his face. He probably had never heard of a place being haunted before, except in a movie or television show. Nor had he heard about protection. Of course, neither had I before I started at Annabelle's Angels.

"She's not really mean," I said. "But she doesn't like us there." I proceeded to tell him the history behind the woman, and he nodded but didn't say anything.

When I was finished, we walked a few strides before he said, "It's kind of too bad she was trapped here on earth."

"You believe me, then?"

"Yeah, I do."

Suddenly, he reached over and grabbed my hand. "Keep walking and talking," he whispered firmly.

My heart began to race when I saw two guys loitering on the other side of the street. As soon as they saw us, they began walking toward us. I heard one guy mutter under his breath, "Easy prey." They crossed the street on an angle, obviously trying to cut us off, and we just continued walking. Beside me, Paul appeared cool and casual, although I knew he was anything but by how tightly he gripped my hand. But he didn't pick up his pace, and he continued walking as if nothing were wrong.

My muscles tensed, and the sounds of my high heels seemed louder and louder. *Click. Click.* The noise tapped inside my head. This was the danger I had felt in the bar. If I had been by myself, who knew what would have happened? I definitely wouldn't have been walking this calmly. By now, I would have been running like an idiot down the street.

The guys appeared in front of us, and Paul squeezed my hand as if to say everything would be okay. I squeezed back, letting him know I understood.

"You got a smoke?" said one of them. His eyes were red and had that bloodshot, high look. He wore a baseball cap backward, a sweat-stained white muscle shirt, baggy jeans, and high-top runners.

"Sorry," Paul said confidently.

We didn't break stride, and they fell into step beside us. Suddenly, the other guy, who was dressed quite similarly to his friend but wore an oversize Los Angeles Lakers mesh jersey, jumped in front of us and skipped backward in front of me. He sneered and looked me up and down. "How about you? I bet you got a smoke."

"She doesn't smoke," snapped Paul.

"I just quit a few weeks ago," I added.

Again, Paul squeezed my hand. I felt a certain reassurance in his gesture, which was a bit of a shock, because we were no match for these two.

"I said I want a smoke," Lakers hissed in my ear.

"Sorry, pal." Paul didn't give me time to answer. "She said she doesn't have one." He spoke loudly.

"You being a smart-ass?" Muscle Shirt grabbed Paul's shoulder, just as Lakers tried to snatch my purse. I held on to it and screamed.

As quick as lightning, Paul dropped my hand and chopped Muscle Shirt's arm. Then Paul spun and high-kicked Lakers. Lakers gasped for breath, holding his stomach.

"You asked for it now!" Muscle Shirt had regained his footing. He lifted his fist for a punch. But Paul was much quicker— he grabbed his arm and flung him over and onto his back. He landed with a thud.

Everything happened so fast.

And I just stood there, stunned and holding on to my purse. While both muggers were reeling, Paul grabbed my hand and said, "Run!"

We took off down the street. I didn't look back. I just ran, holding his hand. We ran at least two blocks before I started to slow down, my lungs bursting, my feet aching in my high heels.

Gasping, I said, "I need to stop."

Paul also slowed down and glanced behind him, but he didn't loosen the tight grip he had on my hand. "We're okay." His breath came out in rasps, too. "We lost them."

Our pace slowed to a walk. I listened for sounds. No footsteps followed us. Insects once again could be heard buzzing in the night air.

"What was that?" I asked. "Where did you learn to kick like that?"

"I guess I know how to protect myself, but in a different way."

I stopped walking. "You guess?!" I held my free hand to my chest to feel my beating heart. "That was insane." My heart started to slow, and that's when I felt the pain in my feet. I grimaced. "I *have* to take off my shoes."

"Okay." He let go of my hand and once again looked over his shoulder. "They're definitely gone," he said. He ran his hand through his sweaty hair and exhaled.

I bent over and unstrapped the clasps on my shoes and, when I had them off, heaved a sigh of relief. I still couldn't believe what had just happened. "I've never run like that in heels," I said.

"Me either," he replied. "Heels are a killer."

With my shoes dangling in my fingers, I looked at him, and even though we had just been through a frightening experience, I started laughing. "You were like a ninja back there."

"Yeah." He shrugged. "What can I say? I grew up watching *Teenage Mutant Ninja Turtles.*"

I laughed even harder. "So that's where you learned to kick like that." I shook my head at him.

"Are you really going to walk in bare feet?"

"Yup," I said. I started walking, and he fell into pace beside me. "You wanna wear heels, you learn to walk barefoot." I glanced at him out of the corner of my eye. "So . . . you never answered me. Where did you learn to kick like that?"

"I have a brown belt in karate," he said. "My mother thought I was too skinny for my own good, so she made me take karate. I happened to like it, and I was good at it."

I playfully nudged him with my shoulder. "You're just being modest. You could have taken on a whole group of those guys."

He laughed. "Nope. We would have gotten creamed. Two was enough for me." He paused for a moment. "That's the first time I've ever used my karate on anyone. Well, except in class. I have to say, I still feel a bit lightheaded. I guess my mom was right." He rubbed shoulders with me. "Little did she know I'd actually protect a girl, too. I can't wait to tell her."

This time, I took *his* hand. By now, we were almost at my apartment. I slowed my steps, liking the feel of his hand in mine. I had to work in the morning, but I didn't want the night to end. I really liked being with Paul. He was full of surprises.

We stopped in front of my apartment, right by the bus stop. I'd only ever had one boyfriend in my life, and I wasn't the type to go around having casual flings, so I was totally unsure about what to do next. Did I ask him to come upstairs? Did he need a drink of water after all that running? I was parched. But . . . would that be too forward? Would he want more from me?

Words sat on the tip of my tongue, but nothing came out. I was saved from speaking when he suddenly ran toward a garden that was in the yard beside our apartment.

"Paul! What are you doing?" I laughed.

He quickly picked a daisy, then ran back to me. "Here," he said. "For you."

"How did you know daisies are my favorite flower?" I took that daisy from him and put it to my cheek and smiled.

He shrugged and grinned. "I didn't. It was the first flower I saw."

He stepped toward me, and I didn't move away. We stood not even a foot apart. In the distance, I heard a bus barreling down the street, the rumbling loud in the quiet night air.

"There's my bus," said Paul, sounding a bit relieved.

He started fishing around in his pockets for some change.

When he was unsuccessful, I quickly pulled my wallet out of my purse. "I have some," I said. I handed him the coins he needed.

"Thanks." He kissed the coins. "If they had taken your purse, I wouldn't have bus fare."

Again, I laughed. His lighthearted attitude was like a cool glass of water, totally refreshing. As we waited for the bus to come to a full stop, he ever so gently pulled one tiny wisp of hair off my face. How he saw the little piece of hair shocked me. The touch from his fingers felt like comfortable worn leather on my skin.

"Can I pay you back for the bus fare with a coffee tomorrow?" he asked.

"I'd like that," I replied.

"We can go to Starbucks." His face lit up into a smile. "My soon-to-be new place of employment, according to you." He touched my nose. Then he took the daisy and put it behind my ear. "It suits you," he said. "Always sunny and bright."

I laughed and playfully punched his chest. He grabbed my hand and held it in his.

His face was close to mine, and I wanted him to kiss me, I really did.

The bus lurched to a stop in front of us, the doors blasted open, and he gestured to my apartment. "You better go inside."

Without another word, Paul climbed the stairs, and the bus doors clapped shut. From the other side of the doors, I saw him point at my apartment, telling me to get inside.

Of course, I didn't listen to him. Instead, I stood on the street and watched the red taillights of the bus get smaller and smaller. And the entire time I stood there, with the daisy still tucked behind my ear, I touched my face at exactly the spot where he had moved that one little strand of hair.

Chapter Ten

"So . . . what's up with you and Paul?" Sarah popped a piece of popcorn into her mouth. Jewel played on our stereo.

"What do you mean?" I asked nonchalantly, taking a handful of popcorn just to seem at ease. What *was* going on between Paul and me? Even I wasn't sure. One thing I knew for certain, he was fun to be with. Even heavy conversations were light. And . . . there was the fact he had a brown belt in karate.

"You spent the entire *weekend* with him," whispered Sarah. "That's what's up. And he's still here." She pointed down the hall to the washroom.

"We're friends," I whispered back. "He never stayed overnight. And he's leaving in, like, five minutes."

"He's a really nice guy," Natalie piped in. "I like him. I'd like a boyfriend like him. I still can't believe he kicked those thugs."

"He's not my boyfriend," I stated, maybe a little too adamantly.

"Indie needs a nice guy after John." Sarah curled her lip and made a snarky face. "That guy was sooo controlling." She looked at me. "Paul is good for you, Indie. Why are you holding back? And I can tell you are. I bet he hasn't even kissed you yet."

Just then, Paul walked into the living room. I jumped up. I so hoped our conversation had been drowned out by the loud music.

"I'm gonna head out," he said.

"I'll walk you downstairs," I replied.

When we hit the street, the sun was just setting, so a beautiful lavender hue tinted the horizon. We leaned against Mable, and our shoulders touched. Paul took my hand in his.

"I had a great weekend."

"Me too." I let him hold my hand.

"You're really fun to be with."

"You too." I sounded like a chirping parrot.

He squeezed my hand, then dropped it. I could tell he wanted to kiss me, just like on Friday night, but he jingled his car keys instead.

"I guess I should go," he said.

I lowered my head and let my hair hang in front of my face. I felt a hand on the side of my face, pushing my hair behind my ear. Paul leaned over and kissed me on the cheek. "I can wait," he whispered. "See you next week."

✤ ✤ ✤

When I walked back into the apartment, Sarah said, "So?"

"So. What?"

"Did you let him kiss you?"

"It's none of your business," Natalie chided Sarah. "Leave her alone."

"Why are you holding back?" Sarah moaned.

"I'm not holding back," I replied. "I'm just . . . taking my time. I like our friendship. What's wrong with that?"

Sarah rolled her eyes and threw a piece of popcorn in the air, catching it in her mouth. Sunday evenings we often spent hanging out, just the three of us, with popcorn and diet soda. It was a time when we could catch up on the week. I flopped on the sofa.

"Indie," said Sarah. She was obviously not going to let up on the Paul conversation. "I've seen you with guy friends. You've had tons. I know how you act around all the guys who are your friends. And that is not how you are acting with Paul. I still don't understand how you just caved with John but you're holding back with Paul."

I looked away. "John wasn't that bad," I said. Why was I defending him? Something bristled inside me when Sarah talked badly about him. His dysfunctional home life played a part in his mood swings, of that I was certain. Sarah was right; I hadn't held back with John.

And no, Paul and I hadn't kissed yet, but maybe we never would.

"I've never met John, so I can't comment." Natalie picked up her guitar and strummed a few chords. "But from the sound of it, I don't think I want to." Suddenly Natalie put her guitar down. "I'm gonna change topics." She held up her glass. "Let's have a good ole Newfoundland toast. Green Lady is gone!"

We clinked our glasses.

"To Green Lady's disappearance into thin air. Like, *literally* into thin air," said Sarah. "May she have a wonderful time in heaven." Sarah grinned at me. "That is where she will go, isn't it, Indie?"

"I hope so." I tried to smile.

"I haven't seen her all weekend," said Sarah.

"Or heard her crying," said Natalie. "I think she really is gone. I hope she is with her family. That's where she should be."

"Your boss is one smart lady," said Sarah.

"Yeah," I said. "Annabelle is pretty incredible."

Natalie tilted her head and glanced at me. "What else has she been teaching you?"

All week I had been waiting for the moment when I could pull out my cards and practice my readings with Sarah and Natalie. Annabelle had told me that once I felt confident in my own readings, to try practicing on friends. Feeling shy about it all, I had been waiting for the exact right moment. I jumped up. "I'll be right back."

I ran to my room, grabbed my cards and books, and sped back to the living room. I hurried so I wouldn't lose my nerve.

"Annabelle gave me these, and I'm supposed to practice on people. Read for them."

Sarah held up her hand. "Read for them? Read what?"

I shrugged. "I dunno, really. Read their future. See things that might happen for them."

Natalie clapped. "Ohhhh. That sounds fun."

"You can go first," said Sarah to Natalie.

I plunked down on the floor and sat cross-legged. Natalie sat in front of me.

First, I went through what Annabelle had taught me and made Natalie knock the cards. Then, I got her to shuffle them. She was a lot better at shuffling than I was. Once she was finished, I said, "Okay, you will pull three cards. The first will be your past, the second the present, and the third your future."

I fanned the cards out and told her to try and feel for sensations. Natalie closed her eyes, and ran her hand over the cards. Suddenly, she squealed. "This one is hot!"

"Pick it," I said.

After she had picked three, she flipped them all over.

"Okay," I began, "your first card is *Forgiveness,* and this is your past."

I knew Sarah was staring at me. And Natalie was waiting for me to say something. I glanced down at the card, at the pretty flower on the front. Suddenly, my body stilled and the flower seemed to flutter in a light breeze. I saw a mother and child. The mother was hanging laundry on a clothesline, and the child ran underneath the sheets holding the exact flower that was on the card. The child was happy until the mother just vanished.

I blew out a rush of air.

"What is it?" Natalie asked.

I looked up and into her eyes. "You have to forgive your mother," I said quietly. "You've never talked about her, but you have to forgive her for leaving."

Silence blanketed us for a few moments.

Finally Natalie whispered, "You can see my mother?"

"I just saw a mother with a child. And then she vanished." I looked up. "Did she leave when you were little?"

Natalie nodded. "When I was five. I've never seen her since. She lives somewhere in Ottawa." Natalie paused. "That's . . .

that's why I came here. To find her." Tears welled in Natalie's eyes. "When I got an apartment and a job right away, I knew it was meant to be."

Sarah put her arm around Natalie. "You never told us any of this."

Natalie swiped at her tears. "I haven't told anyone. Not even my grandmother. She raised me after my mother left. I don't know what I would do without her."

"Your grandma knows why you're here," I said.

Natalie pointed to the second card. "This is my present card, right?"

I glanced down at the second card she'd picked. *Truth.*

"Does this mean my mom will tell me the truth?" Natalie asked.

I looked at the card for a second, hoping for a *yes* to sound in my mind, but nothing came. I inhaled, because Annabelle had told me that breathing was freeing and allowed the senses to be alerted. On my third inhale, I heard the word *no.*

I almost gasped out loud. How was I going to tell Natalie that I didn't think her mother was going to come clean?

I reached for the book. "Sometimes the book can help," I said. As I flipped to the right page I said, "I don't think this card is about your mother, but more about you."

As soon as I looked at the page, one sentence just jumped out at me. I read out loud, "This is a powerful card of healing, and you have drawn it because you are seeking to understand the significance of your present challenges and to clearly determine the course of action that will best support all aspects of your well-being."

I took Natalie's hand in mine. "If your mom doesn't tell the truth, or the meeting with her isn't good, it's not your fault. You are to forgive her and walk away from her." I paused. "Natalie," I said, "I don't know if this reunion is going to be what you want it to be. She might still be really messed up." I looked at Natalie. "Did you set the meeting up with her already?"

Natalie lowered her head and nodded. "When I arrived in Ottawa, I did some searching. I went through about 20 phone numbers before she answered. But when she did and I heard her voice, I thought that was a sign that we were meant to meet. She said she would like to see me."

"Did she sound messed up?"

"Not too bad. I mean, I'm not totally in the dark. My grandmother told me she left me because she was an addict. Heroin, I think. But . . . on the phone she said she stopped. We're supposed to meet next week."

I put my hand on top of hers. "Natalie, don't be disappointed if it doesn't work out how you planned."

"Okay." Her voice sounded small.

I picked up the last card. *Self-Worth*. I heard music playing in my head, and I closed my eyes. It wasn't Jewel, like we had playing in the background. This was Celtic music. I opened my eyes and put my hand on her hand. "You are going to do something wonderful with your music."

Natalie shook her head. "I'm going into engineering at Queen's next year."

"Yes," I said. "But all this pain you feel right now will be used to write songs. You will sing in coffeehouses while you're at school."

"Wow," said Natalie. She sighed. "This is so freaky."

Suddenly, a wave of reality washed over me, and I realized that while I was reading the cards, I had been somewhere far away. And now . . . I was back in my living room, in my apartment. And I was just Indigo Russell. I gathered the cards up and started to put them back in the box, when Natalie touched my arm.

"Thank you," she said. "You have no idea how you have helped me."

"We'll be here for you, Natalie," said Sarah.

"I know. I love you guys. You've made my move to Ottawa."

We had a group hug, and when we pulled apart, Natalie shook her finger at Sarah. "Your turn now."

"Do you need a break, Indie?" Sarah paused for a moment, wringing her hands together. "I have to admit, I'm a little scared of what you might find out about me." She laughed nervously.

The laugh sounded so familiar. So many people had the same jitters when they came to see Annabelle.

"Aren't yah interested to know about you and Tyler?" Natalie urged.

"No!" Sarah shot back. "Why jinx it? If I would ask anything, I would ask about what the hell is going to happen to me with my work. I am so sick of my job serving eggs and sausage. And I need something new and I have ideas, but they're so dumb and don't make much sense. I want to know what to do with my life."

"Knock the cards, then shuffle them," I said.

"You're on, girl."

I ate popcorn as I watched her shuffle. When she spilled the cards all over the floor, like I had the first time I'd shuffled them, Natalie and I laughed.

Sarah must have shuffled the cards for five minutes straight. Natalie and I kept looking at each other and rolling our eyes and shaking our heads.

I started off the same way as I had with Natalie, telling Sarah to pick three cards. "Now, if you want to ask a question, go ahead. I didn't do that with Natalie, but I can do that with you. Go ahead, Sarah."

"What kind of work am I supposed to go into?"

"Pick three cards," I said.

Sarah closed her eyes and in a matter of seconds, had picked three cards. I couldn't help but wonder if that would make a difference to the reading.

She flipped them over. The first card was *Awareness*. For some reason, a couple of nights ago, I had studied the book and loved this card. The photo was a close-up shot of the inside of a peach-colored flower. Little tentacles seemed to be fluttering out of the center. The inside of the flower was the focal point. It made me think that our insides were more important than our outsides, and I knew the card meant the person was longing for some kind of awakening that would assure her of her path. As I stared at the flower, particularly the heart of the flower, I saw the petals opening to allow the center to flourish.

I could hear Sarah and Natalie breathing beside me. I took a deep breath of my own and said, "All the stuff you show the world, all your toughness, is a mask. At your center, you have a huge heart."

"That doesn't mean anything," moaned Sarah. "You know me too well."

I held up my hand. "Let me finish." I closed my eyes and breathed in and out. "Your shell is going to crumble to let your heart out. You will use this to help people."

I opened my eyes and glanced down at the second card, because the first one was making me draw a blank. *Attention.*

I pointed to the second card. "This is a card about accepting your abilities and about release and freedom." I thought again how weird it was that I could remember what I read. If only I'd been able to do that in science class! I tapped the center of the card. "Once you open up your heart, you are going to figure out what you are supposed to do."

I saw a piece of paper floating across the cards. It made no sense, but I could hear Annabelle in my head, telling me to say what I saw and not to try and figure it out. "I'm seeing a piece of paper, and I don't know what it means, but it is important."

Sarah had a blank look on her face. Was I totally blowing this reading?

I considered the third card. *Power.* There were five petals on the card—fat, fuzzy petals that were green but rather dull. I couldn't figure out what kind of flower they came from, because they looked more like slices of sugared green gumdrops than petals. As I kept my gaze focused on them, they changed and became . . . fingers. The fingers moved in this undulating rhythm. Mesmerized, I didn't say anything until, without warning, I blurted out, "You are going to help people using your hands."

After my revelation, I shook my head. Why had I said that? It was such a broad, general statement. Again, I heard Annabelle's voice in my head. "Sometimes you have to put everything together."

But as hard as I tried, I couldn't put the last two cards together.

Are you going to give up?

I snatched the cards off the floor and started putting them away. I wanted to go to bed. Forget that I had tried to do this.

Sarah stopped my movement by touching me on the arm. Although I wanted to jerk my hand away, I didn't. Instead, I lowered my head and let my hair hang in front of my eyes. I didn't want the girls to see my reddened, embarrassed face. "I'm sorry," I said. "I didn't read you very well. I have no idea what the paper means."

"It's okay, Indie. You're just learning. It's your first week at this."

Natalie put her hand on my shoulder. "You got me perfectly," she chimed in.

Not everything comes true right away, Indie. Be patient. Isaiah spoke in a calm, clear voice.

I smiled at Sarah and Natalie. "Thanks for your vote of confidence."

❖ ❖ ❖

On Monday morning, I went to work deep in thought. The night before had been a bit of a bust. I had been right with Natalie but off with Sarah. When I walked into the store, Annabelle was wearing her fuzzy pink slippers. Immediately, my mood brightened.

"They look fabulous," I said.

She lifted her leg and pointed her toe. "I love them." When she put her foot down, she eyed me. "What's up?"

"Nothing," I said.

"Nothing is something." She sang her words.

"I read for my friends last night, and the last reading," I mumbled, "wasn't as clear as I thought it should be."

She patted my back. "What happened?"

I filled her in on both readings.

When I was finished, she said, "Indie, be patient. That last reading could still come true. Don't worry about it. I'm really happy you're trying. It takes time to learn how to focus completely. And . . . we are human. We do make some mistakes sometimes."

I glanced at her. "You do?"

She shrugged. "Sure. I just heard that a woman who I told would have a boy when she was pregnant had a girl."

"Doesn't that bother you?"

"Yeah. I get mad at God when he proves me to be human." She laughed. "But I knew she wanted a boy. She already had two girls. She wouldn't say it, but I knew it, so I kind of got sucked in and told her what she wanted to hear."

I shook my head. "But what I said was so general."

"Who knows when what you said will come true? Maybe it will be a week or a year or ten years. Let it go."

I nodded and exhaled. "Okay. This is harder than I thought."

"How do you like those cards?" She pushed a strand of my hair off my face, just like a mother would do.

"I like them."

She winked at me. "You learn on them, and you're as good as gold." She glanced at her watch. "I've got to go to the back. You know the drill."

"Annabelle," I said as she was leaving the room.

She turned to face me.

"Thanks."

"Come here, you. Give me a hug." Annabelle walked back to me with open arms, and I fell into them, resting my head on her shoulder. This woman was becoming someone I trusted and loved, and in this moment, I knew she felt exactly the same about me. I was so lucky to have met her.

It's called divine intervention, my dear.

❖ ❖ ❖

The week sped by, and I enjoyed my time at the store. It was fun, and I was learning something. But on Friday, I was anxious for four o'clock.

"What's up with you?" Annabelle asked when I started organizing my purse at five minutes before closing.

"I'm going out this weekend. Tonight and tomorrow night. There's a big party tomorrow night at the river. I can't wait. It will be the party of the summer."

She pointed her finger at me. "I have been meaning to talk to you about this for weeks now. You need to learn how to protect yourself. When you give readings, everything in your body opens, which makes you a sponge for spirits to penetrate. And believe me, you don't want that to happen. Also, when you are out with a lot of people, you will need the protection, because it can turn your mind so no visions come to you. You definitely do not want to give readings when you are partying."

I nodded, trying to absorb what she was saying.

"I know I gave you some ways to protect yourself but . . . I think I need to make it easier for you. Every day in the morning and then again before you go out, you should do these simple exercises. I tend to do my protection in the shower. I close my eyes and imagine myself being covered in white light. Then I ask out loud for protection. How you want to think of the white light is up to you. I think of a bubble surrounding me. But that's because I love my bubble baths."

"Okay," I said. "Thanks. I'll give that a try. Every day?"

"Yes, my dear. Every day."

"Okay."

"Good girl—oh, and watch combining readings with alcohol. You may think it numbs you and even protects you, but it has the opposite effect." She held up her hand. "I'm not saying don't drink, because I like a glass of wine now and again, but shut yourself off when you indulge. Don't allow visions or voices to come through. Just tell them to go away."

"I can do that?"

"Yes. And you should. If you're at a party and drinking and someone asks you to read for them, just say no. You're not working tonight."

"Okay," I replied. "That's good to know."

"People will think you know things about them *all* the time. And the fact is if you make a conscious effort to turn off, you won't get anything coming through."

We turned when the door tinkled. Paul stood there looking awkward, like a little boy who had interrupted something.

"Hi, Paul," said Annabelle.

"I'm almost done." I glanced at the clock. "Five minutes."

Annabelle gestured to the door. "Get your things and get out of here. And have a good weekend."

❖ ❖ ❖

As soon as Paul and I left, we drove to Britannia Beach, blasting tunes in Mable's stereo. I patted the dashboard. "I think she likes her name."

Paul laughed.

I rolled down the window, allowing the summer air to flow through Mable. "You going to the river party tomorrow night?" I asked him. "Everyone is going. We could go together."

He looked at me and grinned. "I have to work. At Starbucks!"

"Ha ha. You got the job. When did that happen?"

"They phoned today, and I have to go in for training tomorrow night. I think they're short staffed." He reached for my hand. "I can't believe you knew."

"Yeah, crazy, eh?" I shrugged.

"So . . . how does it happen? If you don't mind me asking."

"I don't mind," I said. I paused for a second to let the breeze flow through my hair. Instead of looking at him, I stared straight ahead out the window. "My mind goes blank, and I feel as if I'm looking through a telescope into a fishbowl, and inside the fishbowl is a picture." I couldn't believe I said that in one sentence. But it felt good, and I wasn't at all embarrassed.

"Is it like a movie? Or a photo?"

"Can be either. But usually like a movie."

"Did that happen when you saw me working at Starbucks?" He grinned. "Was I being a *cool* barista?"

I laughed. "For that one, I just heard a word. You said something to me, I can't remember what now, and I heard the word *Starbucks* in my head."

When we arrived at the beach, we immediately went to the water, and I waded while Paul dunked his entire body and tried to splash me.

After about ten minutes in the water, we hit the conces-
sion stand and ordered a soft-serve ice cream. As I observed the
girl behind the counter twirling the ice cream into the cone,
I almost laughed. Annabelle had said I should pick something
white to protect me. I was going to pick soft-serve ice cream.
What a pleasant thought.

Paul and I wandered over to a picnic table and sat down.
As we licked our ice creams, we talked about music and summer and new movies. We both agreed the summer's funniest
movie, *There's Something About Mary,* was hilarious, and nothing else out this year even compared.

"My favorite by far this summer," said Paul. "I saw it three
times in the theater."

"Three times?" I asked. "That's crazy."

"Yeah. I know. But I laughed every time. . . . We're kind of
like them." Paul finished the last bite of his cone.

"Like who?" I asked.

"You're like Cameron Diaz, and I'm like Ben Stiller. The
nerdy guy who wants the pretty girl."

"You're not the nerdy guy." I playfully slapped his chest.

He took my hand in his and kissed my knuckles. My body
stilled. Slowly, he put his fingers on my cheek. "Ice cream,"
he said.

I touched his cheek, too, even though it didn't have any
ice cream on it. "You too," I whispered. "Just a little right here."

"You are so beautiful," he whispered.

I leaned into his hand and looked into his clear, blue, hon-
est eyes. There was no darkness to them at all. It was different,
and a little scary. I guess I liked darkness and not knowing.

Then it happened.

In broad daylight.

Paul leaned forward and kissed me, right there in the park.

And I responded.

With his arms circling my shoulders and his lips pressed
against mine, I felt perfectly safe, like I'd been wrapped in a
soft-serve ice cream cone.

Part Two

Chapter Eleven

August 1998

"Indie, let's get a move on," Sarah yelled from the front door. "Tyler is ready to go."

"Coming," I yelled from my room as I hobbled around, trying to do up my sandal. They were cute wedge sandals with buckles that were hard to fasten. After I had the sandal on, I quickly glanced around. I was forgetting something. What was it? I wore jeans and a shirt and . . . oh, yeah. I should take a sweater or jacket. I snatched my jean jacket off the hanger. I was almost at the front door when I felt the niggling feeling again. I was forgetting something.

"In-die!" Sarah screamed from the bottom of the stairs.

With my purse slapping against my thigh, I ran down the stairs.

"Finally," Sarah huffed.

"Sorry." I slid into the back of Tyler's car and buckled my seat belt. "I just keep feeling like I'm forgetting something." I opened my purse and searched through it looking for the answer, but there wasn't one. I obviously hadn't forgotten any-thing. Again, the pinching feeling. I shook it off.

"Is Paul coming later?" Tyler glanced at me in his rearview mirror before he pulled away from the curb.

"Maybe. He has to stay until closing and do the crap jobs because he is training." Tyler and Paul had really hit it off. While we girls were playing music in the park last week-end, they tossed around a football. "So he won't be done until around 11:30. Said he might come and give me a ride home."

"He's got lots of time to show up and have fun," said Sarah. "Natalie is coming later, too, after she gets off from work. I bet this par-tee goes until the wee hours of the morning. I'm plan-ning to stay there until dawn. Everyone is going."

"Yeah, even Lacey called me today," I said. I hadn't seen Lacey since that night in the Royal Oak at the beginning of the summer. I couldn't wait to see her and catch up, and I wanted her to come to the store and meet Annabelle.

"What about Burke?" Sarah asked.

"I'm not sure."

Sarah turned around and stared at me from the front seat. "I heard John might be there."

"John?" My pulse quickened. "Where'd you hear that?"

"He came in the restaurant this morning. He was with a couple of his buddies, and, man, did they look rough."

"He doesn't drink much." I defended him.

"I didn't say they were hungover. It was soooo obvious that they were higher than kites. Probably hadn't been to bed all night."

I slouched in my seat and stared out the window. I hated hearing stuff like that about John. John. I hadn't talked to him in well over two months or seen him in almost three months. How would I react when I saw him again?

Last time he'd called, I'd just moved into the apartment and it was two days after the phone had been installed. I had picked it up and almost keeled over when I heard his voice.

❖ ❖ ❖

"Indie," he'd said softly.

"John! Where did you get this number?"

"Your dad."

Next, there were a few seconds of silence before he said, "I miss you."

"I miss you, too."

"Let's go to England. You and me. Just the two of us."

"John, why are you doing this? Why are you saying this to me? You know it will never come true."

"It could, Indie."

"No, it can't."

"Why not? We love each other. And miss each other. You just told me you missed me."

A snapshot of a castle appeared in my mind, and I blurted out, "Because . . . I'm going to travel somewhere. I've already made plans." But I hadn't. That was the first time I'd ever thought about going anywhere besides England. I didn't have enough money for a trip overseas; I could hardly pay my rent. How could I even say I was going to Scotland?

"Oh," he'd said. Hurt pinched his voice.

"I'm sorry, John."

"Yeah. Me too. Well, I got to go. Bye, Indie."

And he'd hung up.

❖ ❖ ❖

That was it. The last time we'd spoken. And now he was going to be at the party.

We stopped at the liquor store, and I stayed in the car and didn't buy anything, but Sarah and Tyler did. I decided that I didn't want to drink. We stopped at a small supermarket, and I went in and bought some hot dog buns, a package of wieners, and a bottle of soda.

When we got to the riverbank, cars were already parked and music could be heard from an open area that was just past the bushes and the trees. It was a good place for a party, because there were no neighbors to call the cops.

I got out of the car and immediately smelled the bonfire. I walked with Tyler and Sarah through the bushes to the stone riverbank, the crackling sound of fire getting louder and louder with each step. The first person I spotted when I reached the opening and the stone bed was Lacey. I smiled and waved.

"Indie!" She came toward me and we hugged. "I'm so glad you're here."

"Should be fun." I held up the plastic supermarket bag. "Hot dogs," I said.

"I've missed you. All those hot dogs over the years. Come on." She linked her arm through mine. "Let's join the fun." Arm in arm, we walked toward the party, which was at around 30 people so far, but it was only 10 P.M. By midnight, the area would be packed with upward of 100 kids.

"What are you drinking?" she asked.

"Nothing tonight. I might have to drive later."

"You turning over a new leaf?" Lacey hip-checked me.

"Um. Maybe." I proceeded to tell Lacey about Annabelle's Angels and how I was learning to work with cards.

"Indie," she exclaimed, "that is so exciting. Can you read my cards?"

"Sure. Come over some night. It would be fun."

"You've always had a gift, you know," she said softly. "I still feel awful about last year and how I treated you."

"Forget about it," I said. "And . . . it's not a gift. Annabelle has been teaching me that everyone is intuitive. She calls it 'ability.'"

"Uh-oh," said Lacey. "Don't look now, but there's John."

"Keep talking to me." My heart sped up. Lacey and I chatted about what we were doing with our summer, and I didn't look John's way. Finally, I said, "Where is he now?"

Lacey scanned the crowd, which was suddenly bigger. In a matter of minutes, carloads of kids had shown up. "Can't see him," she said.

I heaved a sigh of relief and also viewed the crowd. Amazing how it could grow so fast. I couldn't see John either.

Lacey and I continued talking for a little while about nothing really, just crazy stuff from years ago. Then she made a grimacing face. "Oh, no. He's on his way over here."

I exhaled and stood tall.

I heard his flip-flops smacking the stones before I heard his voice.

"Indie." He drawled out the word. My body reacted as it always did when I was near him: my heart raced uncontrollably, my palms got clammy, and electricity jolted through me.

I sucked in a deep breath and tried to meet his eyes, which were piercing me.

"Hi, John." The words barely escaped my mouth. I really did try to look up at him, return his gaze, but it was hard, so hard. He fixed his eyes on me, and I shivered and glanced away at the party and the people. How could he do this to me? Make me melt and cave and feel flustered.

"Indie. I haven't seen you all summer."

I tried to act casual and cool when I said, "Um, remember we talked on the phone in early July?"

"Oh, right. How's your summer been?" he said, ignoring my answer, as if I didn't even have an effect on him.

"Good. Yours?"

"Great," he said. "Trying to save enough to go to England at the end of the summer."

A pang of pain thwacked my chest. "Cool," I said.

I finally made eye contact. He stared at me. Deeply. Almost through me. Lacey coughed and turned her head slightly. His gaze reached far inside me, to the core of my heart, my soul. I couldn't look away, although I desperately wanted to. He slowly reached his hand over, stroked my hair, and murmured, "You still haven't lost your innocence."

And . . . just like that, I let my face fall into his hand, and I stilled beneath his touch, as if a comfort passed over me. We stood there for a few seconds before . . . he just walked away.

I exhaled and put my hand to my chest. My heart was beating uncontrollably.

"Why would he say that and just leave?" Lacey snarled.

My heart thudded. He *had* just walked away. And he hadn't acknowledged that we'd even talked last month. Why did I care about him when he cared so little about me?

Lacey put her hand on my shoulder. "Don't give that asshole another thought."

"I've been hanging out with this guy," I blurted out, my words just tumbling out of my mouth. "Paul. He's really nice. He might come later tonight." I looked at my watch. It was already after 11. Paul had said he would be at the party by 11:30.

"I'm happy for you, Indie," said Lacey. "I really am. You deserve the best." She put her hand on my shoulder. "Let's go stand by the bonfire. I could eat a hot dog."

"Yeah, me too. I'm starving." I wasn't, really, because my stomach felt a little sick, but it wouldn't hurt to cook one. It would give me something to do.

We headed over to the fire, and within minutes, we were circled by old high-school friends, acquaintances, and strangers. The conversation turned to summer plans, fall plans, music, and trivial stuff. Stars winked above, and the tepid night air circled me, giving me that lazy summer fun feeling that made life seem as if it stood still. The bonfire shot sparks into the sky, lighting it up, crackling the air—I loved the look and sounds of a fire, because every second was different. The crackles were like music, only without a steady beat, more random. It was all like magic to me. I put my plastic bag, with my soda bottle in it, on the ground and pulled out the hot dogs. Lacey and I giggled as we each found a stick and put our wieners on the fire to roast.

I pulled mine out of the fire when it was black and almost charred. Just how I liked it. I shoved it in a bun and dabbed ketchup on it.

As I munched on my hot dog, I laughed with Lacey and listened to the chatter around me. Everyone had a plan. Inside I smiled. That included even me, although I didn't talk about my plans to learn as much as I could from Annabelle so I could help people. Not yet. It was too early. Most people probably wouldn't understand.

The entire time I was talking and trying to keep up with the conversation and the laughter, I had the nagging feeling that I had felt at the house, that I had forgotten something. I had just finished my hot dog when it hit me. I hadn't protected myself like Annabelle had ordered me to do. Shit! That was important.

I wondered if I could still protect myself here. Find somewhere quiet. I wasn't drinking, so it might be okay. I had just started to walk away from the bonfire, trying to find a safe spot where I might be able to have a few seconds to myself, when I bumped into this guy from high school.

"Hey, Indie," he said. His glassy eyes had huge pupils. He was known to deal drugs, which was one of the reasons I probably didn't know him that well. I tried to steer away from the drug crowd. "How the hell are you?" he asked.

"Good."

"I see you're still as good-looking as ever. I bet you don't remember my name."

I actually didn't, and I had no idea what to say, so I started up some small conversation about high school and how I was lousy with memorizing anything. As we were talking, I felt weird. Like, really spacey and as if I was taking in something dark about this guy. I didn't want to be around him.

I excused myself and went right back to the fire and the crowd.

By now, the music was blaring and the crowd had multiplied, and for that I was glad, because I could hide and forget about the guy and his weird vibes. I scanned the crowd for Paul but didn't see him. I really wanted him there by my side. For a few minutes, I walked around the party looking for him, hoping to find him just arriving, coming through the bushes. I even asked a few people, but no one had seen him. Deep down, I knew he would look for me as soon as he arrived.

Finally, I went back to the fire and looked for my drink. I had written my name on it with a black marker. When I couldn't find it, I just assumed someone must have thrown it out. I took once last glance and that's when I saw it, but not in the place where I had left it. Lacey must have moved it. I filled my plastic cup with the soda and, as I sipped, I observed the actions of the party. Was I the only sober one?

I had slurped down half my drink before I started to feel kind of funny. I felt a hand on my arm.

"Indie," a voice whispered, "I need to talk to you. It's important."

"Okay," I replied.

It was the guy I had run into earlier. What could he need to talk to me about? "It's about John," he said.

"What about John?" I think my words came out slurred. What was wrong with me?

"It's important, okay? Just walk a few steps with me, and I'll tell you."

With his hand on my elbow, he guided me toward the bushes and a place that was quieter and less populated. I began stumbling as I walked, tripping over stones. My knees were weak, and my limbs seemed floppy and loose, like they were made of rubber. Something was wrong. I went to speak, but he clamped his hand on my mouth.

"She's gonna puke," he said to the few people we walked by. "I'm holding it in her until we get to the bushes."

I heard the laughter. I tried to jerk away, but he had my arm in a viselike grip. Anyway, I didn't have any strength in my body. My vision was blurry, and I just wanted to lie down and sleep.

With every step, we walked farther from the light and more into the dark. The light from the bonfire became part of the distance. And the noises from the party faded away. Everything I saw was double. I wanted to scream, but nothing would come out.

He kept leading me into the bushes. Farther and farther. My feet got heavier and heavier. Branches scratched my ankles and feet and arms. I tripped and fell a few times. He held me up by my armpits. My head swam, and I was so dizzy I wanted to curl up into a ball.

Fight, Indie, fight.

I tried to thrash, but I just felt as if I was falling down a big tunnel. My legs gave out, and I slid to the ground.

And that's when everything went black.

❖ ❖ ❖

"Indie!" I felt someone shaking me. The person screamed loudly, a shrill, haunting scream.

"Someone, help! Please, someone has to help us!"

I opened my eyes and saw Lacey; her pupils were huge, and the whites of her eyes shone in the dark. She looked panic-stricken. My throat was scratchy, my body ached, and something was really wrong. I reached down—my pants were by my knees, and Lacey was struggling to pull them up.

"What's happening?" I managed to croak out the words.

"We have to get you to the hospital." Lacey pushed hair off my face. "Indie, I'm so glad you're awake. I really am." Lacey started crying. "We've been so worried!"

The bushes rustled, and footsteps stomped through them, running. "What the hell happened?" Paul's voice.

Lacey quickly pulled on my jeans again. "I found her like this. We have to get her to the hospital."

"I've got my car." Paul rushed over to me. "Indie," he said softly, "I'm going to carry you to the car."

In one quick movement, he reached under my legs and lifted me up. I rested my head on his shoulder, and he walked through the bushes to the area where the cars had been parked. Not many were left.

He put me in the backseat, and I immediately flopped down and curled into a tiny ball. My chin hit my knees.

What had happened? My body started to shake.

Had something really bad happened? This couldn't be. I couldn't be going through this.

Lacey got in beside me and put her hand on my arm. "We'll call your parents when we get to the hospital. And your roommates, too. When we couldn't find you, they went back to the apartment, thinking you might be there. Everyone has been frantic looking for you."

"Call Annabelle, too," I murmured. My throat felt like I had swallowed sand, but at least I could speak. Annabelle needed to answer my questions.

"I don't have her number," said Lacey. "Let's just get you to the hospital first."

The car lurched forward, hurling stones and dirt as Paul drove onto the road. Once he hit pavement, he floored the gas. I just lay on the backseat, unable to get up.

I tried to think.

Someone took me into the woods.

My pants. Down around my knees. Maybe nothing happened? Maybe I was going to pee in the bushes and had fallen and hit my head. Maybe this was all a dream.

I could feel the tears on my face, but . . . if nothing was wrong, why was I crying?

"Lacey," I murmured, "I don't remember anything. And if I don't remember, then I'm okay. Right? Lacey. Right?"

"Shhhh." Lacey stroked my hair.

By the time Paul pulled into the hospital parking lot, I had woken up a bit. I was so confused that I couldn't grasp why they had brought me to the hospital. Lacey and Paul walked on either side of me, helping me into the emergency room. Lacey took charge and spoke to the woman at admitting. They took me in right away, leading me to a private room, where they gave me a blue gown. Lacey helped me put it on, but I didn't speak to her. I couldn't. No words would form.

It was only when my mother walked through the door that I burst out crying again. My mom thanked Lacey, and she quietly stepped out, leaving us alone.

Mom put her hand on my face. "Oh, Indie."

I hung my head. "I don't know what's wrong. I wasn't drinking."

She put her finger under my chin and lifted my head. "This is not your fault, Indie. We will find out who did this to you."

Tears streamed down my face. What had happened to me? I couldn't remember anything. Maybe nothing. Maybe they would find nothing.

"Nothing happened, Mom. Nothing."

"They have to check you out anyway." She stroked my hair. "You have to do a rape kit, honey. The doctor will have to examine you. Do you understand that?"

"Not really," I whispered.

The door opened, and a young man dressed in a white medical coat and wearing a stethoscope around his neck walked in.

"Indigo," he said gently, "my name is Dr. Theissen." He sounded genuinely kind and concerned.

"Do you want me to stay in the room?" Mom asked.

"It's okay." I hung my head.

Mom left, and the doctor had me lie on my back on the table. He said his hands might be cold when he placed them in between my legs, but I didn't actually feel anything, because my entire body was numb. It only took him a few minutes to complete the test and tell me that I could sit up. I pulled the blue gown as far down my legs as I could, in a desperate effort to get it past my knees.

"Would you like me to get your mother?" he asked with a concern that made the tears start again.

I nodded.

Mom came back in the room, and I overheard them talking about me. "She has definite tearing and bruising and semen in her vagina," the doctor said. "The police need to be called."

I closed my eyes.

"Yes, her father and I would like to press charges," said my mother.

Charges? "Where is Dad?" I interrupted.

Mom turned away from the doctor and stepped toward me, putting her hand on my arm. "Indie, Dad is still out of town and would have been here if there were any flights. He will be back tomorrow."

I lowered my head, letting my hair fall in front of my face. I heard her exhale loudly. "If he saw you like this, he would kill whoever did this to you." She moved her hand off my arm and gently put her arm around my shoulder. "Perhaps it's good he's not here. I've called him and talked to him. We can call him later from home."

"Indigo," said the doctor from across the room. To me his voice sounded tinny and really far away. "I will be handing your medical records to the police, and I will be available to testify on your behalf. I'm also going to give you a sedative for tonight."

Mom squeezed my shoulder. "I want you to come home."

"I think that's wise," said the doctor. "She will need close observation."

I finally lifted my head to stare at both of them. The doctor fixed his gaze on me. "None of this is your fault. You're a brave girl to be here." He gathered his file, put it under his arm, and said, "You can get dressed now."

He left the room and Mom handed me my clothes. As she helped me into what I had been wearing earlier, a part of me reverted back to being a little girl—my mommy helping me dress because I couldn't do it myself. Once on, my clothes scratched my skin, making me itch, and I felt dirty, cheap, gross. I wanted a hot bath and clean pajamas.

Outside the waiting room, Lacey and Paul sat on chairs. They both jumped up when they saw me, and Lacey immediately ran over to me, but Paul hung back a bit.

Did he think less of me because of this? I couldn't look him in the eyes. I wanted to hide in a hole somewhere or even just behind the four walls of my childhood bedroom. I felt as if I was in a fog and couldn't see.

"Thanks for bringing her here," said Mom.

"Did you meet Paul?" I looked up at my mother. Why was I concerned about introductions? Stupid. Stupid. Stupid. What a stupid thing to say. I'm sure I sounded ridiculous.

"Yes." She smiled a little at me before glancing at Paul. "Thank you, Paul, for driving Indie."

He moved closer to me and said, "No problem."

"Yeah, thanks." I lowered my head again so I was staring at the tiled floor.

"Can I call you tomorrow?" he asked.

"Yeah. I'll be at home, though. Not the apartment."

"Indie, I'll do anything to help."

I turned away. No one could help now.

❖ ❖ ❖

The police showed up just as Lacey and Paul had decided to leave. One police officer wanted them to stay so he could ask them questions about the party and who was there. Another officer, a woman from the Special Victims Unit, took me to a private room and asked me question after question. She was pleasant and treated me with kindness, but I still felt as if I was being grilled and had done something horribly wrong.

What did I remember? Did I know the guy? Could I recognize him? Who was I with? Who else was there? Could I give names? They would have to question as many people as possible to get answers, and anything I could tell them would be helpful, even though I'd been through a lot. I explained everything to the best of my ability, but there were segments of time that I couldn't remember. This might sound weird, but I wanted to remember, thought it would make it all easier to answer the questions. I hated saying "I don't know" over and over.

As I answered the questions I could answer, my pulse quickened, and I thought I was going to choke on my words. Suddenly, it became clear to me, and I realized exactly what had happened.

It has really happened. I have been raped.

My blood surged inside me. *How could God have done this to me?*

Why would he do this? I had tried to be good. He had no right. At this moment, I hated the person who did this to me. And I hated God.

❖ ❖ ❖

Finally, at around four in the morning, the police told Mom and me that we could leave but that we would have to go to the station later on for more questioning. Dad was flying home that morning, and Mom wanted him to be with us for the next round. How many more questions would I have to endure? I dreaded the entire ordeal. I just wanted to sleep.

Exhausted, I got in the front seat of the car and just sat there staring out at the darkness.

We arrived home, and Mom helped me walk into the house and get out of my clothes and into a bath. Warm water surrounded me, and I let it cover me.

"Will you be okay?" Mom asked.

I met her gaze. "Yes. I will be fine."

"You're sure?"

"You can leave the door unlocked if you want." I sank into the tub and stared at the ceiling. I was allowed to clean up now. Get his smell off me. His dirt. His grime. His grossness.

She shut the door, leaving me alone, surrounded by water. As I lay in the tub, I ran my fingertips over my skin. *His dirt. His grime. His grossness.* It stuck to me like glue that couldn't be erased.

Where had he touched me? I shuddered and pulled my hands out of the water. I didn't want to know. Within seconds, I got out of the tub and wrapped myself in a towel. Would I ever get his dirt and grime and grossness off me?

Of course, Mom was waiting outside the bathroom door.

"I'm going to bed," I said.

"Okay," she said quietly.

"I want Sasha and Sheena with me tonight."

She pulled me in her arms. "We will get through this together," she said.

When I got in my room, I immediately saw Cedar on my bed. I patted her back and hoped the girls would take care of Henry.

"Why did it happen to me?" I asked Cedar. "No one protected me. No one."

She meowed.

Mom opened the door, and my dogs bounded into the room, wagging their tails, without a care in the world. After I rubbed their ears and bellies, they flopped down at the foot of my bed.

I curled under the covers and pulled the blankets up over my head, leaving only a little peephole so I could breathe.

Then I started the prayer I always said when I was little to keep me safe.

"Matthew, Mark, Luke, and John,

"Bless the bed I lie upon.

"Four corners to my bed . . ."

I stopped speaking out loud and sucked in the stale air from a bedroom that no one had been in for months.

God hadn't protected me tonight. No one had.

Tears started sliding down my face, and I could hardly say the words I had said so often as a child.

Four angels around my head . . .

Sobs racked my body. My shoulders shook. My words came out in rasps. There were no angels there for me tonight when I was in the woods. Not one angel came to help me.

"Where were you?" I spoke out loud.

What did I do to deserve this? I've tried to be good. I was doing what was right, wasn't I? Why didn't I see this before it happened? That's not fair to give me visions but not allow me to see something like this.

Four angels around my head . . .

Suddenly, I remembered the word *rape* flashing twice. Was that supposed to mean something? It had been so long ago. Why didn't that vision come to me yesterday or two days ago so I could have guarded myself? If it was meant to mean something, that was cruel. It was like teasing a starving dog with a crumb.

One to sing . . .

I felt myself crying again. I stuck my fist in my mouth.

One to pray . . .

I would never pray again.

And two to watch until the day.

I hate you, God. I hate you. You didn't watch over me. Hate you. Hate you. Hate you.

Chapter Twelve

I woke up the next morning to rain and gloom and gray. No sunlight shone through my window, streaking my floor, shedding light. The day was as dark as I felt. New physical pains had surfaced, and now other parts of my body, like my back, ached, bringing back the horror of the night before. But it was inside where the pain was the deepest, and I couldn't help but wonder if my blood was even flowing. I was hoping it had all been a dream, some awful nightmare, but every hurt told me otherwise. I rolled over and wished I could lie in bed all day with the covers over my head, hiding from the outside world. I didn't want to talk to anyone.

But I had to. I had to get up, get dressed, and relive it all over again. If I didn't go to the police station and file a report against him, he would just keep treating other girls like garbage and doing whatever he wanted with them, because he had gotten away with it.

When I entered the kitchen, my mother quickly glanced at me.

"I'm fine," I said.

"Your boss called," she said.

"Annabelle?" I answered. "What did she say?"

"She was genuinely concerned. She wants you to call her back at the store. She said she's working today." Mom opened the bread box. "You should eat something. Even a piece of toast."

"I'm not hungry."

She popped one in the toaster anyway. "Paul called, too." She paused. "And John."

"I can't believe this," I said. "Does everyone know?"

Mom set a glass of orange juice in front of me. "Drink this. It's full of vitamin C."

"What did they say?" I asked after downing the glass.

"Both boys are concerned about how you are. It was nice of them to call. Paul seems very sweet."

The toast popped, and the sound seemed to bounce off the walls. "I'm going back to the apartment tonight," I said.

Mom turned to face me. "Indie, I don't think that's a good idea."

"I need to have a life, Mom. My life." I got up and went over to the toaster. "I can make my own toast. I do just fine living away from here."

"I didn't say you didn't, honey. It's just . . ." Mom pulled the toast out, slathered peanut butter on it, and put it in a napkin. "You've been through something horrible, and you might need support. I'm here for you. And Dad will be, too."

"I know. And I love you for it. It's just that I . . . have to deal with this my way."

She handed me the toast. "You can eat this in the car," she said. "Your dad is meeting us there. He managed to get an early flight in."

When we got to the police station, Dad was standing outside with his arms crossed and his body tense. His jaw appeared tight, and his eyes, well, they were sad and angry all at the same time. The first thing he did was hug me, and the embrace lasted a lot longer than our usual hugs. His strong arms tightened around me as if he didn't ever want to let me go. His overnight stubble rubbed against my cheek. His cologne smelled safe and warm. I felt little again, like a child who had scraped her knee and Daddy was reassuring her that it would stop bleeding soon. Only this was so much more than a scraped knee.

When we broke apart, he scratched the back of his neck and exhaled loudly. "I want to kill the bastard." Dad spoke in a low, forced voice.

My daddy didn't just want to comfort me; he also wanted revenge.

By the pained look on his face, I knew he meant it. If he had the opportunity, I was quite certain he would throw a few punches and might not know when to stop.

"No one hurts my little girl and gets away with it." He took my arm and guided me toward the front doors of the police station.

We didn't speak as we walked up the stairs.

We got to the door, but before entering, he stopped. "I know this will be hard." He spoke with a tenderness I had never heard in my dad's voice before. "But you have to do this. He has to be caught, and he has to pay for his actions. We have to press charges."

Once inside the noisy police station, we filled out form after form, then we were ushered into an office. I sat between my mother and my father. They each held one of my hands. The policeman on duty opened a file and pulled out a photograph. He shoved it across the table. "Can you identify this man?"

I looked down and saw the guy who had dragged me in the woods. His name, I now knew, was Dennis. There was no doubt in my mind that it was him. "Yes. That's him." My voice sounded monotone.

"You're certain."

"Yes," I whispered.

The police officer went on to explain that they would be asking more questions of all the partygoers, and it was possible that if it went to trial, I would have to testify against him in a court of law.

"Can you do that?" He sat back in his chair and looked directly at me.

"Yes," I answered.

"It won't be easy."

"I know."

My dad squeezed my hand. "I'm proud of you, Indie."

The policeman fixed his gaze on me again. "Good," he said to me as if my parents weren't in the room. "It's important for us that you do this, too. He can't keep getting away with this. We are also after whoever sold him the drugs."

My throat constricted, and I wiggled my hands from out of my parents' grasp and clasped them in my lap to stop myself from shaking. "I wouldn't know who sold him the drugs or if he sold anything at the party."

For the rest of the meeting, I answered each question with as few words as I could get away with. After another half hour, we were allowed to leave. I walked out into the gloomy day and got back into the car. Mom and I didn't talk much on the way home.

Back at the house, I went right to my room. I could hear Mom and Dad in the kitchen talking, my dad angry and, I was sure, ready to punch a wall. My mom cried and cried.

No matter how hard I tried to sleep, I couldn't.

✤ ✤ ✤

For the rest of the day, I lay prone on my bed, unable to do anything except think about how messed up my life was.

Finally, after being in my room for a few hours, I rolled over, picked up the phone, and dialed Annabelle. I needed to talk to her. She answered after the first ring.

"I've been waiting for your call. How are you?" she asked quietly.

"Why didn't I see this?" I played with the telephone cord.

I heard her exhale before she said, "I don't know the answer to that. Perhaps . . . you did but it was too hard to read. I really don't know, Indie."

A picture of Miles's fat, greasy face crashed through my mind. "I listened before," I said. "I did what I was supposed to do with a creepy boss. Followed my intuition. And it worked.

So what? That wasn't enough for God? He decides he will do it to me again? Was this supposed to be a joke?"

"It's not a joke."

"I hate God right now."

There was a pause on the line.

Finally, she said, "Indie, don't give up. You are here for a reason."

"God is mean." I knew I sounded like a stubborn child, but I didn't care. "And there are no real angels. Or divine teams. No one helped me. They weren't there for me."

"I think you should take some time off. I can get someone to cover for you." She spoke softly. I hesitated for a second. I had to go to work tomorrow, because I needed money for rent. I needed to go back to the apartment, to feel as if I had a life of my own, so I would need to work for a paycheck. And now more than ever, I wanted to get away, travel, get out of this city. Maybe I would go and never come back.

If only I could go back in time, even 24 hours. I had been happy, felt fulfilled. I thought I had a purpose. Why had God taken it away from me? I wanted to go back to the way my life was. Before the party. Before Dennis had taken advantage of me when I was passed out, violating my body, my mind, my soul. Who does that? Who?

"Indie, you still there?"

"Yes," I replied. "I want to come back tomorrow."

"Tomorrow? So soon?"

"Yes."

"Okay. But how about we skip my work with you and you just man the store?"

"Sure. That's fine with me."

Another moment of silence passed over us like a heavy cloud, similar to the ones outside that didn't let an ounce of sunshine through, the ones that made the world damp and cold.

Finally, Annabelle spoke. "Indie, I will help you through this."

"Thanks," I replied.

"See you tomorrow, sweetie. And if you change your mind about coming in, just call me."

"Yeah, okay. See you."

When I hung up the phone, I wondered if Annabelle had seen something about this and maybe she hadn't bothered to tell me. Could she be trusted? Could anyone be trusted? Forget it. I couldn't think like that. I couldn't trust anyone but my family. I flopped back on my bed and slept.

❖ ❖ ❖

I must have been out for hours, because when I woke up, it was early evening. I rolled over on my back and stared at my ceiling, at the plain white paint. The white started to swirl in circles, and although it made me nauseous, I kept looking at it. That is until I heard a rap on my door.

"Who is it?"

"You have company," said Mom. She opened my door a crack. "John is here."

I sat up. "Why is he here?"

Mom stepped in my room. "Do you want me to tell him you're sleeping?"

I rubbed my temples. If he had made the trip over here, it was the least I could do to say hello. "It's okay. I'll come out."

"You're sure." She sounded concerned.

"Yeah. It will be okay."

I made my way down the hallway, and there he was, standing in my front entrance. Memories flooded through me, and a slideshow of pictures skipped through my mind: me running into his arms on our first, and only, Christmas together. Our first kiss after we had walked by the Rideau Canal. Our bodies woven together in my basement during the big ice storm.

At least I hadn't been a virgin last night. At least God had allowed me to experience first love.

"I had to see you," he said.

I nodded, unable to speak.

He stepped toward me. "I still care about you." He took my hand and kissed my knuckles.

I felt nothing. No sweaty palms, racing heart, or tingles. I felt nothing at all but skin on skin. Was my entire body void of feeling?

He placed his hand on my face, and this time, his warm touch did stir something, but it was like a spark that within seconds of igniting fizzled.

"I'm going to beat the shit out of the guy," he said.

"He drugged me."

"He's an asshole."

I eyed John.

"I heard he's a drug dealer," I said, flatly.

John didn't respond to that comment.

I continued. "But the police told me that what they really want from him is *his* dealer, because that would mean a big arrest."

John dropped my hand but then immediately placed his hands on my shoulders. Instead of pulling me toward him in a comforting hug, he held on to me firmly, stared me straight in the eye, and asked, "Why did you go in the woods with someone like him? What were you thinking?"

I shook myself away from John. How could he say that to me?

"Indie, don't cry." John wrapped his arms around me and hugged me tight to his body, stroking his hand up and down my back. This time I didn't push him away. I let myself mold into his familiarity. How many times had he held me like this? Too many to count.

Moments later, we went into the kitchen to talk. John stayed another 30 minutes or so, and we chatted, mostly about trivial things. I told him a little bit about my job, but not about my card readings, and he told me about how horrible his night dishwashing job was and how it didn't pay enough. Then he went on a bit of a government tirade about how minimum wage wasn't enough. In a way, his rant made me feel good, because that was the old John. The guy I fell in love with.

"Well, I should get going," he said. "I have to drop something off for my mom."

"How is your mom?" I asked.

"She's okay." He flicked his hair back, trying to be cool. I knew the gesture; she wasn't good.

"She's been going to the doctor a lot," he said. "She's been having pains in her abdomen. She says they're sharp pains."

I could tell he was worried about her, but then he was always worried about her. I wondered if she was drinking a lot.

"What does the doctor say?"

He shrugged. "Nothing yet. When I ask her about it, she says it's nothing."

"I'm sorry to hear that," I said.

"I tried to talk to her about my dad, but she just freaks on me. I've stopped asking." Anger filled his eyes, and he made a fist with his hand. "I'm going to get answers."

I didn't say anything.

He looked into my eyes. Suddenly, his shoulders sagged, as if the anger he had just felt had hissed out of him like a flat tire. "I meant it when I said I care about you, Indie. I can't talk to anyone like I talk to you. You always listen."

Again, I didn't speak. My heart pounded. We stayed like that, staring into each other's eyes for a few seconds. Then the spell broke.

"I've got to go," he said quickly.

I walked him to the door and stepped outside. Gray rain clouds still stalked the sky. Parked by the curb in front of our house sat a shiny silver car. "Nice car," I said.

He shrugged, almost sheepishly. "My uncle bought it for me." He averted his eyes and wouldn't meet my gaze.

He was lying.

He walked down the cement sidewalk toward his car, but before he got to it, rusty old Mable pulled up and parked behind his spiffy silver car.

John stopped in his tracks and squinted, watching Paul's every move as he got out, carrying a bouquet of daisies. John turned to look at me, then back at Paul. He smacked his fist on the hood of Paul's car, the noise echoing down my neighborhood street. Paul didn't flinch. If he was scared, he sure wasn't going to show it. But then he hadn't shown it that night on the way home either, when we had almost been attacked. When he'd picked a daisy for me.

John looked back at me one more time, his face in a scowl, before he yanked open his car door and sped away from the curb, sending small stones flying.

Paul didn't even glance at John's car, nor did he break his stride as we walked toward me, holding the flowers in his hands.

He handed the daisies to me, and that's when I saw his hands shaking.

"I remember you telling me daisies were your favorite flower," he said.

"Thanks." I took the flowers and brought them to my nose, taking in their sweet smell. "You want to come in?" I asked.

"Sure," he replied. "I won't stay long, though. You are probably really tired."

Once inside my house, I led him into the kitchen, and we sat down at the kitchen table. Mom fussed about, getting a vase for the flowers and filling it with water.

"How are you doing?" he asked with such gentleness I had to lower my head. I liked that he didn't mention John or ask about him.

"I'm okay," I whispered.

Mom placed the daisies on the kitchen table. "I'm going outside for a bit," she said. "If you need anything, you know where I am."

As soon as the back door slammed, Paul said, "I'm so sorry I wasn't there earlier. I've thought about this all day. If I had gotten off work even thirty minutes earlier, I could have been with you, and none of this would have happened."

"Paul," I said, "this is not your fault."

"I should have been there. I could have been there earlier. You wanted me to come. I'm such an idiot."

"It's not your fault."

"And it's not yours either." He put his hand over mine. I liked his tender touch.

"I heard the police know who it is," he said. "I know him, too. He went to my high school for a year before he got kicked out."

A stab hit my stomach, and I glanced up. "He got kicked out?"

Paul nodded. "He was a friend of your . . ." He let his words trail off as if he couldn't say the word *boyfriend* in front of me.

"Did they get kicked out at the same time?" I asked.

Paul nodded. "He's a year older, and he was in grade twelve, so he just quit. I don't think he ever graduated. He had his means to make money. When John went over to your school, everyone thought he'd straighten out." He withdrew his hand, and I watched him flatten it, like he wanted to chop someone. When I looked at his face, I immediately saw that he had clamped his mouth shut, and I swore he was gritting his teeth behind his lips.

"Let's talk about something else," I said.

He sucked in a huge breath of air, exhaled, and said, "Good idea."

Silence loomed over us. What else did I have to talk about? Today I had nothing to talk about. Nothing at all.

He spoke first. "I learned how to make a latte yesterday." He winked at me.

For the second time that day, I attempted to smile.

"Next time you're in," he said in a trying-hard-to-be-jovial voice, "I'll make you a free one."

He reached across the table and took my hand in his again, gently squeezing my fingers. "I hate seeing you so sad."

"I'm sorry," I said.

"Indie, you have nothing to be sorry about. What happened was wrong. If I met the guy on the street, I could do some real damage."

"My dad has first dibs on that one."

"Okay, then I'll karate kick him so he won't get up again and make it all easier for your dad."

I had to smile.

And he smiled back. And just like that, the thought of Paul and my father, the most unlikely duo, working together hit me, and I laughed. And for a few seconds my numbness disappeared and something pleasant flowed through me.

But it didn't last long.

✤ ✤ ✤

The next morning I walked into work and headed right to the cash register, storing my bag under the counter as I had on my first day. Immediately, I opened up the schedule book. "You have four bookings today," I said quietly. My hair hung in front of my face, and I didn't want to look Annabelle in the eyes. "Usually you only do three. I'm worried about you."

Annabelle came over to stand beside me. "Indie, look at me," she said.

I lifted my head a little.

"Please, this is not the time to worry about me," she said. "You've been through something awful." Her voice was soft and soothing. "Do you want to be here today? Because I can close up during my readings and you can go home."

I busied myself by arranging the pens on the counter. "I want to be here," I mumbled.

She put her hands on mine to still them. "Sweetie, I'll help you through this."

I could feel tears stinging my eyes, so I hung my head again. "Why didn't I see this before it happened?" I mumbled.

She wrapped her arms around me. "Sometimes you just can't," she said. "It's just the way it is."

"That's not an answer." I sniffled. "I'm doing all this work with you and then something like this happens. What good is anything that I've been doing?"

She stroked my back. "I know that it seems unfair now."

I pulled away from her and shook my head. "Unfair?"

Annabelle picked up a pair of feathered angel wings and touched them as if they would give her answers. I watched her actions and wondered how I had even gotten involved with her and any of this. It didn't help in the long run.

It will all work out okay. Isaiah's voice cut through my thoughts.

But I didn't want him talking to me. Suddenly, I could feel anger stirring inside me. I couldn't control how I felt anymore. One minute I was sad, the next angry, the next despondent. And in this moment, I didn't want Isaiah in my life. If he was part of my so-called divine team, then he wasn't a very good team member. Where was he on Saturday night? He certainly wasn't my knight in shining armor when I was being drugged and dragged into the bushes.

No one was there for you.

You were meant to meet Annabelle. Don't push her away.

If I could have told him to shut up, I would have, but Annabelle would ask questions, and I was tired of questions.

"One day you will understand the reason," she said with an assured calmness.

I glanced down at the schedule book. The words in front of me got blurry and seemed to be swimming in a pool of water.

"That makes no sense," I whispered. I continued staring at the book.

"I know," she said.

I heard her inhale through her nose and exhale through her mouth. I waited for her to speak, because I knew she had more to say.

"I've felt like that many times."

I finally looked up from the book. I secured my gaze on her hands, instead of her face, and watched carefully as she wove her fingers together, making a steeple with her pointer fingers. For some reason, I was mesmerized by all her small gestures.

"When my marriage failed," she continued, "I wondered why I had married such a jerk. Why hadn't I seen what a louse he really was? He felt he could push me around. I asked myself the same thing you're asking yourself. How could I have not seen that he was going to be so abusive?"

I just looked at her and listened.

"Just because we have this ability to help people around us doesn't mean we can always help ourselves. I'm glad you came to work today."

"Me too," I said finally.

"Can you promise me something, Indigo?"

"What?"

"You won't give up just yet."

I swiped at my tears with the cuff of my shirt. "I don't know if I can do that."

"Okay." She held up her hand, palm toward me. "How about this: we won't do any more sessions in the afternoons, but you keep your cards and practice at home."

I shrugged. "Maybe."

I reached under the counter for my purse. "Do you mind if I step out for a minute? It's only ten to nine. I need a smoke."

—⁓⁓⁓—

Chapter Thirteen

The rest of the summer passed in a blur, or should I say daze. I went to work, I went home, I ate sometimes, I drank wine and beer to dull my pain, and I smoked at least a pack of cigarettes a day. They did the same thing, dulled the pain.

Sometimes I sat on my bed and petted Henry for hours on end.

I tried to read but couldn't concentrate.

I could watch mindless television, because then I didn't have to concentrate.

And I drank coffee. With Paul. But that was as far as our relationship went—or as far as I allowed it go—even though I enjoyed his carefree company.

I refused to let him get close or touch me; I knew he wanted more, but being the nice guy that he was, he didn't try to even kiss me again.

On the last weekend of the summer, which was a long weekend, I was sitting at the kitchen table drinking a glass of wine when the phone rang. Being the closest to the phone, Natalie picked it up.

"Just a second," she said. She pulled the phone away from her face. "Indie, it's your mom."

"Right on cue," I said. My mother called me every day and sometimes twice a day. For once, I liked her hovering, and I looked forward to her often simple, hello-how-are-you calls.

"Hi, Mom," I said.

"Honey, I have some good news," she said. "Dennis Neufeld has been charged with drug possession. And from what I can gather, the police interrogated him so hard that he also confessed to the attack. You won't have to testify against him."

I closed my eyes and leaned my forehead against the wall. The weight I had been carrying for the month of August lifted, a little anyway, and I have to admit a feeling of relief engulfed me. I hadn't realized how much the thought of going to a court had worn me down.

"Thanks," I finally said. We chatted for a few more seconds, then I hung up.

"So?" Sarah looked at me wide-eyed. "What was that about?"

"Spill," said Natalie.

"They got him," I said. "Dennis Neufeld got picked up for drugs and confessed to raping me, so I won't have to testify against him." I still had a hard time saying the word *rape* out loud.

Natalie and Sarah hugged me hard.

Although a big part of me was relieved, I still ached inside. Sarah flung her arm around me. "Let's go out tonight."

"I have to phone Lacey first," I said. "And tell her."

Of course, Lacey and I ended up talking for 30 minutes. It reminded me of the old times, and for a second, I felt that we were in grade eight again.

But those days were gone.

"So that's my news," I said to her at the end of the call. "You must be excited for school."

"I can't believe I'm leaving so soon," she said. "This time next week, I'll be living in a dorm."

"I have to see you before you go. What are you doing tonight?"

"Nothing."

"Come over. We're going to go out for a few drinks. You can sleep over."

✦ ✦ ✦

Lacey arrived looking like a model, dressed in jeans, high strappy sandals, and a cute little shirt she had just picked up at Le Château with her lifeguarding money. She hugged me.

"I'm so glad a part of this is behind you," she said.

"I don't want to talk about it," I said. "Let's just go out and have fun."

The Royal Oak was jammed, but we managed to find a spot on the patio. In late August, the nights cooled considerably, and although it was still nice to be outside, you needed some sort of jacket. My cigarettes were securely stashed in the pocket of my jean jacket, and as soon as we were settled against the railing, I pulled them out.

"I thought you quit," said Lacey.

I shrugged. "I started again." I lit my cigarette off Sarah's and inhaled.

After blowing out a smoke ring, I said, "So . . . you packed yet?"

"I'm ready. We're driving up next week." Lacey rolled her eyes. "My mom insists on coming and crying, even though I'm only going to be an hour from home. When are you going to visit me?"

I shrugged and looked at Natalie. "What do you think? You're the driver."

"Anytime," said Natalie. Her usually bright eyes looked dull, and her voice lacked enthusiasm. My heart suddenly ached. *She'd met her mother but hadn't said anything because of me and my problems. When had that happened?*

I had been so absorbed in my own feelings that I had totally forgotten about that. And Lacey talking about her own mother probably reminded Natalie of hers.

"How about October? Just before Thanksgiving?" I said. "Does that work for you, Natalie?" I wanted to cheer her up, give her something to look forward to.

"Sure does," she answered.

"That works for me, too," said Lacey. "Well, I think it does. If I have an exam that week, I'll let you know. Exams, ugh! What a horrible thought."

We stayed at the Royal Oak until almost closing time, and by then, I'd had more than my share of beer. We all had. Walking home, we sang and laughed, and I didn't care about anything. When we got back to the apartment, I opened a bottle of wine.

"Let's have another drink," I said.

"Tell me about your card readings," slurred Lacey.

I clapped my hands. "Let's do a reading right now." I ran to my room and got my cards from the back of my dresser drawer, where they had been stashed since before that awful night. I yanked them out and they tingled in my hands.

Not like this. Isaiah spoke to me. *Not after you've had alcohol.*

"Shut up," I whispered, closing the dresser drawer. "I'll do what I want."

Yes, you will. You always do, and that's a good thing. He doesn't know what he's talking about. But you do.

I ran down the hall and back to the living room, where I poured myself a big glass of wine and lit all the candles we had in the living room before turning out the lights.

"Ohhh," squealed Lacey. "This is spooky. But so fun. It's like we're having a séance."

The four of us sat cross-legged on the floor with a big fat candle in the middle of our circle so we could see the cards.

Sarah laughed. "What are those boards called? The ones that you do séances with?"

"What boards?" Lacey asked.

"The ones where you push the little thing around and it answers questions." Sarah pretended to push something with her fingers.

Natalie laughed. "Ouija boards. My grandmother had one. My brother and I would steal it and go to our rooms, shut off all the lights, and ask really stupid questions."

I laid my cards down on the floor. "Knock them with your fist," I said to Lacey. "To get all the energy out."

"Indie's really good," whispered Natalie. "I met my mom, you know."

"Why didn't you tell us?" Sarah asked.

I put my hand on Natalie's. "Are you okay?"

Her eyes glistened in the candlelight. "Because of you, Indie, I am," she said softly. "If you hadn't warned me what to expect, I would have never survived. She's a drug addict, always has been, and that's why she gave me up. She'll never be the mother I want her to be. She can't. She put off our meeting for over two weeks. Kept making excuses. Then after *finally* meeting her, I realized something. I'm glad she gave me up. I'm glad my grandmother raised me. My life would have been awful with her."

"I'm sorry," I said. "It still must hurt."

"It does. But we all have our pain." She wiped her eyes with the sleeve of her pajamas. "I can handle it." She pointed to the cards. "Let's play cards."

As Lacey shuffled, I thought about John and his mother and how neither of them could deal with their addictions either. My cigarette package flashed in my mind, and I shook my head to get rid of that thought.

"Indie *is* amazing," said Sarah, breaking my thoughts.

I frowned at her. "I didn't read you very well at all."

Sarah grinned and ran to her room. When she came flying out, she slid across the floor in her socks. "I picked up this *piece of paper* the other day. Well, it's actually a brochure."

"What is it for?" Lacey asked.

"Massage therapy school! I went in this vitamin store 'cause I wanted some green tea, and this brochure was, like, sitting there, and it jumped out at me. Then I picked it up and realized this would be something so cool to do. And I got really excited. I looked it up online, and I'm going to register for next fall. I can work really hard this year to save money."

"I was here when Indie read for Sarah," said Natalie with excitement. "She talked about how she would do something with her fingers!"

We all high-fived, telling Sarah how wonderful that was. I truly was happy for her.

"Let's get this séance started," said Lacey. She pointed to the cards. "Read for me! Tell me if I'm going to find a new boyfriend."

As we polished off a bottle of wine, I told Lacey that she was going to meet a guy at Queen's and he would be a musician.

"Musician?" Lacey put her hand to her mouth and giggled. "I've always loved jocks. A musician! Are you sure?"

"Yup," I said. "A musician. And you're going to get A's but one C in some stupid course."

Lacey smacked her thighs. "I bet it will be that dumb stats course I have to take. I've heard it's soooo hard." She tapped the cards. "Let's talk more about the guy!"

I read her cards for another hour, then the four of us polished off all the alcohol in the apartment. Sarah and Natalie called it quits at three, but Lacey and I finally fell into bed around four o'clock. With just a single bed in my room, Lacey and I were really squished, but it was what we used to do when we were little, except now we had Henry nestled at the foot of my bed instead of Cedar.

Our shoulders touched as we both lay on our backs staring at the ceiling. The streetlight shone through my bedroom window creating shadows on my walls, jiving one minute, dancing seductively the next.

"Do you ever wish we could just be little again?" Lacey asked.

"Yup. When I didn't know I was weird."

"Indie, you're not weird. You were so good tonight. Do you know you can make a ton of money giving readings like that?"

"It's stupid."

"No, it's not."

"You're going to rock Queen's."

"I hope so. I'm nervous."

"I wish I hadn't gone to that party."

"It wasn't your fault. Now he's going to jail, and he deserves it."

"That's a good thing, I guess. Still doesn't take away what happened."

"You're going to do amazing things, Indie."

You should not have read the cards when you were drunk.

You were just having fun. You're good at this.

Could that be true? Could I be good at it?

"I'm tired," I said. "Let's try to sleep."

❖ ❖ ❖

September rolled around, Lacey left for school, and I continued working at Annabelle's. Paul started university, and we didn't see each other as much. I missed him but knew it was for the best. Since the river party, I didn't want him to touch me.

"I bought you this," Annabelle said to me one beautiful September day, when the leaves had started turning color so the outside world was full of vibrant reds and yellows and oranges. She handed me a little brown book similar to the one she carried around all the time.

I furrowed my brow. "What is this for?"

"You need to start writing stuff down and also journaling your thoughts. You can write things about the cards and keep track of anything you might read in books. Are you still practicing with your cards?"

I shrugged. "Sometimes." The last reading I had done was the one with Lacey, when we were drunk. I didn't dare tell Annabelle about that one.

"Just remember not to read when you've been drinking, okay?"

How did she know? Sometimes it drove me crazy that she just knew everything about me, like, all the time.

"Okay," I replied.

"That's good," she said casually. I expected her to say more about it, lecture me, but she didn't.

"Would you like to start back on the cards?" she asked. "I have another deck I'd like you to work with."

I didn't answer.

"The cards are just for help, though," she continued. "They're like cue cards. When you start doing readings for clients, I want you to rely on your abilities. Not cards."

"I just like reading for my friends," I snapped. "I don't want to meet anyone new." The second the words were out, I wished I could take them back. Annabelle had been so patient with me over the past month.

"What happened to you came from a dark place, Indie."

"It's over now." I shrugged as if I didn't care.

"It's not over. It never will be, because it's part of you."

"I wish it would go away."

"Indie, you have to be careful, because right now you are like an open vessel for spirits. This darkness that surrounds you is like glue for dark beings who don't want to leave the earth. Are you protecting yourself?"

"Sometimes," I answered. Again, she always knew. I hadn't protected myself when I read for Lacey, the one and only time I had even looked at my cards in the past month.

"By the way, what happened with the ghost? I know you protected your apartment a while ago, and she left, but sometimes they can return."

I shrugged. "She's gone."

"Did you see her walk through the light?"

"Not exactly. She left through a window."

Annabelle scrunched up her face. "Okay, sweetie. I know you did what I told you, and that's great, but she could still be around, living somewhere else."

"I think she's gone," I said. "It's been ages since any of us have seen her."

Annabelle nodded. "Okay. Now . . . one more thing. I hate to be a nag tonight, but there is a dark side to the cards, too, Indie. I worry about you. It is what we call the occult, and if you use and abuse the cards, you can open yourself to all sorts of bad things. The same goes with stuff like the Ouija board." She wagged her finger at me. "Am I getting through?"

"Yes." Why was she talking about Ouija boards? The woman wasn't making sense.

"All right, beautiful," she said. "I've given you enough to chew on for one day."

She was only trying to help me. I knew that. I looked at her and smiled. "Thanks," I said.

"I'm here for you," she said.

Suddenly, my vision blurred.

I saw white, and I was sliding down my long tunnel. In my telescopic lens, I saw an aqua river with a streak of red blood flowing through it. I had seen this before. But this time the blood stopped and pooled, and it thumped and bubbled, but not in any kind of rhythm.

Sadness flowed through me, and I had to lower my head.

"It will all be okay," said Annabelle.

"Will it?" I lifted my head to stare into her eyes.

"Yes." She smiled broadly, a fake smile I could tell, but a smile, and it didn't look good at all. Her teeth had a funny color to them.

I held up the brown book. "Thanks for this," I said.

"You're welcome." Then she winked at me. "Promise me you'll use it."

"Sure. Okay. I'll try." I said, wanting to lighten the mood. I glanced at the clock. "You have a client in thirty minutes."

"I'd better get prepared." She gave me an impish grin. "I need to protect myself first."

"You do that," I said.

As she was leaving the room, she turned to me and said, "I keep hearing the word *Paul*. I know I've told you this before, but it keeps coming back."

"Stop matchmaking."

"I'm not." She waved her hands, and I smiled, happy to see her animated again. "It might not even have to do with Paul. Your *friend*."

"Thirty minutes." I tapped the book.

"I'm going." She walked to the back, to her pink room.

❖ ❖ ❖

The day cruised by, and as hard as it was to admit, I liked my job and I liked the store. I almost felt more at home in the store than I did anywhere in my life. Annabelle knocked off early, at two, and I was left alone for the last two hours. I cleaned and tidied and talked to customers.

At exactly 4 P.M., the door chimed, and in walked Paul, which surprised me. I hadn't seen him in a week or so. I immediately smiled. The guy did have a way of lighting up a room and making me sing a little happy song inside.

"You need a ride?" he asked.

"I thought you had school." He had started at Carleton, so we didn't see each other as much. His daily trips to the store had dwindled. Because of being in school full-time, he'd had to quit his sandwich job.

"I'm pulling a few short day shifts at Starbucks. I worked three hours this afternoon. I was in the neighborhood, so I thought I might as well drive you home. Timing was perfect. I got off just before four."

"Thanks," I said. "Just let me lock up."

The brilliant sun shone in a beautiful azure sky, and although the air was warm, there was this hint of crispness to it. Time was moving forward, and the seasons were changing. Ottawa had four distinct seasons, and I loved the fall because every day was different. Summer fun was now over, and it was time to do something.

We strolled slowly to his car, chatting about his classes. I got into his car and immediately rolled down the window; he threw on some tunes. We pulled away from the curb, and comfort set in. We didn't have to talk. The music was enough.

When he pulled up in front of my apartment, around 15 minutes later, I gasped.

A FOR SALE sign hung in the window of George's antique store.

"George is selling already?" I asked out loud.

"That's the antique's guy, right? Your friend."

I turned to Paul. "Yeah. He's a great guy. I got to go. Thanks for the ride."

"No problem. See yah," he said.

I hopped out of the car and ran toward the store. The door tinkled when I bounded in. George was behind the counter, shining jewelry.

"George, I saw the sign on the door." I walked toward the counter.

"Indie." He put down the necklace and wiped his hands on his apron. He always wore the same checked apron when he cleaned.

"This is so sudden," I said. "When you said Claire wanted you to retire, I didn't think you meant this winter."

"Ahh, Indie. It's time."

"I'm going to miss you," I said.

"You're one sweet girl."

"You love this so much," I said. "Won't you miss it?"

"Of course I'll miss it and your smile, of course. But I'm having some health issues." He laughed. "Claire thinks I'm getting dementia. Every time I try to find something, I discover it somewhere else. She thinks I'm losing my memory, and she wants me to sell before it's too late and she has to do all the work. We might get a place in Florida for the winter."

"What do you mean, things have been moved?"

"I just forget where I put things. I think they're one place and then I find them somewhere else."

"We all do that when we're busy," I said.

He laughed and winked at me. "I've saved something for you."

"What?"

He pulled out an exact replica of the ring that he had cut off my finger. "I looked high and low for this and finally I found it. I wanted you to have another one. I know it's not the one your mother gave you, but since it is a family thing, I still think it will be something you can cherish." He winked at me. "Plus, I think it means something that you believe in. Afterlife."

Little did George know, I wasn't sure what I believed in anymore. But I wouldn't tell him that, not after he had given me such a nice gift.

"Thank you," I exclaimed. I took the ring and slipped it on my finger. "Perfect fit. Thank you again, George."

We chatted for a few more minutes before I decided to browse around the room, knowing soon I wouldn't have this opportunity. I leafed through old books and magazines and carefully, almost reverently, touched old lamps and furniture.

When I spotted a brown box that looked like a game of some sort, shoved to the back of a shelf, I pulled it out. Although the black scrolling letters were a bit smeared because of age, I could still read *Ouija Board* on the front of the box.

I gasped out loud. And stared at it. Annabelle.

"That it is one of the first editions of the Ouija boards," said George from across the room.

I turned to him. "What do you know about it?"

"Well, it was a game that was created in the 1800s and has an incredible history."

"Tell me," I urged.

"In the late 1800s, people were crazy about séances and trying to contact the dead through spirit mediums. They loved automatic writing and sitting around a table calling out to the dead, and they thought if the chair tipped or the table rocked, some spirit was in the room." He motioned for me to bring the game over.

Once it was on the counter, he opened up the box and pulled out the wooden board. "But then someone had the great idea to create a board game. A businessman named William Fuld bought a company called Kennard Novelty Company in a business takeover, and they had created the final form of the board. So it wasn't really created by Fuld, but like a lot of businessmen, he took the darn credit. Anyway, he took over and renamed the company Ouija Novelty Company, and he promoted the game like crazy. Everyone thinks he was the founder, but he wasn't really."

I waited, hoping to hear more.

He touched the board. "He died young after falling off his factory roof. His family sold it to Parker Brothers."

"I didn't realize the game had been around for that long," I said.

"It had many names, like the talking board or the witch board." He shrugged. "Many believe that it's dangerous because it can allow spirits in."

I gingerly touched the wood, intrigued that the Ouija board had been around for so many years. A hundred. Wow. My fingertips burned as I traced the scrolled alphabet and the words *no* and *yes* that were in the top corners. Twice in one day, I'd heard about this type of board.

Synchronicity.

It had to be.

"How much is it?" I asked.

"I don't think you should buy this. Save your money." George picked up the lid to put it back on the box.

And I reached out and put my hand on top of his. I wanted to know more about this board that had come up twice in one day. "Please," I said. "I bet it's harmless. I think it would be fun for me and my roommates."

"Okay. But I don't want any money for it." He rubbed his chin. "It's all a bit strange how I found it, though." He furrowed his eyebrows, looking perplexed. "It was in the *bottom* of a dresser. In a drawer. I swear I had gone through the dresser when I bought it. I had to fix the hardware on the bottom drawer, and when I pulled it out, I found the board." He laughed. "That's why my wife thinks we need to get a condo in Florida."

"Ahh." I winked at him. "I bet she just wants to spend more time with you in a nice sunny place."

He grinned. "You sure know how to make an old man feel good. Before you go, I have to tell you how to play the game."

I had to hide my smile. Of course he would have to explain it to me. He pulled out the little block that went with the game. "It's really quite simple. This here is called a planchette. And you ask a question and move it around until it hits either *yes* or *no* or hits a letter. If it goes to a letter, you keep going until you spell something. I think it's all staged. Kind of like magicians."

He put the game back in the box, handed it to me, and reluctantly sighed. "It's yours. I never could say no to a pretty young thing like you."

I put the box under my arm and expressed my thanks again.

You're not listening. Isaiah spoke to me as I left the store.

"So?" I said under my breath. "It was a gift. Am I not supposed to take a gift from a friend? Anyway, you didn't listen to me, so why should I listen to anyone? And you're the one always telling me about synchronicity. Isn't that what this is?"

183

Chapter Fourteen

"Look at those guys standing by the bar," Sarah whispered in my ear. "I bet they'd buy us a beer."

"Sarah, no," I pleaded. Natalie was working, so I didn't have her to back me up.

"Come on, please, Indie. I need to do something to forget about jerk-face." She swigged back the rest of her beer, then held up her glass. Last week, Sarah walked in on Tyler in bed with his old girlfriend.

"I bet you could work some of your magic," Sarah continued, scrunching up her face. "Pleeeease. I'm so low on cash because I'm saving so hard for school next fall."

Don't give in. Isaiah spoke to me. I wished he'd leave me alone. I had been ignoring him lately, because he was always trying to ruin my fun.

This isn't the way to use your abilities.

"Okay, let's do it," I said. I needed to help Sarah get through this. Tyler was still living in our building, and she kept running into him. It made her crazy.

I took a deep breath, exhaled, and did that three times as I stared at the guys. Annabelle had taught me that breathing was

185

so important to my visions. And three times in and out was the magic number. I was to inhale through my nose and exhale through my mouth. Breath was life. And perhaps tonight it was free drinks.

After getting a good look at the guys, I closed my eyes.

Blond. I heard the word loud and clear.

I leaned in to Sarah and whispered, "The guy with the blond hair is the one we hit."

"Yes-s-s," said Sarah. "I knew you could do this. Come on. Let's make our way over there."

After ten minutes, Sarah and I each had another beer in our hands, compliments of Stephen, the blond guy. In total, we were surrounded by four guys, who were sort of fun. Sarah flung her head back and laughed loudly at some dumb joke, and I laughed, too, although I didn't think the joke was all that funny.

As we were hanging out, talking about nothing, I kept scanning the bar, in the hopes of *not* seeing Paul here. What would he think if he saw me purposely trying to get guys to buy us beer?

Paul liked me. I knew he did. But I just hadn't been able to get close to him. Not after what had happened at the river party. I shivered, thinking of that awful night. Would the horribleness of it ever go away?

Two more beers later, with a numbness that felt good, I realized that it was already midnight. "I got to go," I said to Sarah. "I have to work in the morning."

"Me too," she replied.

"We're going to go for pizza," said Stephen. "You girls want to come?" He nudged Sarah with his shoulder. "My treat."

"Sure," said Sarah before I could say no.

❖ ❖ ❖

"You look tired," said Annabelle the next morning. She eyed me. "Late night?"

"Not too bad." I went behind the counter and opened up the schedule book. Sarah and I had gone to bed at four. We had gotten home at three and played around with the Ouija board for an hour. It kept spelling out the name Stephen, which made us laugh hysterically and convinced me that it really was just a fun party game, nothing more to it. Natalie had joined us as well when she had come in from a night out with friends. We'd had so much fun we were all keen to play with it again another night. After dark. With candles.

So I'd only had a couple of hours of sleep.

"You only have two clients today," I said ignoring her stares.

"I have an appointment," she said.

Annabelle suddenly grabbed the counter with one hand and pressed the other hand to her chest. Her face drained of color.

"What's wrong?" I came up behind her and put my arm around her to help hold her up.

She shook her head. "Nothing. I'm just having the odd dizzy spell. Too much caffeine perhaps. My periods have been heavy lately, too."

"Maybe you should go to a doctor."

She blew out a rush of air, steadied herself, and pointed to the back door. "I'm okay. I'm going to my room to get ready."

I watched her walk away and noticed her sagging shoulders and heavy footsteps.

❖ ❖ ❖

Annabelle finished her two sessions and left, and I was alone in the store. I tried to stay awake by cleaning and straightening. The minutes ticked by at a snail's pace, and every time I glanced at the clock, it didn't seem to have progressed more than five minutes. In the afternoon, the odd person came in, which made the time go by a little faster. Still, it was the slowest day I'd ever worked.

Finally, it was five to four. I started tidying up when the door tinkled, and I knew before looking up who it was.

"Hi, Paul," I said.

"I was in the neighborhood to pick up my check from Starbucks. I got some cash. You want to go to a movie tonight?"

"Sure!" The thought of sitting in a movie theater sounded great. I needed an early night with no alcohol. Five nights in a row had worn me down. "You don't have homework tonight?"

"I did it all. And"—he gave me a sheepish shrug—"this movie is for film class. I have to write a report on it."

"And you don't want to go alone."

"Going with you will make it feel a lot less like school and a lot more like something fun to do."

I smiled. "Let me lock up."

"You want to get something to eat before the movie?"

"Only if you let me buy dinner."

"Perfect. Let's go to Starbucks for free coffee and muffins."

I shook my finger at him. "No way. You're not getting out of this. I'm a working girl, and you're a student."

"Yeah, but I'm taking you to the movie for a school project. You are helping me get an A."

"Stop arguing with me." I made a playful face.

It was such a beautiful autumn day, the breeze warm and the air crystal clear, that we decided to pick up a cheap takeout pizza and go to the park, knowing that soon it would be winter and the snow would fall. This might be our last chance to sit outside and eat. With soda and pizza, we sat on one of the picnic tables, just under a tree. The leaves above graced us with their magnificent shades of orange and red and yellow.

"The park is always so quiet in the fall." I stared out at the trees. "I like this time of year."

Paul yanked open the box and dove into the pizza, handing me the first piece. "Me too. It always has that feeling of new beginnings. I guess it's because school always starts in the fall. It was always a new grade and a new teacher, and there were new kids to sit beside. That part scared the heck out of me."

"What were you like as a kid?" It occurred to me that I really didn't know much about Paul because I hadn't asked.

"Nerdy." He laughed.

I punched him. "No, really. Tell me."

"Okay," he said. "I liked sports but never made the top teams. Although I was pretty good at soccer 'cause I could run fast. I never played hockey. My mother didn't want me to get in any fights." He laughed. "Then she puts me in karate so I can learn how to fight. Parents do weird things sometimes."

I let our shoulders touch. "Were you . . . bullied?" I asked.

He chuckled. "I could talk my way through the bullies. Promise to give up my homework, stuff like that." He took my hand in his. "What about you?"

"Quiet. Shy. In school anyway."

Again he gently bumped me with his shoulder. "But I bet you were the girl every boy wanted to kiss."

This time I laughed. "Me?" I shook my head. "I don't think so. That was Lacey."

I let go of his hand and took a bite of my pizza. "We better eat this before the cheese gets all gross and congealed."

We ate in silence for a while. Finally, I said, "So tell me about this class you're taking. Sounds interesting and not at all like school."

"It's so easy. All I have to do is watch movies and write reports on them."

"What are we going to see tonight?"

"What do you think? Is there anything you really want to see?"

"It's your class."

"How about *Simon Birch*?"

I shrugged. "I've read a little about it."

"Yeah, me too. From what I've heard, the kid is hilarious." He stopped to pull another slice of pizza from the box. He chewed and sipped his drink.

Again, the air took on a silence, and I liked it because it was comfortable. Easy. No pressure to talk and say anything profound.

After a moment or so, he started back up again. "Has the ghost been back?"

"Nope. Not in our apartment anyway." I took a piece of pepperoni off my pizza and popped it in my mouth.

"That's good. I think it's pretty cool that you got rid of her the way you did. Your roommates must be thrilled."

"Yeah," I replied. "Especially Natalie. Green Lady scared her."

"Did she scare you?"

"Oh yeah. All the time. But that was before I knew about her past," I replied. "Then I felt sorry for her."

"Is Natalie still going to Queen's next year?"

I dotted my mouth with the napkin before I said, "I think so. We are planning a trip to visit Lacey. We're going next weekend. I think she might even have a gig lined up. She's worked on a few songs."

"Queen's is such a good school. Are you going to join her onstage?"

I shook my head. "Nah. I haven't been playing much lately." I sipped my soda. My guitar *was* collecting dust in my room. "Sarah is going to school next year, too," I said to change the subject. "In Toronto. She's going to become a registered massage therapist."

"That's kind of cool. What will you guys do about your apartment? Will you move?"

"I don't know," I answered, thinking about the question. I got up and threw the remains of my pizza in the trash can, then came back to the table and sat down again. "I have no idea what I'll do." I said this as if I were talking to myself in my bedroom. Since the river party, I had kind of given up on all my dreams.

"Something will come to you. Maybe you can open a business. I've been researching, and some psychics make good money. You just have to be an entrepreneur."

"Maybe I'm not that good at it."

"Sure you are."

I hung my head and glanced at him, but only out of the corner of my eye. "I hope so."

More silence.

Paul took a newspaper out of his backpack and unfolded it to the entertainment section. "We should go if we want to make the seven o'clock showing," he said, pointing to the movie. He stood up.

"You're right," I said, glancing at my watch. "It starts in twenty."

I reached down to pick up the pizza box to put in the garbage, but Paul obviously had the same idea. Our hands connected, and for a moment, I let them stay like that. Warmth crept through me and a sense of peace pervaded. I glanced at him, and he looked directly into my eyes. He had these baby blue eyes that always crinkled in the corners when he smiled. They were like pools of tepid water, and I felt as if I could see through them to the bottom. I knew that what was below the surface was safe and that there were no monsters or demons lurking, ready to pounce.

I smiled at him, then slowly withdrew my hand.

He backed away, too, and I saw a flicker of disappointment and perhaps even hurt cross his eyes, but it disappeared right away. "I'll throw this in the garbage," he mumbled.

We walked slowly to the car, and I reached for his hand. He squeezed my fingers, and I sighed. Why couldn't I let him in?

In the movie theater, our thighs touched, and I didn't move away. I think it was the dark of the room that made it easier to stay joined with him. The movie mesmerized me, and within ten minutes, I forgot where I was and concentrated totally on the main character, Simon. He was a boy who was small for his age and always in trouble but he was determined that God had a purpose for him. Did God have a purpose for me, too? Was that why we had picked that movie?

Paul drove me home, and we talked about the movie the entire way. Mostly we laughed at Simon and how mischievous he had been.

"So it's a bit ironic," said Paul when we were almost at my place, "that we chose a movie with that kind of theme after what we talked about earlier."

"You mean because it was about having goals and dreams that you can accomplish? Like a purpose in life?"

"Yeah. Do you believe that?"

"I don't know. I used to. I guess I'll wait and see before I answer that." I glanced over and smiled at him. "I guess I hope so."

"Maybe you should look at what you can do with your visions like a sport or learning to play music. You have to practice it."

I laughed. Paul was so practical all the time. "You're cute when you're serious."

"Hey, just trying to help."

When he pulled up in front of my apartment, I said, "Thanks. I enjoyed the movie."

He held up his thumbs. "I've got so much info for my paper thanks to you." He reached over and touched my hair. "Plus, you're the best company ever."

I lowered my head and let my hair hang in front of my face.

He lifted my chin. "I have to write about six movies for this course," he said. "You want to be my movie partner?"

I playfully slapped his chest. "Only if I can pay for some."

"Maybe one." He touched my cheek with his fingertip. "If it's a chick flick, you pay."

I laughed, and the sound came from deep in my belly. Paul always made me laugh.

❖ ❖ ❖

On Sunday night, I brought the Ouija board out to the living room on Sarah's persistent request. We set it up on the floor and lit the candles. I had bought a bunch of new ones for the occasion. Natalie had bought wine, and Sarah munchies.

We set up the board and placed the little moving piece in the middle of it. Sarah clapped her hands, and Natalie giggled.

"Who wants to ask the first question?" I asked.

"I will," said Natalie. Both Sarah and I looked at her, because it was so unusual for her to speak up and take the first turn.

"Must be important," said Sarah.

"Will my mother ever get clean?" she whispered.

We put our hands on the little planchette and stared down at the board. When it started to move, I got this funny tingling in my arms, and it ran right from my shoulders to my fingertips. It was almost like a buzzing sensation.

The little block started to move below our fingers, and it went right to the word *no*.

"I'm sorry, Natalie," I said. I touched her arm.

"It doesn't matter. I have my grandmother. I just wondered if she ever would. You guys can have a turn."

"We don't have to play anymore," I said. I could see the pain in Natalie's eyes.

"It's okay, Indie," replied Natalie. "I've had some long chats with my grandmother lately, and it has made me realize how lucky I am to have her. My mother has her issues, and they're not mine."

"Okay," I said. "Sarah, you're next."

"Who will be my next boyfriend?" Sarah bopped her head when she said her question, and it was so obvious that she was trying to lighten the mood.

Again, we placed our fingertips on the little block. As it moved to the letter *S*, I again got the buzzing feeling in my arms. I wanted to shake them and get rid of the feeling, but I couldn't take my hands off the moving block, or I would wreck the game. Suddenly, the buzzing seemed to crawl under my skin and into other parts of my body, like my legs and abdomen. The little block kept moving from letter to letter, spelling out the word *Stephen,* and it was all I could do to hang on until the end. When it hit *N*, I swiftly took my fingers off the block and pulled my knees up to my chest, crossing my arms around them. My body felt as if little worms were slithering just under my skin.

"That is such bullshit!" Sarah laughed so hard she fell backward.

Natalie laughed, so I laughed, but the sound out of my mouth was like a horrible chortle.

"It's just a game," I said.

"Your turn," said Sarah to me.

"Okay," I said, relieved that they were oblivious to my reactions. "I'll make this easy, too. Who will be the next boy I kiss?"

"Oh, for God's sake," said Sarah. "You sound as if you're in grade two."

I was going home for a meal, and I would give my dad a kiss on the cheek. I would make sure the planchette would spell *Dad.*

We put our fingertips on the little block.

"Bet it goes right to *P*." Sarah sang her words.

The little block started to move across the board, and it was so obvious that Sarah was pushing it toward the *P*. Natalie too.

"You guys are making it go there." I laughed and tried to push it the other way, toward the letter *D*.

"Hey, stop forcing it." Sarah laughed with me. And we played a little pushing game with Natalie and Sarah going against me.

All of a sudden, the block moved toward the letter *J*.

And it stopped.

"Okay, so that's freaky." Sarah pushed away from the board.

I also scooted away from the board, as I could feel a weird heat coming from it. "I don't want to play anymore," I said.

Natalie stared at me across the candlelight. "You don't look so good."

My forehead burned, and sweat seemed to ooze from every pore. My body started to shake, and I couldn't stop it.

"Indie," said Sarah, "are you okay? You said it yourself. It's just a game."

"I'll get you some water." Natalie ran to the kitchen.

When Natalie returned with a full glass of water, my body temperature had returned to normal, but I still felt shaky. I accepted the water, almost spilling it as I brought it to my mouth and took a big gulp.

Water dribbled down my chin, and I wiped it off. "Thanks," I said.

"Maybe Paul's middle name begins with *J*," said Sarah.

"Let's put it away for tonight." I put the game in its box.

"Let's have a pillow fight instead." Natalie threw a pillow at Sarah, and she ducked so that it hit me. I tried to laugh and pretend that nothing was wrong. I picked up the pillow and threw it back, but my arms were like rubber, and it missed Natalie completely.

"Okay, that's it," said Sarah. "If you're going to throw like a girl, we'd better blow out the candles or we might end up in flames."

We blew out the candles and turned on the lights. The fluorescent shine gave me comfort.

"Let's watch a movie," said Natalie.

"And eat junk food," said Sarah.

"Sounds good to me." I took the board to my room and stashed it in the back of my closet.

✧ ✧ ✧

All week I went to work feeling exhausted. Every morning I would wake up and wonder if today was the day I was going to start feeling better. And every day I came home from work and slept. For the most part, I felt as if I had heavy blankets covering me—not one either, but many—and they swathed me and dragged me down, making every step a plod.

If Annabelle noticed, she didn't say anything—that is, until Friday. The day I was heading down to Kingston to see Lacey. Natalie and I were leaving as soon as I got home from work.

"Something's not right with you," she said. My shift was almost over, and I was getting ready for a fun weekend. I did not need her telling me this.

"What do you mean?" I asked.

"Your energy is off." She walked around my body, keeping her hands about six inches away from me but doing this waving motion.

"What are you doing?" I moved away from her.

"Trying to feel your energy." She stopped and backed away from me. "I have a good friend who is a Reiki healer. I want you to see her ASAP."

"Not this weekend," I replied. "I'm leaving for Kingston as soon as I get off work."

"I think you should reconsider your trip."

"I'll be fine."

"I worry that you don't protect yourself enough."

"I do," I said.

"Indie, please, listen to me."

〰〰〰

Chapter Fifteen

"I love this song." Natalie turned up the volume on the radio and the two of us sang along with Jewel's song "Who Will Save Your Soul?"

I rolled down my window to let the breeze flow through the car, and it whipped my hair everywhere. Everything in me had shifted, and I felt free and alive, buzzed and ready for a good time. Sure, my stomach was a bit queasy because of what Annabelle had said before I left, and my nerves were crackling for some strange reason, but I wasn't going to let any of that ruin my trip. My tiredness had been replaced with this crazy electrical energy, but that was a good thing, seeing as it was the weekend.

I sang as loudly as I could until the song ended. When the ads came on, I turned down the radio.

"I called Lacey on her new cell phone," I said. "She's excited. We are hitting the university pub tonight."

"Lacey has a cell phone?" Natalie switched lanes as we drove down the 401 Highway.

"She's my only friend that does." I loved the wind flowing through the car.

"She's so lucky." Natalie looked relaxed in the driver's seat. "I want one, but they're stupid expensive."

"She's always had the best phone before anyone else. When we were little, she was the first of us to have a phone in her room." I turned down the radio even more because the DJ was still talking about what was happening in Ottawa this weekend. I didn't care! I wasn't going to be there.

"So you excited for the open mic at the coffee shop?" I asked.

"Nervous is more the word."

"You'll be great. I feel it with every fiber of my being."

✤ ✤ ✤

When we arrived at Queen's, I felt as if I'd stepped into another time in history. Built in the mid-1800s, the main limestone building at the center of campus stood like a majestic statue. With our weekend bags slung over our shoulders, Natalie and I walked down the concrete path, in awe of all the other heritage stone structures, modeled after old British universities. The entire campus had a back-in-time feel to it. A tingling and buzzing raced through my body, starting at my head and moving down to my toes. I could barely keep my feet on the ground.

We found Lacey's dorm building, and inside, it had a bit of a musty smell, but that was dorm living, or so Lacey had told me, especially in a university that was well over 100 years old. As I walked down the hall, I felt removed from time, and it intrigued me, made me want to time travel.

Lacey's dorm room was one-quarter, if not one-eighth, of the size of her room at her house in Ottawa, and I burst out laughing. "Where are all your clothes?"

She yanked open the closet door. "Voilà."

Every inch was jammed with sweaters and T-shirts and skirts and blouses and winter jackets and everything else she could cram in there.

"And look under here." Lacey dropped to her knees by her little single bed and pulled out a canvas bag that had a zipper on the top. "This is where I keep the stuff I occasionally wear. You know, like scarves and belts and crap like that."

I sat on her bed and bounced up and down. "I'm so excited to be here. But where are we going to sleep?"

"On the floor. We'll put your bags on my desk, because I'm not doing any work this weekend. I'm borrowing a foam mattress. I can't wait for you to meet my friends." Then she leaned over and whispered, "Did you bring your cards?"

I tugged them out of my bag. "Sure did."

She clapped her hands. "Come on, let's go find everyone."

Natalie and I traipsed down the hall, following Lacey, and the spring in my step was almost surreal. Students passed us, and Lacey seemed to wave at everyone.

"Trust you to know a ton of people already," I said.

"Frosh week was soooo fun, Indie. I met so many people there. We had tug-of-wars and toga parties, and it was such a blast."

I thought about how fun it would be at a school like this, in a dorm, hanging out until all hours of the night with people my own age who were going through the same stuff I was. We took the stairs up to the third floor and walked down the hall and around the corner until Lacey stopped at a door and knocked.

A girl yelled, "Come on in. Door's open."

We walked into a room that was bigger than Lacey's, but there were two of everything, so that made it the same size.

"Kristen and Paige, these are my friends from Ottawa." She slung her arm through mine. "This is Indie, my bestest friend ever, and Natalie. Natalie wants to come to Queen's next year. They have the cutest apartment in Ottawa."

"I bet your bedrooms are bigger than ours," said Paige, a striking brunette who was all muscle. I wondered if she was an athlete.

Kristen, a tiny little Asian girl with the cutest face, looked at me. "Are you the one who reads cards?"

I shoved my hands in my back pockets. "Yeah. I try."

"Try? You're awesome," said Lacey.

Paige laughed. "She told us what you said about her going out with a musician. And it *almost* came true!"

I stared wide-eyed at Lacey. "You didn't tell me that."

"Well, it's not true yet, but I really like him. I wanted you to meet him this weekend, but now he's gone," she moaned. "He was going to do the open mic, but he had to go home because of some family function. He's from Kitchener. He plays guitar and sings country music."

"Too bad," I said. "Next time." I turned to Natalie. "Natalie is doing the open mic, too." I smiled proudly at her.

"That's brave," said Paige with a horrified look on her face. "I could never do that."

"Or just stupid." Natalie laughed, and I could tell it was a nervous laugh.

"Predrink in my room," said Lacey. She looked at her watch. "Let's say 8:30."

✤ ✤ ✤

By ten that night, with no food in my stomach, I knew I had to slow down or I wouldn't make it past midnight. Natalie was pacing herself because of her big night tomorrow. Lacey was full throttle ahead, as were her friends. University living.

We sat on her bed, and I enjoyed hearing the stories of different professors and how they were good or bad and all the chatter about the school football team and the games and the fun they were having on campus. Natalie lapped up every word.

We hit the campus pub around 11, and you could hear the loud music before entering. The few drinks I'd had in Lacey's dorm room had buzzed me, and now I felt as if I were walking a foot off the ground.

I met so many people in one evening that by the time we walked back to Lacey's dorm, my head was swimming. We arrived just after one and ordered pizzas, which we took to Paige and Kristen's room because it was bigger.

I sat cross-legged on Paige's bed and waved my cards in the air. "Who wants a reading?"

"I do! I do!" Paige sat down across from me on the bed.

"Someone give Indie another beer," yelled Lacey.

"Shh," said Kristen. "We're not supposed to have beer, and we're past curfew. If we get caught, we're in deep trouble."

"I know the resident supervisor," slurred Lacey. "We'll be okay."

I accepted the beer and took a big swig before I said, "Knock three times."

Paige knocked, shuffled, then picked her three cards. I tried to remember what the cards were about, but I couldn't, so I just went with the visions that kept flipping through my brain like flash cards. One after the other. And voices, too, speaking on top of one another. I spoke quickly, trying to say everything, and I could hear them all laughing around me.

"Indie, slow down," said Lacey. She held her stomach she was laughing so hard.

"I'm trying," I said. "But there's so much coming at me."

"This is *sooo* freaky," said Kristen.

I saw a man, very good-looking and a business man. I told Paige she was going to meet a guy and get married when she was 28. Then I heard the words *Texas* and *Dallas* and I saw a swimming pool, so I told her she was going to live in Texas and . . . the words just kept spilling out of my mouth. She would have two children, a boy and a girl; she would get a master's degree; her life would be successful; and she would live in a nice house. Then I heard the word *drowning,* and it kept hammering my brain like a skipping CD. I put my hands to my ears and stopped talking.

"What's wrong?" Paige asked.

"Nothing," I said. "Everything is going to be great for you." I forced a smile. "I just have a crazy ringing in my ear. They are talking so fast."

"Who is talking fast?" Paige asked.

"Angels."

They're not angels. Isaiah said. *They're lower spirits.*

"I'm next," said Kristen.

Good for you. You're having fun.

"I'm shaking," said Paige holding out her hands. Then she hopped off the bed. "I have to write it all down." She grabbed a lined notebook off her desk and began writing.

"My boss tapes her readings and gives the tapes to her clients," I said.

Act normal. Act normal. No one could know about the bizarre words mobbing my brain.

"That's a great idea," said Paige, without looking up. She kept scribbling in her book.

The same thing happened when I read for Kristen. My mind became like this huge computer downloading information that I just spewed out. One thing after another. I told her she would be a dentist and go to India and treat little children. I could see them playing and talking another language, and I could see her studying and working, but then I saw her insides. And I saw a bunch of eggs bopping up and down, but they were empty. There was no yolk. Suddenly, they flattened and started floating like light paper.

"Am I going to have children, too?" she asked. "I've always wanted kids. I've always wanted a big family."

I swigged back some beer. "You are surrounded by children," I said.

She clapped her hands. "I always tell my mother that I want four kids, just like she had."

I wanted to tell her that wasn't what I meant, but I couldn't, because I didn't really understand what I was seeing. The eggs were flat. Empty. Did that mean what I thought it meant?

Was she not going to have any children of her own?

Fortunately, Lacey was listening to the reading and piped up, "No more talk of kids. We're only in first year! Who wants another drink?"

We crawled into bed at three, and my body almost felt as if it were levitating off the thin foam mattress. I didn't know what to do. I couldn't stop the palpitations or the droning that was inside me, flowing through my veins. I had never taken drugs in my life, but I wondered if this was what people felt like who did. Who shot up and sent crap into their veins? It made no sense to me. I wanted this buzzing to go away.

Lacey and Natalie fell asleep right away, but I just lay there sizzling.

Finally, I got up and slipped on my shoes and tiptoed outside for a cigarette. The night air circled me, and the inferno inside me cooled a little anyway. I had no idea what was wrong with me or why I felt so jittery. I leaned against the wall, lit my cigarette, and inhaled. As the smoke sank into my lungs, I closed my eyes. The first time I'd ever really talked to John, we had smoked a cigarette together.

I opened my eyes and looked at the glimmering stars and the round, full globe of the moon, and sucked on my cigarette. The smoke seemed to calm me down a little.

For the longest time, I remained outside, in the cool and the quiet. A few students walked by me, and a few said hello. I smoked another cigarette. And another. The air brushed my skin but didn't make me drowsy.

Because I wasn't tired.

Not in the least.

❖ ❖ ❖

The next day I woke up after two hours of sleep, feeling buzzed again. Last week I had been so exhausted that I must have slept enough for the weekend. When I glanced at myself in the mirror, I saw that my eyes were wide and bright, and my pupils were dilated. I didn't have bags under my eyes. I certainly didn't look exhausted.

We spent the rest of the morning wandering around campus, with Lacey showing us which buildings she had to go to for her classes. I loved the old stone buildings and wondered if any of them were haunted. I wished I were smart enough to go to university. I thought about Paul. I thought about John. My mind just seemed to be all over the map. My energy seemed to be working on high gear. It went from thought to thought with no order and no reason, and I couldn't seem to stop it from going up and down like a yo-yo and back and forth like a Ping-Pong ball.

After the campus tour, we went into historic Kingston for lunch at a funky little restaurant inside an old redbrick building down by the pier. I ate a bit of salad, but I was too hyped to eat much. Perhaps I was nervous for Natalie?

Or maybe I was taking on her energy.

Natalie and I split the lunch bill, and we all headed back outside to walk along the pier. The waterway in Kingston was where the St. Lawrence River flowed into Lake Ontario. Here, closer to the water, the air was a bit chillier, and I wrapped my sweater around my shoulders. Sailboats docked in stalls swayed in the slight breeze, and the sky shone blue and clear. Kingston was a city full of life and energy and history. It also had that real university feel to it.

As we strolled, Natalie hummed her tunes, and I knew she was going to be a huge success. So why was I feeling so weird and buzzed?

❖ ❖ ❖

That night we got ready to go in Lacey's small room, and by the time we were dressed, her room was a total disaster, with piles of clothes everywhere.

"You look great, Natalie," said Lacey. "Like a musician."

Natalie was dressed in jeans and a yellow, red, and green gauzy shirt, and she wore the funkiest jewelry. Drawn to her necklace, I reached out and touched it. I didn't think I'd ever seen it before. It was a thick silver Celtic cross on a black leather rope. "This is beautiful."

"It was my grandmother's. She gave it to me before I left. I was saving it to wear on a special occasion. She got it in Ireland. One day I'm going to Ireland to learn about Celtic music history."

Like a flash, I saw the two of us walking down a road, and we were surrounded by green hills. The picture left as soon as it appeared. "I've always dreamed of visiting the Scottish ruins," I said.

"Maybe we can go there together," said Natalie.

A waft of flowers hit my nostrils. "In the spring," I blurted.

"Oh, wow. That would be so fun." She smiled at me with a glint in her eyes. "I'd go to Scotland with you if you'd go to Ireland with me. We could visit England as well."

I lifted my chin. "I'd love to do England first."

Natalie hugged me hard, and my body vibrated. It was happening. We were going to Europe.

She pulled back, squared her shoulders, picked up her guitar, and exhaled. "Shall we go?" she said. "If I don't get to that coffee shop soon, I won't go at all."

I glanced at her fiddle sitting in the corner. "Take that too."

"Why? I'm only up for one song."

I smiled. "I'll carry it."

❖ ❖ ❖

The coffee shop, Grinds, was packed when we got there, and we had to take a table at the back. I couldn't believe how busy it was. Natalie placed her guitar in between her legs and held on to it as if it were her baby.

"Good crowd," said Lacey.

"Really good," said Natalie, glancing around. She leaned into me and whispered, "Too good."

I touched her arm. "You're going to be amazing."

She put her hand on her stomach. "I think I might throw up."

"You're going to be great."

"When they call my name, I could just stay seated. Or run to the bathroom and hide."

"When you get on stage, just try to forget about everyone and sing to your grandmother. You wore the necklace she gave you, and she deserves to hear you sing."

"You think she'll hear me all the way in Newfoundland?" She held on to her necklace.

"I know she will," I whispered.

A young guy with a wild, dark afro, dressed in black jeans and a white T-shirt with some logo I couldn't read, went over to the stand-up microphone onstage and tapped it. The noise screeched through the small room, and everyone groaned and covered their ears.

"It's on," someone yelled.

"I guess it's on," he joked, his voice projecting through the microphone and off the walls.

"Turn it down!" another person yelled. Then the crowd laughed.

Natalie leaned in to me and whispered. "Are they going to heckle me, too?"

"Of course not."

"Welcome to open mic! And my name is Mike."

The crowd booed.

He held up his hand. "Okay, I get it. Enough of the bad jokes. Our first performer tonight is all the way from Toronto. Please welcome him to the stage."

A rocker guy with hair down to his waist and an electric guitar got onstage and walked to the microphone, adjusting it to fit his height. "Hi, my name's Mike."

Everyone laughed.

"No, seriously. My name *is* Mike." He plugged in his guitar, and it screeched louder than the microphone had.

"Too much static, dude!"

Horrified, Natalie's eyes grew wide, and she glanced back at the person who had made the comment. "They should kick him out," she said. "That's so disrespectful."

The guy onstage started playing and singing, and once he got going, he was okay. I actually liked his rock music and thought he had a decent voice, but I wondered if he shouldn't have tried a different venue. Coffee clubs were for music like Jewel and . . . Natalie.

When he was done, the crowd cheered and clapped; a few heckled, but not many.

"See?" I said to Natalie. "They liked him."

Lacey leaned across the table. "When are you on?"

Natalie lifted her hand and put up four fingers. Lacey nodded, sat back, and picked up a menu. "Let's get lattes and some sandwiches. They have yummy food here."

When the lattes arrived, I sipped mine, even though I knew caffeine was the last thing I needed. My body was still pulsing, almost like a throbbing heartbeat, and I couldn't figure it out.

Keep calm for Natalie. This is her night.

I listened to the next couple of acts: a country singer and a young girl with an amazing voice who sang an Alanis

Morissette song. Our sandwiches arrived on little wicker plates just before Natalie was up.

When Natalie looked at the plate of food, her beautiful pale skin turned a shade of olive green. "Don't look at it," I said. "You're next."

The emcee got up and told another lame joke, which some people laughed at and some booed. Natalie's leg shook up and down. She tapped her fingers on the table. I could hear her breathing beside me.

"And next on the stage we have a young woman from Ottawa. She is here to sing a song she wrote herself. Give it up for Natalie O'Reilly!"

Natalie picked up her guitar and walked toward the stage, looking exotic with her lanky body, sculpted face, wide eyes, and smile that could melt the ice in a glass. Calmly, she pulled up a stool, sat down, and lowered the microphone. Her guitar rested on her lap and looked as if it were a part of her, an extension.

"How yah gettin' on?" she asked, smiling.

"A fellow Newfie!" someone yelled from the audience.

"That's right! All the way from St. John's." Natalie peered into the crowd, shielding her eyes with her hand, trying to spot her fellow Newfoundlander. "Where yah from?" She sounded so casual. The stage was almost like her friend.

"Goose Bay!" the guy yelled.

"Lard Jesus. You're *barely* a Newfie."

Everyone laughed. Natalie charmed the crowd with her smile as she gently strummed a few chords on her guitar, obviously warming up. When the audience had quieted, her smile vanished, and she leaned toward the microphone. "I wrote this song for my mother." Her voice, although barely a whisper, projected to every person in the crowd. "It's called 'Red Eyes.'"

The room went silent, and I held my breath. That is, until the first clear note came out of her mouth. Her haunting voice rang pure, and even though I had heard her sing many times, tonight she sounded so different. Melancholy. Sad.

And unbelievably amazing.

"They mean more than me,

those red eyes."

Her voice hit every bone in my body. I glanced at the crowd, and they were as enthralled as I was.

"Did you ever try to love me more . . .

than those red eyes?"

As she sang, a deep sorrow enveloped me, and a few times I had to look down because I thought I might break into tears. Why was I so emotional? It was just a song, and I was this close to sobbing. One minute I was happy, one minute hyper, one minute sad.

"Red eyes . . . red eyes.

They greet the sunrise, and wave to the sunset . . ."

The audience hung on her every note.

". . . but forget about me.

Those red eyes."

When she finished, the room hushed for a second then burst out into the biggest applause of the night. I stood and clapped vigorously, and Paige, Kristen, and Lacey also stood, which got the rest of the crowd on their feet.

Lacey pinched my arm. "That was phenomenal!" she shouted over the noise. "I can't believe she wrote it, and her voice, it is just so . . . so magnificent."

Whistles sounded from the crowd. Natalie leaned forward and in a soft demure voice said, "Thank you."

The emcee came back on the stage. "Well, I think we have a star in the making. Ladies and gents, one day we will see Natalie O'Reilly's name on a CD cover, and you can say you heard her here." He turned to Natalie. "That was an incredible performance."

"Let's hear another one from her," yelled someone from the crowd.

He held up his hand. "We have a long lineup waiting."

"Come on. Just one more from the Newfie for the Newfie."

The emcee looked at Natalie, and she looked over at me, horror written all over her face. I raised her fiddle in the air, and she grinned and nodded. Once she had her fiddle under her chin, she started tapping her foot and broke into a Celtic song that rocked the place. She had everyone clapping and dancing in their seats.

We stayed and listened to the rest of the performers, and when there was one left, I suddenly felt my heart start to race again. The buzzing in my blood returned, and this time it was worse. Way worse. Too much caffeine. I needed water. I tapped my fingers on my thighs. I jiggled my leg. I bopped in my seat. I couldn't stop my body from moving.

What was wrong with me? I had been feeling so good. Now I was off again.

It had been like this all weekend. Good. Bad. Good. Bad.

Dizzy, I closed my eyes, but vertigo took over my body, spinning me around and around, so I opened them.

Something had shifted. The energy in the room was different. What was it?

Lacey leaned over and whispered in my ear. "I don't want you to freak out, but You Know Who just walked in."

My throat instantly dried. My palms started to sweat. And an electrical current jolted through my body.

Just like it used to.

I slowly turned my head, and there he was, staring at me, his face a web of distress and anguish and his eyes a red mess.

John.

Chapter Sixteen

The minute I saw him I got up and went to him. Almost as if I were on automatic pilot. "What . . . what are you doing here?"

John's red eyes pierced me, like a sharp blade. The vibrations my body had felt all weekend had escalated, and I was visibly trembling.

He put his hand on my shoulder. "I could ask you the same question."

"I came to see Lacey." I looked away. I didn't want to see his red eyes.

He leaned over, and the smell of soap and cigarettes made my pulse quicken and a current surge through my body. His warm breath circled me when he whispered in my ear. "Indie, I need to talk to you."

My parched throat made swallowing hard, and I tried to create some moisture that would allow me to speak. "Let's go outside," I muttered.

"You still smoke?" he asked when we were out in the cool night air. He pulled a pack out of the pocket of his purple buttoned shirt. I'd never seen him wear such a bright color before.

"Sure do," I said.

He lit one and handed it to me. And I accepted without hesitation. I inhaled deeply, wanting the smoke to calm me, but it didn't and my mind raced as I wondered what I was doing, standing outside with him.

"What are you doing in Kingston?" I asked.

He shrugged. "Seeing friends."

Silence drifted over us and became intertwined with the cigarette smoke with each inhalation and exhalation.

Finally he spoke. "My mother has cancer."

I stared at him. "What?"

He tilted his head back and gazed at the sky. "Ovarian cancer." He blew out smoke, then looked my way. The desolate expression in his eyes punctured my heart, and I didn't know if I should cry or reach out and hold him in my arms.

"I told you I had to talk to you," he said, his voice barely a whisper. He ran his hand through his hair. "She found out a few weeks ago."

"Can it be treated?" I asked.

He shook his head. "I don't know. The doctor said it's already at stage four, and it's spreading fast."

"John, I'm so sorry." I stubbed my cigarette out in a metal bin that stood beside me before I reached for his hand. It was cold. I remembered when I first read my cards, alone in my bedroom, and I asked about John, I had felt the pains in my abdomen. That must have been what that was, pains for his mother.

He butted out his cigarette and pulled me toward him and hugged me hard. Wrapped in his arms, my heart beat against his, and I knew he needed me to be strong.

"She's going to die," he whispered in my ear.

I desperately wanted to tell him that she was going to be okay, but I couldn't speak. The words wouldn't come out, because in that moment, I knew John's mother wanted to die.

Suddenly, he pulled away from me and held me by my shoulders. His sharp gaze went right through my eyes and deep into my body. "She's going to die, isn't she, Indie?"

I didn't answer.

"You know things before they happen." He put his hand under my chin so I couldn't look away. "Can you see her dying, Indie?"

"Death isn't something I can see," I said, holding his stare. "She's tired, John."

He dropped his hand from my jaw and kicked the ground. "She won't live for me."

"She's trying."

His shoulders slumped, and he looked off into the dark night. "Not hard enough."

I had seen things about John's mother, horrible things, and I knew that no matter how much she loved her son, she was dying because she couldn't live with the guilt. So many times, I had thought about telling John about my vision . . . that I saw his mother kill his father. But I couldn't. It wasn't my secret to tell.

I looked into John's sad, red eyes. He didn't need to know. I had been right not to tell. It wasn't my place.

"I've got a hotel room tonight," he said. "Will you stay with me?"

"Just for an hour or so."

❖ ❖ ❖

I went back into the coffee shop and tapped Lacey on the shoulder. "I'm going to spend a little time with John and catch up," I said. "I'll be back in about an hour."

Lacey shook her head at me. "Don't," she said.

"I have to, Lacey," I said. "His mother has cancer. He needs a friend."

Natalie put her hand on my arm. "Lacey's right. Think about my song."

All the weird jitters in my body had returned, and it was as if someone inside me had flipped a switch to make me vibrate. "I have to," I said.

Lacey hugged me. "See you later."

"Okay." I nodded.

John and I left the coffee shop, and at first we just walked side by side without touching, but once we were away from the crowd and alone, he reached for my hand. I didn't pull away. I liked his touch.

"My hotel isn't far from here," he said.

"I just want to walk for a bit," I said.

"I have to go back there," he said. "Come with me. Please, Indie. I need you. I'll walk you back in a little while."

"Okay," I conceded.

The grungy hotel room reminded me of Miles and my horrible maid job. I grimaced when I entered and immediately felt the bugs under my skin.

Leave, Indie. This time Isaiah spoke firmly.

I knew I should leave. All my gut instincts said get out.

Be a friend, Indie. You can handle this.

I stiffly sat down on the end of the bed. John sat beside me, and our thighs and shoulders touched. Everything in my body quickened, and my heart squeezed. He stroked my hair and kissed the top of my head.

"You're the only person I've wanted since I found out about my mom."

I didn't answer.

He lifted my chin, tenderly this time, and made me look into his eyes. In all the time I went out with him, I could never see through his dense gray eyes. Not once. He was a mystery to me, someone dark and deep, and his eyes were like blurry pools with demons lurking below the surface.

Finally, I said, "I have to go."

"No," he murmured in my ear. "Stay. Just a little longer."

Unexpectedly, I felt his lips on mine, and my body ignited into fiery flames. I kissed him back with a shocking intensity, as if it wasn't even me. We fell back on the bed, and he touched me everywhere, and I thought I was going to explode.

"You want me?"

Out of my mouth came the word *yes.*

❖ ❖ ❖

A few hours later, I awoke to voices outside the motel door. I reached for John, but the other side of the bed was empty. I sat up. Where was he? The door creaked open, and I snuggled under the covers, pulling them over my naked body. The draft from the outside entered the room, and I curled into a ball. When I touched my bare skin, I felt dirt. Cold, ugly dirt.

John tiptoed back into the room and shut the door very quietly. Then he sat on the chair by the little wooden table. I pretended to sleep but kept my gaze on him. He emptied the contents of a little pouch onto a mirror and took a rolled-up bill and stuck it in his nose.

My heart raced. All the rumors were true. I didn't want to believe it. I closed my eyes when he snorted. The sound echoed off the cheap walls.

I had to leave.

But he wouldn't sleep now.

After he snorted, he sat up in his chair and tilted his head back, his hair falling back behind him. Within minutes, he was tapping his foot. He got up and started pacing. In time, minutes perhaps, he would want me again.

"John?" I tried to sound as sleepy as possible. "Are you awake?"

"Indie." He shoved the rolled-up bill in the drawer before he came over to my side of the bed and sat down. He stroked my hair. "I didn't mean to wake you," he said gently. "I can't sleep. I can't sleep, thinking about my mother."

"It's okay," I whispered. I touched his arm. "Can you get me a soda? I'm so thirsty." I knew the machine was down the sidewalk and behind a carport area by the front lobby.

"Sure," he said.

Of course he would. At this point, being so high on cocaine, he would do anything to be outside, smoking a cigarette, just to keep moving. As soon as I heard the door latch, I quickly put on my clothes, grabbed my purse, and opened the door a crack. I peered outside, and when I couldn't see him, I ran out the door and into the dark night.

❖ ❖ ❖

215

"What happened last night?" Lacey asked me the next morning as Natalie and I were packing. She sat on her bed in her pajamas, watching us get our stuff together.

"Nothing. We just talked." I couldn't look at her. Lacey, my friend. I was lying to her because I was ashamed. What had I done? Why had I slept with John? I'd been awake all night. How could I have gotten so sucked in? My heart felt as if it weighed a million pounds.

What would Paul think of me now?

The guy cared and had never, ever been anything but kind to me. Would I have to make up lies for him as well? Was I falling deeper and deeper into a well of darkness?

"What time was it when you came in?" Natalie rolled up the foam mattress.

I picked up the tie for it. "Not too late," I replied. "Around three." As Natalie held the mattress, I wrapped the tie around it. "What did you guys get up to?" I couldn't meet her gaze.

"We came back here." Natalie gently tossed the foam to Lacey who caught it like a football. "And talked for bit. Then we went to bed."

"We missed you," said Lacey.

"I need a shower before we head back." I picked up my towel and shampoo and walked out of the room.

✤ ✤ ✤

Natalie and I barely talked on the drive home. All the energy I'd had over the weekend had disappeared, and I leaned my head on the back of the seat and closed my eyes. Exhaustion seemed to seep from every pore in my body.

Why had I done it? He was wrong for me. Why had I gone back to John? I still felt dirty and cheap.

It was as if it hadn't been me in that hotel room. Not me at all. I wasn't someone who fell into bed with anyone.

John isn't just anyone.

Paul would be devastated if he knew. Sure, we hadn't agreed to be exclusive, but this would hurt him so much. So not only did I hurt John by doing something I shouldn't have, but I would also hurt Paul. Why was I causing so many people so much pain?

"So," Natalie broke my thoughts, "are you really keen on a trip to Scotland and Ireland like we talked about yesterday? I'm game if you are." Natalie sounded serious.

"Absolutely." I tried to exude some enthusiasm, but I think I fell flat. Reviving my plans for a trip *would* give me something to concentrate on. If I took on two jobs to pay for it, I wouldn't have to see anyone, and I could just work. "Let's start planning," I said.

She held up her thumb. "You betcha."

"You can take your guitar and sing in the pubs."

"Oh, yeah. And get material for new songs. And you can visit ruins and commune with the dead."

I tried to laugh.

We drove another couple of miles before she spoke again. "It's none of my business," she said carefully. "I don't know John . . . very well . . . but I don't get a good vibe from him."

"His mother is dying."

"I know you wanted to be a friend."

"I was . . . more than a friend," I said quietly.

"You slept with him?" Natalie almost swerved off the side of the road. She slammed on the brakes, and we pulled over.

I nodded. "I hate myself."

Natalie put her hand on my shoulder. "Don't. You made a mistake, that's all."

"A big mistake." I slouched in my seat and stared out the window.

For the rest of the drive, I gazed outside at the passing trees and listened to the radio. I turned it up full blast, and neither of us talked. Around two in the afternoon, we pulled up in front of the apartment and I saw the SOLD sign in the front window of George's store.

"Wow," I said. "That was fast."

"That's for sure," replied Natalie.

"I'm going to miss George so much."

"I didn't really know him," said Natalie. She cranked the wheel and parked the car.

We got out, and Natalie pulled her guitar and fiddle out from the backseat.

"You were amazing last night," I said.

"Thanks," she replied. "And, Indie, thanks for believing in me. If it wasn't for you, I wouldn't have gotten on that stage." She paused and glanced at me. "Promise me something? Don't throw *your* dreams away for a guy, especially one who will never make you happy."

"Okay." The one word barely made it out of my mouth, but she heard me.

I lowered my head. Tears were again on the surface of my eyes. "See you upstairs. I want to visit George," I muttered before I turned and walked quickly toward the store.

The OPEN sign for the store wasn't turned around, but I could see a light in the back of the store, so I tried the door, and it opened. The bell tinkled when I entered, but I didn't see George.

"George," I called out.

No answer.

Perhaps he was working on something in the back? Why would he leave his door open, though? That was unlike him.

I glanced around. "George," I called again.

Screech. Screech. The sound was slow but steady.

My heart constricted, my body broke out in a sweat, and all the bizarre twitching and pulsing that I had felt over the weekend returned. My frayed nerves hummed inside my body as if they were alive and ready to zap.

Screech. Screech.

The noise came from the back of the store. I stepped forward, looking through the furniture to see where the light was coming from.

Suddenly, I saw her in the rocking chair: Green Lady. She rocked back and forth. Back and forth. The noise was the sound of the chair.

She hadn't left. Why? Annabelle had warned me that she might not have gone. Why hadn't I listened?

I started to shake, and my knees were ready to buckle. "I thought you had gone to see your baby." My voice trembled.

She sang a lullaby. And rocked back and forth.

"George," I whispered, "are you here?"

When he didn't come running, I knew he wasn't even in the store. She had probably opened the door. She had been the one moving things on him! She'd left our place and come to stay in the store.

I would have to tell George about her the next time I saw him. But right now I had to help her.

Annabelle had told me to just tell the ghost to go. "You need to go through the light," I said.

Screech. Screech. Back and forth.

"Please," I begged. "Your boy is there."

She stood up and looked at me. "He is?"

"Yes," I said. "Go to the light. He's waiting for you."

Suddenly, behind her something glowed, almost as if a huge flashlight had been turned on.

"Go," I said softly. "Please, go."

She turned, tilted her head, and stared at the light. Then a little boy appeared and held out his hand. She walked forward. And disappeared.

The room turned dark and cold. My body shook and trembled. My stomach heaved. My head ached. And I felt as if I had little bugs crawling on my skin. I had helped Green Lady, but I hadn't protected myself, and now I was open. Wide open. I was doing everything wrong.

I ran outside, gasping, and leaned against the wall to catch my breath. Then I collapsed in a heap on the ground, wrapping my arms around my knees.

❖ ❖ ❖

I entered Annabelle's Angels the next day, and as soon as Annabelle saw me, she held up her hands for me to stop moving toward her.

"Your energy is worse than it was on Friday," she uttered.

"I'm so sorry." I hung my head. Last night I'd gone to bed at seven and slept all night. When I woke up in the morning, after 12 full hours of sleep, every jitter in my body was gone but I was exhausted beyond belief. Yes, I had sent Green Lady to the light, but that didn't take away the fact that I was an absolute mess.

Why had I slept with John? What would Annabelle think of me?

"Go to the back room." Annabelle pointed to the door. Then she moved around me in a big circle to get to the front so she could turn her OPEN sign to CLOSED.

My feet were glued to the floor, and I didn't move.

"Indie, you have to do this. Go. Okay?"

I hurried to the back room and flopped down in the pink chair. I'm not sure how long I sat there, with my head resting on the back of the chair, but my mind wouldn't turn off.

I had slept with John. Probably hurt Paul. Lied to Lacey. And George was leaving because I didn't get rid of Green Lady the first time. She had been the one moving things. I had pushed her aside instead of helping her.

Indie, George wanted to sell his store. Isaiah spoke to me.

"Why do you care about me?" I asked.

Face it, Indie. You're just a fuck-up.

"And why do you keep bugging me? Sometimes you help me, like with Miles, and sometimes you just make everything worse." I put my hands over my ears and rocked back and forth. "I should never have listened to you."

"Indie." Annabelle spoke from the door.

I sat up straight.

"This is Judy. She is going to help you. She is a Reiki healer. She will know what to do with you."

Judy was a heavyset woman, and she wore these massive gemstone rings. Unlike Annabelle, *she* looked like a psychic. I stared at Judy for a second before I turned to Annabelle. "I'm sorry." The words barely escaped my lips. And I really was sorry.

"I don't want to hear you say that again," said Annabelle with such tenderness that I wanted to crawl in a hole and cover myself with dirt. "We'll fix this."

She didn't move toward me. "I can't be near you right now. I'm sorry. But I just can't."

Judy led me to the room where Annabelle had taken me the first day I came to see her, and she had me lie down on my back on a massage table. She placed her hands over my heart. "From what Annabelle tells me, you have some blockages. I'm going to run my hands over your body in an effort to release whatever it is that is attached to you. I will be concentrating on your chakras to see if any of them are blocked. You can close your eyes if you want. It might help you relax."

I did as she said and closed my eyes, and although Judy wasn't touching my skin, I could feel her hands above me. She placed them above my stomach. It was the weirdest feeling ever, like a huge leech was stuck inside me and wouldn't come off.

"Oh, wow," she said. "You are really blocked."

Then out of the blue, she burped this really loud, belching sound. Normally, that would have made me laugh, but the sound almost came from me, and it made me feel relieved. Above me, Judy made a sound, almost a whooshing, like someone was being sucked through a straw. Involuntarily, my body twitched, and suddenly I felt lighter than I had for a long time.

As Judy moved her hands up my body toward my heart, I gasped. Again, she let out this really gross burp, then the sucking sound started, and this time it was deafening. My body almost levitated off the table because the pull was so intense.

"That one was huge," said Judy. "Incredible. I've never seen anything like this. Working on you like this is something out of this world. And I mean that literally."

She continued to clear all my chakras, and every time the whooshing sound began, a feeling of relief would wash over me. I have no idea how long I lay there and let her work her magic.

Finally, she broke the silence. "How do you feel?"

I opened my eyes and stared up at her. "Better. But woozy."

"That's to be expected," she replied. "You have been through a thorough cleansing. You need to breathe—inhale and exhale—to clear your body. Keep doing that until you feel that you are steady enough to walk. I don't want you leaving this room until then."

I sat on the end of the table, just sitting there and breathing. After a few minutes, I felt almost normal. Almost normal?

That was a joke. I just had spirits sucked out of my body. That was not even close to normal.

And that was the reality of my life.

"You also need to drink a lot of water today." Judy interrupted my thoughts. "And avoid coffee, cigarettes, and alcohol. I would actually do that for a good month."

I lowered my head.

She stroked my back. "Take it easy." Then she stepped back from me and looked at me with a quizzical expression.

"You know you have someone beside you."

"I do?" I looked to my left then to my right but didn't see anyone. But I could smell something really familiar. A pipe.

She nodded her head. "Frank is with you."

"That's my papa," I said. "My grandfather."

She nodded. Then she squinted. "Someone else is with you, too."

Isaiah. "Who is he?" I blurted out.

She smiled. "He says he's your guide and part of your divine team. He's chosen you, honey." She paused. "He's got a few angels with him, too, so . . . you've got quite the team, girl." She winked and left the room, her long, flowing dress trailing behind her.

I slid off the table, and my legs almost gave out they were so rubbery.

Judy had made me feel better. The nervous vibrations were gone.

When I went out to the front of the store, Annabelle immediately embraced me in a huge hug. "Come hell or high water, girl, you are going to learn to protect yourself."

"I did something really stupid over the weekend." I hung my head just thinking about John. Why? Why had I comforted him that way? But more to the point, why had I wanted him?

"I know," said Annabelle. "But we all do stupid things. It's how we deal with them later that matters."

"Of course you know." I kept staring at the ground, unable to lift my head to look at Annabelle. I wished I were a turtle and could hide my entire head.

"You can't take it back, so move forward and learn from it," continued Annabelle. "We all have to learn from our mistakes."

I blew out some air. Finally, I looked at her. "I have this voice in my head, and it won't go away. Sometimes it helps me, and other times . . . it tells me I'm no good or to do the wrong thing."

"Ah. We all have that little voice that tells us how *crappy* we are at things."

"I guess so." I rubbed my temples. She had just said I was a *fuck-up*, though. That was pretty harsh. "Sometimes she uses words that are a lot worse than *crappy*," I said, shaking my head. "It's so loud in my head. How do I get rid of her?"

"Good question. Because you don't want to all the time. Tell me, has the voice ever been helpful?"

I nodded. "With this boss I had at my last job. He was creepy and wanted me . . . sexually. The voice told me to 'beat him at his own game.'"

"Did you?"

"Yup. I kicked him where it hurts."

Annabelle laughed. "Okay, that's good. So, believe it or not, that voice can be used sometimes." Annabelle held me by the shoulders. She looked me directly in the eyes. "You just need to control her and use your own intuition to guide you as to when she is right and wrong. She is your ego talking to you."

"How do I do that? Control her?"

"You have two voices. You have your intuitive voice and your ego voice. Your intuitive speaks first. Ego second. The ego will try to make you see what isn't true but will also help you have confidence."

"I think I get that." I turned away from Annabelle. When I was in John's motel room, my gut instinct was to leave. Annabelle was right. It had spoken to me first. But then that ego voice had come in and told me to be a friend.

"Lately," I mumbled, "the ego voice has been really strong, though."

Annabelle gently touched my arm. "Indie, it's okay. You have to move on from whatever happened this weekend. Now, this might be hard to understand, but we all need our egos to be successful. If you let her take over, though, you won't have any success."

"Okay." I lowered my head.

"You've had a lot of lower energy spirits inside you so she took advantage of you. But now that you have been totally cleaned up inside, she can help you. She can get you through a door for an interview or give you the confidence to push forward with something you want to do. You just can't let her control you. That's what has been happening."

"But sometimes she tells me to do the wrong things."

"She's overpowering your intuitive voice. Don't let her do that. Listen carefully to the two voices because your intuitive voice will speak first. That is the one you listen to."

✤ ✤ ✤

The day passed quicker than I thought it would, and by closing, I had some of my energy back. Sleep was on my agenda, but I definitely felt as if all the creepy-crawly things were gone.

At four o'clock, I heard the bell tinkle. My body turned cold. I knew who it was.

"Hey, Indie," said Paul. "How was your weekend?"

John crashed through my mind. Wafts of the cheap hotel room hit my nostrils. What would Paul think of me?

"Um," I said, knowing he was waiting for an answer. "It was okay." My voice went up an octave, even though I was desperately trying to sound normal.

"How was Natalie's debut?" His eyes shone like bright blue water.

"She was amazing." I smiled, nodding my head. Now this was something I could talk about with passion. "Absolutely amazing," I repeated. "She sang a song she wrote."

"Wow," he said. "That's impressive." He stepped toward me. "You still up for the movie tonight?"

I stepped back from him. I had totally forgotten that I had agreed to go out with him. "I'm pretty tired." I placed a strand of my hair behind my ear.

"Oh, okay. No problem." He shoved his hands in his pockets and shrugged. "I'll go alone, then." He furrowed his eyebrows at me for a moment before he nodded, once, as if he knew something.

"Sorry," I said. I genuinely meant it.

He gave me a sad little smile before he turned and walked toward the door. He was almost outside when I said, "Paul."

He glanced over his shoulder at me, his hand still on the doorknob.

"Thanks for asking." I didn't want him to go. And I wanted to go to the movie with him, but if he knew what I had done, he wouldn't want to go with me. Why was I pushing away the only good thing in my life? "Maybe another time, though."

"Sure. Call me anytime." He mimicked calling on the telephone. I smiled and gave him a little wave.

"See yah later, Indie."

And then before I could blink, he was gone.

I locked up and walked out into the sunshine. It was a beautiful day, and I put on my sunglasses as I waited for the bus. Paul. He was the nicest guy. And I liked him, I really did. But he wouldn't want me if he knew what had happened. I didn't want him to know, and if we were together, I would have to tell him. He was someone I couldn't lie to.

The bus jerked to a stop in front of me, and I climbed the steps and tossed my money down the little drain. I found a seat at the back of the bus and sat down.

A black man sat across from me, and he smiled at me, his eyes crinkling in the corners of his face, showing his weathered lines.

"Hi, Indie," he said.

Confused, I looked over. His voice sounded familiar, but I was sure I had never seen him before. How did he know my name?

I lowered my head and tried to stare at him out of the corner of my eye. Was he a friend of my parents? His face was lit with a perma-grin, and he had these amazing white teeth that seemed to shine and gleam. Everything about this man oozed kindness, and although I knew I should be afraid of him, a stranger on the bus talking to me, I wasn't.

He met my gaze again and smiled. This time I smiled back before I looked forward. Suddenly, my body was encased in a blanket of warm, comforting air. I didn't look at him again until it was time to get off. I rang the cord, and when the bus stopped, I walked to the door. He got up, too.

Was he following me?

Weirdly, I felt no fear. I felt calm and completely at ease. I stepped down and outside, and the bus doors shut. Then I turned. "You're Isaiah," I said.

He nodded. "Yes, Indie. I am."

"Where did you come from?"

"We were friends in a past life. And still are."

"If you're my friend, why didn't you help me?"

"Well, sometimes we're not allowed to help. If we do, we will stop your growth as a spiritual being." He winked at me. "And sometimes you are one stubborn Taurus and you don't ask for help. You need to learn to ask."

I reached out to touch him, but he disappeared.

I'll show you the way.

✤ ✤ ✤

When I got back to the apartment I saw the light on in George's store and through the window I saw him, packing boxes. I wanted to say good-bye.

"Hi, George," I said as I entered the store. Immediately, I felt the clear energy in the room. Green Lady was gone.

"Indie!" he said with a smile. He put a book in a box and the dust flew in front of him. He waved a hand in front of his face and laughed.

"When do you actually move?" I asked.

"Two weeks." He placed another book in the box.

"You're going to love Florida," I said.

"I hope so—it's a good place for a crazy old geezer like me," he chuckled.

"George, you're not crazy. You don't have dementia."

He turned to look at me. "Now how would you know that?"

I clenched my hands together. "There was a ghost in the store," I blurted out the words. "The English woman who owned the house, whose son died."

"Mrs. Schmidt?"

"Yes, her. She was moving things on you."

"So I'm okay?"

I laughed. "You're more than okay. I'm going to miss you."

"C'mere, you."

I stepped toward George and hugged him like I would hug my grandpa. I would miss him, but I knew Florida was going to add years to his life.

❖ ❖ ❖

That night, I sat in my bedroom and thought about what Isaiah had said to me about asking for help. I put my head in my hands. What should I do? Should I talk to Paul about what had happened?

"Help me." I said out loud.

Don't tell him. You weren't exclusive.

"Shut up," I said with authority. Then I sat on my bed with my arms crossed and waited. Nothing came. Nothing. This was stupid. Both Isaiah and Annabelle had told me to listen. And here I was listening, and all I heard was white noise.

I sat on my bed and kept sitting there.

There was a knock on my door, and I almost jumped out of my skin. I'd been sitting on my bed for more than an hour waiting for a sign. Enough waiting around.

I got off my bed. "What's up?"

Natalie opened my door. "Phone for you."

I hadn't heard the phone. "Thanks," I said and went to the kitchen and picked up the receiver.

"Hello."

"Hi, Indie."

"Paul," I said. "I thought you were going to the movie."

"I did. It's over. I caught the early show."

I glanced up at the clock George had given me, and sure enough, it was 9:30 already. "What did you see?" I played with the telephone cord.

"*Rush Hour.* It was awesome."

"Are you home already?"

"Nah. I'm calling from the pay phone at the theater."

"You called to tell me about the movie?"

"Yeah. And to hear your voice."

This was my sign. Thank you, Isaiah.

"Did you want to pop by?" I asked.

"Sure. But I thought you were tired."

"I want to see you," I said.

After I hung up the phone, I sighed. I wanted to see him, but would he still like me after what I had done? I had to tell him the truth. I had asked and listened, and now I had to follow through. Paul had called for a reason.

I waited for Paul downstairs, and when I saw Mable, I waved. "Let's go to a coffee shop," I said. We needed privacy.

We went to a little coffee shop around the corner. It had quiet tables and cushy seats. I ordered an herbal tea, and Paul got an iced coffee and a huge cookie.

"You want some?" He broke off a hunk.

"I'm good," I said. I twirled my mug. *Speak, Indie, speak.*

"The movie was so great," said Paul. "Jackie Chan is so funny."

"Yeah, he is," I replied.

"There was one part in the movie that was so hilarious—"

"Paul." I put my hand on top of his. If I let him continue, he would talk about the movie, and I would lose my nerve. "I have something to tell you."

His face dropped, and he pulled his hand away. The look on his face said he knew what I had to say wasn't good. *His* intuition had kicked in. "What?" he asked.

"Over the weekend," I said. "I, uh, I ran into John."

Paul leaned back in his seat, moving away from me. "And," he said.

"He told me his mother was dying of cancer."

"That's terrible. I'm so sorry."

"I ended up back at his hotel room."

He narrowed his eyes and stared intently at me. "Is this going where I think it's going? 'Cause if it is, I don't want to hear the rest."

Tears pooled behind my eyes. "I'm sorry," I whispered.

"You're sorry?" He shook his head at me. "That's all you can say?" Paul crumpled his wrapper and stood. "We should go."

Part Three

Chapter Seventeen

December 1998

Large, fluffy snowflakes were falling from a gray sky, and all I wanted to do was run outside and lift my face so I could taste the fresh and pure snow. Instead, I flipped the *Ottawa Citizen* open to the help-wanted section.

Annabelle was already in the back, reading for one of her regular clients, and because of the storm, the store was empty. It had been crazy busy up until today, with all kinds of people shopping for Christmas presents, especially stocking stuffers. With my help, Annabelle had purchased the most amazing angel wing tree ornaments from a seller in the United States, and they had sold out in just days.

And *also* with my help, and my insistence, we had decorated the store at the beginning of December, even putting up a fake Christmas tree trimmed with beautiful angels and with wrapped colorful boxes underneath.

Annabelle had kept the store open late on Thursday and Friday nights to extend the shopping hours, so I had managed to work lots of extra hours and earn some additional cash. I'd put some away, but . . . most I'd spent on Christmas gifts for friends, family, and my pets. Henry was getting a new jeweled collar with the cutest bell and some catnip treats that he loved.

Yesterday, Natalie flew home to Newfoundland to spend the holidays with her grandmother. Before she left, we'd exchanged gifts. She gave me a beautiful blue turtleneck sweater, and I surprised her with a silver necklace that had a music note on it. Both Natalie and I had thought Sarah would get us something like a six-pack of beer, but she had surprised us each with a travel book—mine was on Scotland, and Natalie's was on Ireland. For the entire evening, we sat on the sofa and picked the places and things we wanted to see on our trip, bookmarking pages and circling all the sights that looked like must-sees.

But I needed money, or I wasn't going anywhere. And right now the thought of a trip to Scotland was the only thing that was keeping me going.

I scanned down the help-wanted ads and found nothing at all that I could apply for. I groaned. I tapped my pen on the counter.

Maybe I could babysit. Or dog-sit. Or house-sit. Or anything.

I had to get to Scotland. Get away. Do something with my life. Forget about how I had treated Paul like crap. My stomach flip-flopped. I missed him, and it was a different feeling from how I had missed John. Paul had talked to me, not *at* me. And he listened to me, even when I was whiny or sad or boring. Best of all, he made me laugh. Annabelle was teaching me about something called manifesting; it was about trying to make things come true by thinking positively about them. I took out a piece of paper and started writing.

I am in Scotland.

I am in Scotland.

I wrote and wrote the same line until my hand cramped and I heard Annabelle's door creak in the back.

I quickly shut the newspaper, crumpled up the paper I'd been scrawling on, and shoved it all under the counter and into my purse. I'd only saved $100, and that wasn't nearly enough. Natalie and I were so serious about the trip and had done a ton of research, but I just couldn't seem to put money in the bank. What was wrong with me?

After getting my book last night from Sarah, and after hashing everything over with Natalie, I had gone to bed and kept Henry up by reading about Scotland until three in the morning. He liked it when I read out loud to him. Something was drawing me there. I wasn't even sure what. The Scottish ruins begged me to visit.

Would they heal me of the pain I was still in, months later?

Voices sounded from the hallway, and I stood up and straightened my jeans. I didn't want Annabelle knowing that I needed more work, because she would give me grief for spending too much money on her present. "It's so quiet today," said Annabelle when she came into the storefront with her client Susan. She was a regular.

I pointed to the window. "It's snowing like crazy."

Susan did up the buttons on her long, black wool coat and wrapped her tartan scarf around her neck. "Well, ladies. Time to brave the snow."

"I like your scarf," said Annabelle.

"Thank you," she said. "I got it in Edinburgh." She hugged Annabelle. "Merry Christmas. And thank you so much for all you've done for me. What would I do without you?"

I watched the interaction, and it warmed me inside. Annabelle walked Susan to the door, and when she opened it, a waft of cold air and snow blew in.

When the door was shut and Susan was gone, I started singing "White Christmas" in my best Bing Crosby impersonation. Annabelle joined in, and we made it to the chorus before Annabelle grimaced and put her hand to her chest.

I immediately stopped singing and moved toward her, putting my arm around her shoulder. "What's the matter?"

"I'm not feeling great." Annabelle scratched the back of her neck. "I'm sure it's just the flu."

"Are you sure?" I asked. "It seems like more than the flu to me."

"I think I'll lock up for the day. I doubt it is going to be very busy because of the snow."

"Lock up?" That meant no overtime for me. I worked by the hour, and I was getting used to the extra time. "I can keep the store open," I said. "You can go home."

As if reading my mind, Annabelle said, "I'll pay you. Take the day off." She glanced out the window. "I don't like the look of the snow anyway and don't want to risk driving in it later. I'd rather get home. And you need to go, too." She wagged her finger at me. "Go see Paul. You have a present for him."

I tried to speak, but no words would come out. I *had* bought Paul a gift. But I had no idea when I would give it to him. I hadn't seen him since the day we'd gone to the coffee shop, just after I got home from Kingston. Every time the phone rang, I ran to answer it. And every time I was in the pub, I would look for him. The days had folded into weeks, and nothing. A few times I'd tried to call him, but I hung up before leaving a voice message. To ease the void I felt without him, I spent my time planning my trip with Natalie. For both of us, it was an escape from our pain.

"He's a nice kid," said Annabelle, breaking the silence. "I think you two might have been together in a past life."

"Me and Paul?" I laughed. Annabelle had been teaching me about past lives. I wasn't quite sure yet whether I thought they could be possible. Could it be that I had lived in the past with a different body and experience?

I eyed Annabelle. "You really believe in past lives, don't you?"

"I do," she said. "We are old souls, my girl. We've been around a few times. There are those who are new souls, and it is their first time on earth, but not us. We've had many, many lives, my dear."

"Do you know who you have been?"

She laughed. "Oh, yeah. I was a nasty old man in Germany who treated his children horribly. I think that's why I don't have children in this life. Sometimes we come back to rectify something we did in a past life."

"How do you know that?" I asked.

She wagged her finger at me. "You're driven to go to Scotland for a reason, my dear. Often it's that kind of feeling. Almost like you've been there before."

"Do you think Paul and I were together in Scotland?"

She laughed. "I didn't say that. Could have been anywhere." She tapped her fingers and stared at me. Then she said, "You might have been brother and sister somewhere."

Brother and sister. I had sort of treated him like a brother. An uncomfortable silence invaded the room. Why had Annabelle brought up his name? Now I was thinking about him.

And I desperately want to see him.

Suddenly, the smell of his aftershave hit my nostrils. I quickly glanced at the door, but he wasn't there. Hoping Annabelle hadn't noticed anything weird, I bent down and pulled my purse out from below the counter, shoving the newspaper deep inside it, trying not to make any rustling noises. When I straightened up and looked at Annabelle, I realized that I could have screeched my fingers down a chalkboard and she wouldn't have noticed a thing; she was deep in thought.

"What's wrong?" I asked quietly, my words ringing through the room.

She glanced at me, and I looked into her eyes, shocked by the sadness bleeding through her dark brown irises.

"I'm so glad I met you."

"Me too."

"It's nice to have someone around at Christmas. You've brought so much life to the store."

"I have your Christmas gift." I reached below the counter for the small present I had managed to sneak into the store today.

"Here." I handed her a small box wrapped in silver paper.

Just like a lightbulb turning on, Annabelle smiled, her beautiful brown eyes illuminating her face, and a wash of relief flowed through me.

She ran her fingers over the shiny paper. "I have something for you, too, in the back. I'll go get it."

When she returned with a gift wrapped in purple and silver paper, she was having difficulty breathing. I said, "You need to see a doctor."

"I did," she answered.

"What's wrong?"

"I need to quit smoking." She pointed to the gift she had given me. "I think you're going to like what I got you."

I shook the present like I did every Christmas gift that was for me. She laughed and rolled her eyes. "You are one crazy girl. But I love you."

Immediately, I stopped shaking my gift and looked at her. "I love you, too," I whispered.

✤ ✤ ✤

That afternoon, as I was packing to head home for at least a week over Christmas, and getting Henry ready to meet Cedar, Sasha, and Sheena, I was surprised by a knock on the apartment door. Both Natalie and Sarah had already gone home, and I was the last one to head out. Who would have ventured out in the snow?

I picked Henry up and headed to the door.

"Who is it?" I asked before turning the latch to unlock the door.

"Paul."

My heart almost stopped beating. My throat dried. And I stood still for a second. Yes, I'd had this weird feeling I was going to see him, but I thought it would be a run-in at the mall.

I pulled at the chain and clicked open the lock to see Paul, his hair dripping wet from melting snow, and holding a huge, and I mean huge, box wrapped in about three different types of Christmas paper.

"Hi" was all he said.

"Hi," I said shyly back.

After more than two months, he was standing in front of me. I had been waiting for this day.

He shook his head, and water flew everywhere. And I laughed. Just like that, I laughed.

"Sorry," he said. "It's really snowing out." He pushed his present toward me. "This is for you."

"You want to come in?"

He shrugged. "Sure."

I ushered him into the apartment.

"I think you told me once that you loved Christmas," he said.

"I have a gift for you, too."

He looked surprised. "You do?" Then he grinned. "Let's open them!"

I took the present and, of course, shook it, back and forth, and up and down. "I can't even guess," I said. "What could be so light in such a big box?"

"You'll have to open it to find out," he said. He laughed.

I led Paul to the living room and the little Christmas tree that we girls had set up a few weeks ago. "Sarah said I was insane to buy a little tree from the Canadian Tire tree lot, but I had insisted. Christmas isn't Christmas without a tree," I said.

"It sure is nice," said Paul a bit sarcastically.

"I like it," I said. Yes, it looked like a Charlie Brown tree with its spindly branches and oversize decorations, but the price had been right, and the cheap silver balls and garland from the Dollar Store made it festive. We'd had fun picking out the decorations and kept the price tag at under $10.

"I like it, too," said Paul. "It's perfect for you guys."

I reached under the tree for a little package. "For you," I said.

He took it and playfully shook it.

"You're just teasing me. Open it."

"You open yours, too." He arched one eyebrow.

I ripped at the paper and he did the same with his gift. He had his opened before me, because his was so small. When I had all the paper torn off, all I had was a big box with nothing in it.

He waved his present in the air. "Movie tickets," he said. "And popcorn gift certificates. Great gift!" He laughed. "Okay, this is sooo funny. Dig to the bottom of yours." He pointed at the box.

I looked deep into the box, and when I saw the envelope in the bottom, I laughed, too. "Movie passes," I said.

"Keep looking."

I peered into the box and pulled out another envelope, waving the contents in the air. "Popcorn gift certificates."

We both fell back on the sofa; we were laughing so hard.

The same gift! We bought each other exactly the same thing without knowing.

I turned my head to look at him at exactly the same time he did, and our faces were suddenly close. Like really close. He reached over and touched my cheek, and I leaned my head toward him.

He kissed the top of my head, and we inched toward each other. And just like that, I was in his arms and his nose was pressed against mine. Warm air encased me, and tingles ran up and down my spine, into my legs and arms. His body shivered beside mine as he stroked my hair, slowly, tenderly. I touched his hand, running my fingers over his knuckles. When he leaned toward me, I didn't back away but moved forward to meet his lips. We connected, and a beautiful heat flowed through me. I opened my lips, allowing his tongue to move inside my mouth. My body trembled, but in a really good way.

When we broke apart from our kiss, he wrapped his arms around me, holding me close, and I relaxed and rested my head against his chest.

"I really am sorry," I whispered.

"It's okay," he whispered back. "I've had a few weeks to think. I'm sorry, too. I should have been there for you that night. You only acted the way you did because of what happened to you. So right now all I want to do is hold you in my arms and keep you safe."

"I want you to kiss me."

❖ ❖ ❖

In the dark of the night, I sat under my family Christmas tree, staring up at the colored lights that twinkled in the magic of the night. I loved our majestic tree. I had awoken at 4:44, like

I did every Christmas Eve since I was a little girl, and tiptoed down to sit under our tree.

As I stared at the tree and the sparkling lights, I thought about everything, and it was as if little snippets of my life flashed through my mind. So much had happened to me this year.

So much good, and so much bad, too.

I had no idea why the bad had been so bad. I wanted to be mad at God still for all the bad stuff, but it was Christmas, and I had a hard time feeling anything but joy. Since all the little demons had been sucked out of me, I felt okay again and not as tired. Green Lady hadn't returned, and I had stopped playing with what Annabelle called the occult. The Ouija board had been thrown in the trash.

As I stared up at the tree, mesmerized by the colors and the glimmering of the little lights, my mind went blank, and I felt myself sliding down my long telescopic lens. I was alone in the room, so I let my mind go, let my body still, allowed the vision to appear.

When I got the bottom and looked into the fishbowl, though, I saw nothing. No vision came. Instead, I saw white, like pure Christmas snow. My body stilled even more. I fixed my gaze on one little white light on the Christmas tree. How long I sat there with my eyes fixed on one bright light I don't know. Time was insignificant.

All was silent and then, like a bang, I heard the word *theology.*

I blinked, and I was back in my living room, sitting cross-legged in front of my Christmas tree.

I shook my head, got up, and went back to bed.

❖ ❖ ❖

I woke up three hours later and ran into Brian's room. There were presents to open.

As usual, we sat around the tree and Dad handed out the gifts, one by one, trying to make it even. My biggest thrill was watching everyone open the gifts I had given them.

But I did notice that I had fewer gifts than Brian, and that shocked me. My parents never did that. Mom counted them out religiously so everything was even.

Finally, after he had opened three to my one, my mom glanced my way. "We have a big gift for you, Indie. That's why you don't have many small ones."

She stood and pulled a card from the tree. "This is for you."

Puzzled, I took the card. I flipped it over and opened the envelope and screamed when I pulled out a plane ticket to London.

"I talked to Natalie and Annabelle about this," said Mom, her eyes beaming with excitement, "and we figured out a time that both of you can go. And we decided that flying to London would be best. Then you can go to Ireland and Scotland from there."

I jumped up and hugged her and my dad. "Thank you. Thank you so much." I twirled around the room. "I can't believe it!" I spun so much I got dizzy and winded, and I ended up toppling onto Brian, who laughed and started wrestling with me and pushing me out of the way.

Chapter Eighteen

Even with the plane ticket paid for, I still had hardly any money in my account to spend on my trip. As usual, I had overspent at Christmas on gifts. Now, I had to save and save big.

Again, I asked Brian if he needed any extra staff at Licks, but the opposite was true: they were letting people go because it wasn't going to be busy enough in January. He promised me something in the summer, but that would be too late. My ticket was for April.

I caught the bus to work, thinking about how I could make extra money. I stared out the window at the streets, just thinking. The white snow of Christmas had turned to gray slush.

When I got to the store, the door was locked, which was odd because Annabelle was always there before me. I opened the store and flipped on the lights.

"Annabelle," I called out.

No answer.

Maybe she got stuck in traffic. The schedule book said she had an appointment at 9:30. I glanced at my watch and saw that it was almost nine. She still had some time.

I busied myself organizing the store, tidying everything. Ten minutes passed, then 15, then 20. The phone rang shrilly, and I answered it.

"Annabelle's Angels," I said in my officious business voice.

"Indie, it's me." Her voice sounded hoarse.

"Annabelle. Hi. Where are you?"

"I can't come in today. I've got a wicked cold. I tried to get ready and was on my way out the door, but I think my fever has spiked."

"I hope you're okay," I said. I worried about her health all the time. She still hadn't quit smoking. I had quit again, just to show her that it could be done, but it hadn't been enough incentive for her.

"I'm fine," she rasped. "Just a nasty flu bug."

I looked down at the book. She had only one client today. "Should I cancel your appointment?"

"No," she stated. "I want you to do the reading."

"Me!" Sweat beaded on my forehead, and my heartbeat quickened. "I, uh, I don't have my cards here."

"You don't need cards. I've told you that before. I want you to use your God-given abilities."

"I, uh, I can't do this yet."

"Indie, yes, you can." She paused. "You need a second job, don't you?"

"Yeah, but this isn't exactly what I was thinking. And who will run the front of the store?"

"Lock the door. Turn the sign around. It's just one client. When you're done, you can open the store back up."

"What am I going to talk about for an *hour?*"

"Believe me, the time will fly by. Call me when you're done. Oh, and, Indie, don't forget to protect yourself before you begin."

"I already did. This morning in the shower."

"Good girl. Okay, call me after."

I hung up the phone, and my body started shaking. I couldn't do this. I had to tell the client that Annabelle was sick. I looked at the book. Catherine. The woman's name was Catherine. Beside her name was *first time.* At least she wasn't

a regular with Annabelle. I wrung my hands. And I paced behind the counter. Back and forth. Little steps. Back and forth.

I couldn't do this!

Sure you can. My ego voice spoke, and she shocked me a
little. Then I remembered what Annabelle said. Sometimes she
was helpful.

I went to the card section in the store. What if I took a
new deck and paid Annabelle back? At least the cards would
give me something to try to read off. I was just about to grab
a package when the bell tinkled, and the door opened, and in
walked my first client.

Don't use the cards.

"Hello," I said. "Welcome to Annabelle's Angels." Oh, crap,
I sounded like a dork, like a perky cruise-ship lady.

"I'm here for a reading," said the woman.

I tried to smile, I really did. "You must be Catherine."

She nodded and wrung her hands together, obviously
nervous.

You're going to be okay, Indie. You can do this.

"Isaiah," I murmured under my breath, wanting him near
me, beside me the entire time. I needed him today.

"What?" The woman frowned at me.

I looked right into her eyes, and something washed over
me—my entire body brightened, if that makes any sense. For
a few seconds, I stood still and thought of a white ice cream
cone swirling down over me, covering me in white light, protecting me.

Once I was covered in white, it was as if another light went
on inside me, and I could see ahead, way down the road. I
didn't need to be afraid.

I walked to the door, turned the OPEN sign to CLOSED, and
smiled at the woman. "Shall we go to the back?"

I led her to the pink room and had her sit on one of the
fluffy chairs. I positioned myself across from her. I'd never sat
in Annabelle's chair before, on this side of the table.

"Are you Annabelle?" she asked, confused.

I shook my head. "Annabelle is sick today. My name is Indigo. I will do your reading, but if you're not satisfied, I can book you an appointment with Annabelle, and there will be no charge for today."

"Okay." Catherine's voice sounded like a little bird chirping.

As if I'd done this a million times, I slowly reached across the table. "Give me your hands."

She placed her hands in mine, and I closed my eyes. When my lids covered my sight, they felt light, like a colorful afghan blanket on a bed. I inhaled through my nose and exhaled through my mouth and let myself slide down my tunnel. I don't know if I smiled, but I think I might have, because the sliding felt so natural and fun. When I got to the bottom, all around me was white. I concentrated on the blank page in front of me and her hands, the feelings I was getting from them, the vibrational energy that went from her to me.

Then it happened.

I saw a pair of boobs. Big boobs.

Boobs?

Yes, boobs.

My eyes popped open, and I stared at Catherine, having no idea what to say. She sat across from me, and she looked at me as if she wanted me to say something. I heard Annabelle's voice in my head: "Say the first thing you see. Don't edit. Don't ever edit."

But I couldn't say what I saw!

This was crazy.

Say the first thing.

You can do this.

Suddenly, I knew that at this moment, my intuition was guiding me and my ego was pushing me forward.

"Okay," I said to Catherine. "This is really weird but . . . I'm seeing a pair of boobs."

And just like that, Catherine nodded as if this was okay. Then she said very softly, "I'm thinking of getting a boob job."

"Don't," I blurted out. "He's not worth it. It won't make you happy or him happy. If you want to do it for you, that's okay. But don't do it for him."

Words spewed out of my mouth like verbal diarrhea. I knew nothing about this woman, yet here I was talking to her as if I did.

Her eyes filled with tears, and she turned away from me. "My boyfriend doesn't like me the way I am. He keeps saying he'll leave me if I don't get a boob job."

I breathed. In and out. I had to help her. But I couldn't let her emotions run mine. My heart rate slowed, and once again I was calm and centered. I squeezed her hands. "He's not worth it. You are beautiful the way you are."

I closed my eyes again and let myself slide. Vision after vision appeared, and I talked nonstop. Letting her energy enter my body, I could see her walking down a long road. I could see what was ahead of her and what to avoid and what to embrace.

When I looked at the clock after what felt like five minutes, I realized we had been in the room for more than an hour. I gave her hands one last squeeze and pulled away. "Are you going to be okay?" I asked.

She tilted her head and gave me a little smile. "Thank you," she said. "You have no idea how you have helped me." Her smile expanded to cover her entire face. "I am going to be okay. And I don't need big boobs to do that."

I laughed. "I had no idea what to do with that vision."

She pulled out her checkbook. "How much do I owe you?"

I didn't charge her as much as Annabelle charged her clients, but still, when I had the check in my hand I was shocked and felt so incredibly grateful because I had helped someone. And I'd done a good job. Could it be possible . . . could I do this as a living? I walked Catherine to the door and flipped the sign back to OPEN.

Then I called Annabelle.

"How did it go?"

"Good, I think." I proceeded to tell her about the boobs vision, and she laughed.

Then she said, "I'm happy to hear about all of this, but if you are going to start reading for people, you will need to cut your cords with them as soon as you finish the reading. It is important to let everything you have seen about them go. You don't want to remember anything."

"Okay . . ."

"It is okay you told me today, but going forward, don't ever tell anyone anything—even me. The information you receive should remain confidential. Right now, wherever you are standing, I want you to envision a bunch of cords. They can be ropes or even computer wires. Just some type of cords."

I closed my eyes and saw cords of wool. Weird. I wasn't a knitter.

"Now snip them," said Annabelle.

In my mind I cut all the cords.

"Now shut the light off. And let your mind go dark."

I sucked in a deep breath and saw myself actually flicking a light switch to the off position, creating a dark room.

"You okay?" Annabelle asked.

"Yes." I opened my eyes, and my world was light again. "I'm good."

It was really weird, because I honestly felt that all the words that had tumbled out of my mouth less than an hour ago were in some foreign language and that I would never be able to decode them.

"Let's move on to real life," said Annabelle. "Real life keeps you grounded on earth. And let's face it, that's where we live. I need you to order more of those rose quartz crystals today."

The reading was over, and I was back in the store with my schedule and cash register.

Had I really just gone somewhere in the universe, on a journey not of this earth, and returned just like that?

When the door tinkled at noon and Paul walked in with two Starbucks cups, I knew I was definitely back on earth. He gave me one of his quirky smiles. "In the neighborhood," he said. "I got you a green tea."

"Thank you," I said.

"Thought you might need it," he said.

I eyed him, slightly taken aback by his comment. No one knew about my reading this morning. I hadn't told a soul.

"Why would I need it?" I asked.

"You . . . don't know?"

"Know what?" Now he had my interest piqued.

He blew air out of his lips, making them vibrate so he sounded like a horse. Then he took the tea out of my hands, placing it on the counter. "I don't want you holding this yet. John Smith was arrested this morning."

"What?" I swear my breath almost stopped.

"Cocaine possession," said Paul. "I heard he's getting charged with dealing."

"He'll go to prison."

Paul nodded. "If he's convicted. But rumor is that he was caught red-handed. It was a bust. A big bust. They hauled him off in cuffs."

My legs were shaking so much that I had to sit on the stool.

"Do you think you'll go see him in jail?" Paul asked.

I glanced at him. "Why would you ask that?"

Paul shrugged before he lifted his coffee to his lips and took a small sip. "You're just the kind of person who would. That's all. I didn't mean anything by it."

I put my fingers to my temples, lowered my head, and closed my eyes. *John. Why would you do something like this?* All his plans to go to England were gone. He was going to prison instead. I felt a warm hand on my back. Without opening my eyes, I reached up and touched Paul's hand.

"Indie," he said quietly as he squeezed my fingers. "I have to tell you this so you don't hear it from someone else. Dennis ratted John out."

"Dennis? Dennis Neufeld?"

"Yeah. They were all selling for the same guy. They got the main guy and three guys working under him, including John and Dennis."

I heard John's words in my head. *Why did you go in the woods with someone like him?*

He knew what Dennis was like, yet he blamed me. In that moment, I knew exactly what I needed to do. "I need a second," I said to Paul. "Don't go, okay?"

I went to the back room, sat down on the fluffy pink chair, and closed my eyes. Then I created a picture in my mind of thick, twisted ropes, the kind sailors used to anchor boats. I snipped them, little by little, until there was not one thread left hanging. After they were severed completely, I hit the light switch and allowed my mind to go dark, pitch-black, and I stayed in that dark for a few moments.

When my body felt light, I popped open my eyes, stood, and walked back to the front of the store. Of course, Paul was still waiting.

"Are you okay?" he asked with such genuine concern.

Instead of answering his question, I asked, "How about a movie tonight?" I took his hand in mine and smiled. "We could treat each other."

❖ ❖ ❖

Over the next few months, I did readings in the back pink room, for all the new clients who phoned in, because Annabelle insisted they go with me. She wanted me to develop my own list of clients. *Clients.* The word sounded so grown-up, but I have to admit I liked the sound. It made me giddy—almost as if I were doing something with my life.

Something good.

Two weeks before I was to leave for Scotland, I finished a reading and walked my client Mary to the door.

"Thank you so much, Indie." Mary gave me a big hug.

"You're welcome. Any time."

She smiled at me. "You've made a difference in my life."

"I'm glad I could help."

"Annabelle's lucky to have you."

"I'm lucky to have her, too," I replied, smiling. And I was lucky. That I knew.

Mary left, and when I turned, Annabelle was gazing at me with a contented look on her face. "You want to go for something to eat? I'm starving."

"Sure," I replied.

❖ ❖ ❖

Annabelle and I went to a funky tapas restaurant, and the waiter brought us menus and two glasses of water with lemon.

"I'm really proud of you," she said, playing with the lemon in her drink.

"Thanks." I picked up my drink and had a sip.

Casually, she glanced at me over the rim of her glass. "You fought it, girl, but you've come around. You still have a lot to learn, but you are definitely on the right path."

"I'm reading those books you gave me." I paused, but just for a second. "Especially the one on past lives."

"Ahh, yes, past lives. A past-life spirit will make you feel as if you're looking into a mirror."

"Because . . . we were them once. Right?"

She winked. "You're a quick learner."

I smiled. "This might be the first time I've heard that."

"You are," she stated. "You need your own store, you know."

"Are you kidding me?" I leaned back and shook my head. "I'm not ready for *that* yet."

"You will be one day." She twirled her fork, and I figured she wanted a cigarette. "How's Paul?"

"Good. We're taking it slow but making progress."

She eyed me. "You're going to miss him when you're away, you know."

Now it was my turn to do something with my hands, and I swirled the lemon in my water glass. "I know," I whispered. "I don't want to, though."

"Why not?"

"I don't ever want to feel dependent again."

Annabelle put her hand on mine. "Indie, it's okay to love. And if that means you might miss him, it doesn't make you dependent. And it doesn't mean you can't have fun on your trip."

I looked directly into her beautiful brown eyes, and she held my gaze. "What about you?" I asked. "Is there anyone special in your life?" Annabelle never talked about her love life, and her eyes often showed such pain.

"Not right now." She pulled away from me, picked up a menu, and scanned it. "I don't have time. But soon I'm going to connect with an old loved one." She scrunched her face at me. "So . . . any questions on your readings? I'm here to help."

I spun my glass around. Lately I had been thinking about death and how to handle it if it came up in a reading. I wanted to be prepared. "Do you see death in your readings?" I blurted out.

She shrugged. "I usually just get a feeling of sooner or later," she said. "But never any specifics." She narrowed her eyes. "Are you seeing death?"

I shook my head. "No. Not really. Sometimes when I'm reading someone, I get a feeling, but it's so unclear that I don't say anything."

"It's better not to say anything. I don't think that's up to us."

"Do you . . . do you know when you're going to die?"

She looked down at her nails, playing with the paint on them for a few moments. When she looked up she said, "I think I'm going sooner rather than later."

"What do you mean by that?"

"Ten, fifteen, twenty years." She took a sip of her drink. She smiled at me and reached across the table. "Let's channel now and find out."

"In here?" In horror, I glanced around the restaurant.

"Sure. I don't care what people think of me." She took my hands, held them tightly, and closed her eyes. I closed mine too, just because.

Within a few seconds, she said, "You're going to live into your eighties." She paused. "I'm going earlier than that."

"Excuse me, ladies," said the waiter.

We opened our eyes and looked at each other.

"Time to order," said Annabelle.

Chapter Nineteen

"I'm going to miss you guys," said Sarah.

Two suitcases sat open on the floor of the living room, and Natalie and I were double checking the contents to make sure we had everything we needed for our trip.

"Group hug." Natalie jumped up, and the three of us hugged and danced in a circle until klutzy me stumbled on an open suitcase.

"Ouch."

Natalie and Sarah laughed, and we toppled to the sofa.

When we had quieted down, Sarah glanced from Natalie to me, then back to Natalie. "I've been thinking," she said quietly, a little too quietly for Sarah. She had something important to say.

"I'm moving back home." Her words came out in a rush. "I've got to save money for school next year."

Natalie looked at Sarah wide-eyed. "Okay," she said, "that is just plain weird, because I was thinking the exact same thing." She shut her suitcase before she said, "I want to spend time with my grandmother before I go to Queen's in the fall."

My heart sank to my big toe, the one I had just painted bright red for the trip. Why hadn't I seen this coming? I was the one who was supposed to see and hear things. Deep inside, if I was to admit it to myself, I had seen the signs—I had just tried to make them not come true. Sure, I had a job and the readings were great but . . . something was missing. This room- mate breakup was going to make me move on, and I wasn't sure I wanted to do that. At least not right now!

Sarah fixed her gaze on me. "I think we should hand in our month notice now and try to be out of here the first of May. Do you want new roommates, Indie? We can always put ads out to get new people to come live with you. Or maybe you have some friends who might want to take over our rooms."

I shook my head. "Don't worry about me. I'll figure some- thing out." I held up two sweaters. "Which one?"

"Definitely blue," said Sarah.

I tossed the blue oversize one in my luggage as the doorbell rang. I jumped up and raced to the door.

"I think someone's in love," Natalie called out to me.

I opened the front door and wrapped my arms around Paul. He grinned. "Are you packing?" he asked. "How many bags? Four?"

"Ha ha. Just one."

"One?" He followed me into the living room and stared at my open bag stuffed full of clothes.

"You're not even close to being ready." He laughed and flopped on our beanbag chair, putting his hands behind his head. "I've got the best view in the house to watch you cram ten pairs of shoes in one bag."

I threw the blue sweater at him.

He caught it in one hand and tossed it back into my suit- case. Then he jerked his head toward my bedroom.

We walked to my room, and once inside, I shut the door. He led me to my bed, and we lay down. I curled my body into his. He pulled me close, and I rested my head on his chest.

"I'm going to miss you," he said, stroking my hair. Then he kissed the top of my head. "But you're going to have so much fun," he whispered.

"I'm going to miss you, too," I whispered.

"I bought you something to take with you."

I sat up, looked down at him, and playfully punched his chest. "You didn't need to buy me anything."

He grinned and also sat up. "It's for me, too." He pulled a little card out of his shirt pocket. "It's an international calling card. You can phone me and tell me what a great time you're having."

❖ ❖ ❖

Natalie and I boarded our plane a few days later, and we settled in for the long trip over the ocean. She pulled out a novel, and I went to pull out my novel, too, but the book on past lives seemed to just pop out of my bag and fall into my lap.

"Whatcha reading?"

I held up the book. "Annabelle gave it to me. It's a book on past lives."

"Cool."

I laughed. "The author believes that many of us were someone else before we were us."

Natalie narrowed her eyes as if she was thinking hard. "I guess I believe that." Then she smiled. "So I could have been someone heroic?"

I shrugged. "Yeah. That's the idea."

Natalie's face broke into a huge smile. "I believe that. I can see myself as some fiddler in a kingdom."

I laughed. "I can play this game. I think I was someone like Mary, Queen of Scots."

"Oh, I could be Joan of Arc, then." Natalie laughed.

"I could have been a witch in Scotland who had to give readings by looking at the swirling water in a big black pot."

Natalie giggled. "Yes, you could have been. I bet you were a good one, too. You would have changed the world."

Our conversation ended at that, because the pilot came over the loudspeaker telling the attendants to prepare for takeoff.

❖ ❖ ❖

We arrived in London, checked into our hostel, and wasted no time, because we had only three days to explore the city.

Our first excursion, so we could get familiar with the city and pretend we were real tourists, was to ride the red double-decker bus. I almost had to pinch myself as I stared out at London, at the busy streets, the cars that drove on the other side, and the old buildings. They were so much older than anything in Canada. I was here. I was really here. And I had done it on my own. I was proud of myself.

We hopped on and off the bus, taking in Trafalgar Square, Downing Street, Tower Bridge, and of course Big Ben and Buckingham Palace. Per usual, Natalie wanted photos. Tons of photos.

We got back on the bus, and when it stopped at the London dungeon, Natalie looked at me. "Do you think it's haunted?"

"Oh, yeah," I said. "And I'm not going in there."

"Me either," said Natalie. "Green Lady was enough for me for a lifetime."

❖ ❖ ❖

The second day in England, we walked along the Thames River. When lunchtime arrived, we bought some fish and chips.

"Paul would love these," I said to Natalie as we sat on a bench eating, the river flowing in front of us.

The chips had been wrapped in newspaper. I dipped one into the little container of mayonnaise they had given me. "He loves mayo."

Natalie had smiled. "I think you like him a whole lot better than you think you do, girl."

"Yeah, maybe I do."

"You're not getting homesick already?" she asked.

"Not a chance," I said. "I'm ready for Ireland."

❖ ❖ ❖

We rode the train to Wales on our way to Ireland, and the view from the windows of the green rolling hills was spectacular. Of course, once we were settled in the hostel, Natalie wanted to hit an Irish pub for music and food and a mug of beer. I was game for that.

As we listened to the Celtic music, I picked at my chicken pot pie. Beside me Natalie tapped her toe and moved to the music. All day I had been having weird feelings that something wasn't right at home, and it irritated me. How could this be happening? My first overseas trip, and I was being nagged by something.

Natalie nudged me with her shoulder. "What's wrong?"

"Nothing," I said. I attempted a smile. "I'm loving this music." I did a little face bob with my head. "But you're as good as they are."

"Ahh, you're too kind."

"I'm telling the truth."

"Okay. So tell me the real truth. What's wrong?"

"I'm sorry. I have a feeling that I can't shake."

"Call him."

"That's not what this is about. It's something else."

She wagged her finger at me. "Call him."

Later that night, I did call Paul from a green telephone booth just outside the pub. Little windows lined the box, and I was able to see people walking in and out of the pub. Natalie sat against a window ledge outside the pub and enjoyed a cigarette. She looked at peace and at home. I wished I could feel like that.

"I don't want to talk too long," I said, after I'd told him all about England. "I will use up all my minutes." I paused for a brief second. "Is everything okay?"

"Yeah, sure. Everything's fine. I'm in the midst of exams. Studying my brain off."

"Okay." I looked outside the phone booth. Natalie had finished her cigarette and was looking pensive and thoughtful.

Paul seemed distant. Or was I imagining things? Was he not happy to talk to me? Did he not miss me? Was he seeing someone else?

"Are you studying by yourself?" I blurted out.

"Sometimes. Other times, I work with some friends."

"What friends?"

"Just people from my class."

Natalie was looking my way. "Well, I should go," I said.

"Great to talk to you," he said. "Drink a pint for me."

When I stepped outside, rain drizzled from the sky, and it felt like little elves creeping across my face.

"So, feeling better now?" Natalie asked.

"Absolutely," I lied.

❖ ❖ ❖

"Let's go to the Urquhart Castle today!"

We were at the end of our trip, and I had saved this castle for my last tourist stop. It was my highlight. We had been to so many amazing castles since we'd been in Scotland, and it had been nothing short of spectacular.

Excitement overwhelmed me and squashed down any worries I had about what was going on at home. The bad feelings had persisted, but I shoved them all aside. I was in Scotland, and nothing was going to ruin that. I would deal with whatever it was when I got home. If Paul was seeing someone else I guess . . . I didn't want to think about it. Not now. Not while I was in Scotland.

If we were meant to be, we would be. Annabelle quoted that line all the time. I hadn't bought her anything yet, because I was waiting to get her a tartan scarf at Urquhart Castle.

Of course, it was raining when we left the cute little B and B we were staying at. Mom had booked it for us as a birthday gift for me and to get us out of the hostels for a few nights. It was built into the old castle walls in St. Andrews, and I loved it because it felt magical. The grass surrounding the B and B was almost fluorescent green, and the hills rolled and looked soft and forgiving. For breakfast we'd had black pudding, sliced sausage, and tattie scones. Natalie had had the grilled tomato, but I just couldn't stomach tomatoes. There was something about their consistency that made me ill. And I was not going to be ill today, or think of anything about home.

"Watch the chicken poop," I said to Natalie, laughing.

Chickens roamed freely in front of the B and B, just like we were in the medieval days, and every time we left the building, Natalie and I dodged the chicken poop.

Natalie hopped from one foot to the next, and we laughed all the way to the spot where we had to catch the bus. Other tourists climbed the bus stairs with us, and Natalie and I found a spot near the back.

Sitting in my seat, my body vibrated with excitement.

Natalie poked. "You have been waiting all trip for this," she said.

"Yup." I bounced on my seat, and we burst out laughing.

Once the bus was full, the driver revved the engine and shoved the bus into gear, launching it forward like a rocket. Then he drove like a maniac through the narrow streets.

Natalie held the arms of the seat. "He's trying to kill us," she whispered.

If I'd opened my window, I swear I could have touched the vehicles traveling on the other side of the road.

Finally, the bus lurched to a stop, and when we stepped off, we were met by a cold gust of wind. I shivered and wrapped my jacket tight around me. Of course, the gift shop was the first thing we passed and would also be the last. That was typical in any tourist attraction.

"Let's get scarves," I said, pulling Natalie's arm. I would get one for me and one for Annabelle.

Once we had our tartan scarves and they were flung around our necks, we made our way down to the water. We stumbled upon a Loch Ness monster sculpture. Natalie ran ahead of me and sidled up to it.

"I'm gonna ride Mr. Loch Ness monster right out of the water," she yelled into the wind, climbing onto its back.

Giddy with excitement, I laughed and starting snapping photos of her. When it was my turn to pose for the camera, a weird sensation flowed through me as I held on to the fake sea monster, and it almost felt as if he were moving beneath my fingers. All the times we'd taken photos of us by the wooden people back home, I'd never felt them come alive. This was so different.

After we had enough photos to fill five pages in an album, we made our way down to the castle by foot. Each step I took, heading down the hill, I had a crazy feeling that I'd been there before. I hadn't felt like this with any other castles. Why this one? I picked up my pace and almost started running down the cobblestone path. It was as if I wanted to run home.

"Whoa," said Natalie, trying to follow me.

Even with her urging, I didn't slow down.

"We should stop and get some information on the castle," she said, breathing heavily from trying to keep up with me.

I shook my head. I didn't want to read about it—I wanted to feel it. I had to get to the castle, get inside, even though there was nothing much left of it. As I ran, I could see it in front of me, tall and stately, and huge and real, and not just some pile of stones. It beckoned to me as if I were heading home.

We hit the ruins of the castle, and it was like I had flipped a switch by my ears and turned my hearing off. I could see people talking, their lips moving, but I couldn't hear anything. My mind was silent. Without even thinking about Natalie and where she was, I headed straight for a set of stairs that led up to the disintegrating castle, with all its crumbling stone. I made it to a lookout point, which I presumed used to be a window, and I stared out at Loch Ness.

My body trembled as I stared at the massive, deep lake, and it was almost as if I could see boats out there. Suddenly, I felt myself sliding, and I grabbed on to the wall for support.

And that's when my mind went blank. And all I saw was white. Pain in my back jolted me. I was at the bottom of my fishbowl.

I was wearing a long robe. I could feel something heavy hanging around my neck—I looked down and saw a big cross. My hands were large and calloused and strong. I was inside a man; he was me. In a flash, I was outside the man, and when I looked into his eyes, I saw my eyes. It was as if I were looking at myself, but I was a different person. Then I got sucked inside of him again and became him. My hands involuntarily reached to my chest, and I pulled at something, hard, something embedded in my heart.

I yanked at it.

The pulling pushed me back, and my back scraped against the stone wall. Finally, whatever had been lodged in me was out of my body. When I looked down at my hands, they were covered in crimson blood. It dripped through my fingers and onto the stone floor. But I didn't scream.

Instead, I glanced upward. I was surrounded by thick, gray castle walls, and stone steps loomed in front of me. Candles, embedded in metal sconces, lit the hallway with their fire, casting shadows on the walls. Torches, burning brightly, stood stoically on the steps.

Noises sounded from somewhere: yelling, screaming. Up the stairs. Women.

"Burn them at the stake!" I heard myself bellow.

I blinked.

"Are you all right?" I felt a hand on my shoulder.

I turned to see a man with a camera around his neck looking at me with concern. "You look awful pale, love."

"I'm fine," I murmured. Had I screamed out loud? "I just need to sit down for a second."

He didn't say anything else, so I figured it was all just in my head. I found a place to sit and put my head in my hands, trying to block out the sounds again, but I could hear everyone talking about the ruins, snapping photos, saying "cheese."

I know this place. I've been here before. Did I burn witches? Was that what this was about? Perhaps I was to change that somehow, fix the wrong I had done years ago. Those witches had been able to see and hear like me. That was all. Some were good, and some had gone to the dark side to practice. Was I supposed to prove that we could use our God-given abilities to spread love and not evil?

Annabelle had come to me to help me move forward. She had taught me so many things, and I hadn't exactly been the easiest student to teach. But I had learned from my experience. I knew all about the dark side and love within the light.

I couldn't wait to tell her my experience at the castle.

Like a big bang, a gunshot, I heard a voice in my head. *Theology.* I quickly opened my eyes and grabbed my chest. It hurt.

I sucked in air. What was wrong with me? Why had I heard and felt such a bang? I placed my head in my hands. This was too weird. All of it. I had heard that word at Christmas as well. Why was it coming back to me now?

"Hey, there you are," said Natalie. She breezed up the stairs to where I was sitting. "I've been looking everywhere for you."

Cold encased me, and I wrapped my arms around my body. I stood up. "I'm freezing," I said. "Let's get out of here."

As we hiked back to the parking lot where our bus was, I got up the courage to ask Natalie, "Do you know what theology is? I heard someone talking about it at the castle."

"I think it might be the study of God," she replied. "All that comes to mind for me, though, are pics of white-haired men with really long beards, spewing religious facts. Or men in long gowns walking around Italy with Bibles under their arms."

I laughed nervously. *I* certainly was *not* going to be walking around in a long robe in Italy any time soon.

✢ ✢ ✢

At the Ottawa airport, Mom greeted me at the baggage carousel. She hugged me hard. When I pulled back, I saw the pained look on her face, the sagging eyes, the droopy mouth, and I knew something was wrong.

"How was your trip?" She tried to sound excited.

"Mom." I looked her in the eyes. "What's wrong?"

"Oh, honey."

"Is it Dad? Brian? Cedar?"

My mother shook her head. "No, sweetie. It's Annabelle."

"Annabelle?" My knees quaked. My heart sped up. Vibrations shuttered through my body.

"I don't know how to tell you this, but . . . she had a heart attack."

The bang. I had felt that in my chest. Was it a sign that I had ignored? What was wrong with me? I hadn't read the signs right when I was overseas. Why?

I quickly scanned the baggage starting to come through the shoot. "Once I have my bag, I want to go straight to the hospital."

My mother wrapped her arms around her body and kept shaking her head. Tears fell down her face. "She's gone, Indie."

"Gone? Gone where?" I searched her eyes for answers.

"Indie, please. Listen to me. She passed away. The funeral is tomorrow."

"What? This can't be. It can't be. I have so much to tell her about my trip. I had, I had a past-life experience. I have to tell her."

She knows. Isaiah spoke softly. I wondered if she was with him now. And Papa.

My mother pulled me into her arms.

I couldn't believe it, though. No matter what I was being told. I was still on earth, and Annabelle wasn't. "I need her," I sobbed. "There's still so much I don't understand."

"I'm so sorry." My mother held me and ran her hand up and down my back.

"Mom." I cried into her shoulder. "I . . . should have figured this out. I would have come home."

"Shh. Indie. There was nothing you could have done. She had a heart attack, and within hours, she died. You wouldn't have gotten to see her anyway."

Sobs racked my body, my stomach heaving and my heart breaking.

Chapter Twenty

I stood in the store. Annabelle's Angels. Annabelle stood in front of me, and she was smiling and looking at the appointment book.

"You can't be here," I said. "You're dead."

But she was there. I could see her. Why was she there? She looked beautiful, more beautiful than ever before. Her skin had this translucent glow, stress lines gone, and her eyes were clear and bright, the brown in them solid, pure, rich, like decadent chocolate. She smiled, and her teeth were now white, straight, and perfect.

"I'm here," she said, her smile wide.

"No, you're not!" I cried. "You're dead. How can you be here?"

"You have to carry on for me. Use your gifts for the good."

❖ ❖ ❖

I woke up in my childhood bedroom, trembling, holding my chest, and gasping for breath. She had come to me in a dream. Today was her funeral, and she had come to tell me that she was okay, that she was happy.

The dream had been so real, as if Annabelle had been at the store and it was still open, but even in the dream, I knew she was dead.

I dressed in a daze and went to the funeral with my mother. I was glad to have her with me.

I cried while the priest talked. Tears and more tears. I couldn't stop them. It was as if a tap were on and leaking and the plumber was too busy to come and fix it. Her ex, Gary, was nowhere to be seen.

The pew was hard. The priest droned as he spoke, his words making no sense. I lowered my head and let the tears fall. This was wrong. All wrong. Yes, she said she would leave sooner rather than later, but . . . did she have to leave this soon? What would happen to Annabelle's Angels? When the funeral was over, I stepped outside and immediately put on my sunglasses to hide my swollen eyes. Sobs caught in my throat again, and I held my stomach.

I had to go to the store. I had to feel her.

Mom wanted to drive me, but I insisted on going alone. I had to do this by myself.

Lights were on inside the store when I pulled up out front. Through the windows, I could see Annabelle's mother standing at the counter, obviously deep in thought. I guess we both had the same idea.

The sign read CLOSED, but when I pushed the door, it opened.

Her mother looked up. "Indie," she said.

"I had to come here," I said.

"Me too. Everyone else is drinking and eating, but I needed to feel her one last time, and I figured this was where she would be." She held up Annabelle's brown book. "I found this in the back," she said. "She wanted you to have it. She talked about you all the time, you know."

I walked toward the counter, took the book, and touched the front cover. The worn brown leather warmed the pads of my fingers. I slowly flipped it open and immediately saw Annabelle's scrawled handwriting. The book had been like an extension of her body, and now I had it. I had a piece of her. The book was full of her ramblings and thoughts.

"Thank you," I whispered.

Her mother gazed around the store. "She never had children, so this store was like her baby."

"What is going to happen to it?" It had been like a second home to me, too.

Tears rolled down her cheeks. She swiped at them. The small movement made my body swell with sadness, and my eyes welled up.

"Annabelle didn't leave a will." She pressed her fingers to her forehead and kept shaking her head. "Gary will get everything, and he is closing the store and selling it. They weren't divorced." Her shoulders started to shake. "Annabelle put too many things off."

"Except leaving the earth," I whispered.

"Yes," said her mother, running her fingers across the feathers of an angel wing. "Except that."

❖ ❖ ❖

I got in my car and drove away from the curb. I was so confused. Why was all this happening? I slammed on my brakes when I hit a yellow light. The brown book slid off the seat and onto the floor. I heard a car behind me slam on its brakes as well, so I looked in my rearview mirror.

That's when I saw her.

Annabelle.

She was wearing her funky tortoiseshell sunglasses, and her wavy hair was blowing in the spring breeze like she didn't have a care in the world. She grinned at me. I quickly turned around to look over my shoulder. But she was gone.

A honk sounded behind me.

I floored the gas pedal, and my car lurched forward.

Leave it to Annabelle to show up and, without saying a word, tell me that everything would be all right. At the next stoplight, I bent over and picked up the brown book.

"I know you're here with me," I said. "I will carry on for you somehow. I can promise you that."

❖ ❖ ❖

Two days later, at the apartment, Sarah had her stuff in boxes.

We were all moving out by May 1, so that meant we had five days left before we parted ways. I had loved living in the apartment. Since I had nowhere to go and no job, I was returning to my house to live with Mom and Dad. In many ways, I felt as if I was going backward.

"I can't believe this is happening," I said to Sarah.

"Yeah. It's sad to leave *us*, but I guess it's time. We all have to move on and do something with our lives. It's called growing up."

"I'm going to cry," said Natalie.

"Me too." I plopped down on the floor.

"Are you okay?" Natalie asked me.

I shrugged. "As good as can be."

"We did have fun at the Royal Oak," said Sarah, changing the topic. She was good at diverting.

"We did," I replied.

"I've got the photos to prove it," said Natalie, holding up her camera.

"Only like a million," said Sarah.

Natalie glanced at me. "Is Paul helping you move?"

"Yup," I said. "Everything will fit in Mable. Henry included."

"I'm glad you're taking him," said Natalie.

"I'm going to miss him," said Sarah. Then she looked at me. "Speaking of missing someone. You ever sneak a trip to jail to see John?"

I shook my head. "I cut my cords with him. We're over."

Sarah held up her hand and I smacked it. "Well done, my friend," she said. "Well done. Maybe we have all grown up." She picked up Henry and rubbed her nose in his face. "Even you, little man. You are no longer the scrawny kitten we found whining in the bushes."

❖ ❖ ❖

That night I sat in my old bedroom with the purple walls, black bedspread, and Jim Morrison poster. It felt so weird to be back in the same house with my parents after living away all year and being independent. The confinement was wrong. All wrong.

The four walls of my childhood bedroom used to give me comfort, but no more. Now I felt trapped. Even Henry seemed a bit out of sorts, as if he wanted to go back to where he was king. There was no way Cedar was giving up her crown.

I sat on my bed cross-legged and put my pointer fingers and thumbs together. And I started to softly chant, just like Annabelle had taught me. My throat clogged. She had taught me so much. I still couldn't believe she was gone.

I let my mind go blank and focused on keeping it white. It stayed white for the longest time. And I breathed; in and out. I kept breathing.

Keep breathing, Indie. Keep breathing.

I was totally bathed in the white light when I was thumped over the head with the word *theology!*

And it was in Annabelle's voice.

Although I was startled, I kept my eyes shut and focused on the blank walls. "You have to give me more," I whispered.

Ottawa, she said.

My eyes popped open, and I ran over to the new computer my parents had bought me for my birthday—it had been set up in my bedroom when I returned home. I turned it on and listened to it hum to life.

I logged on and searched the Internet for *Theology* and *Ottawa.* When it appeared on my screen that there was a Theology program at St. Paul University in Ottawa, I almost fell off my chair.

I read through the requirements and knew I didn't have them. I didn't have the grades to get in or the subjects or anything at all.

"Okay, divine team," I said out loud. "You had better do some magic here 'cause this isn't looking likely."

✣ ✣ ✣

Paul showed up that night on my doorstep, with a big bottle of soda and a huge bag of potato chips that he obviously bought at a convenience store.

"I'm done with exams," he said. "I thought we could have a party."

I laughed and opened the door. "Just the two of us," I said. "Some party."

"Your parents can join us if they want."

"They've gone out."

He followed me into the kitchen, and as soon as he had placed the stuff on the table, he pulled me into his arms. "I know you're not ready to go out to the bar just yet," he whispered in my ear.

"But you should," I said.

"Nah. I want to be with you."

Once I had filled two glasses with ice and soda, we sat at the kitchen table.

"How are you?" He ripped open the bag of chips.

"I'm okay. How were your exams?"

"I'm done. That's all that counts."

"Are you going back to work at the deli?" I asked, twirling my glass around.

He put his hand on mine. "Something will come up for you, too."

"Funny you should say that." I took a chip out of the bag but didn't eat it. "There's this school I might apply to." I slouched in my seat. "But I don't think I'll get in. It's in Ottawa."

"Ottawa!" He pumped his arms. "We'd still be in the same city. You can't get in if you don't apply."

"The application is super long." I almost moaned. "I don't know where to start. And I don't have the qualifications."

"I'm good at that stuff. Why don't we go over it right now? I can help you."

"Seriously?"

"Sure. Why not?"

Paul and I spent the rest of the evening going over the application. He was such a help that it made the job that much easier. He walked me through it step by step, and at the end of the night, I knew exactly what other documents I needed.

"Why do you want to go to this school?" he finally asked at the end of the evening. He stood at my front door, ready to head out. "Not that I'm complaining," he said. "Not even close. You just don't strike me as the nun type."

I playfully slapped him. "I'm not going to be a nun."

I'd been waiting for this question to come up all evening. "I heard the word three times in my head," I said. "Once at Christmas, then in Scotland, and last time was after Annabelle died. I heard her voice in my head."

He touched my hair, running his fingers through it. "That's a good thing," he whispered. "You need to listen to those voices."

I looked into his eyes and the blue of those safe pools instantly calmed me. I smiled.

He put his fingers on my cheek. "Thank you," he said.

"For what?"

"For giving me confidence. I was the school geek. Then I kissed the pretty girl. I thought that only happened in movies."

"It happens in real life, too." I stood on my tiptoes and kissed him, wrapping my arms around him, pulling him toward me.

✧ ✧ ✧

My acceptance to St. Paul University for Theology wasn't without its hiccups, but one thing Annabelle had taught me was if things were meant to be, they would work out. Yes, I received a rejection letter because my grades weren't good enough. That was no surprise. But then at the bottom of the letter, it suggested I should reapply as a mature student.

So I went to Annabelle. "What next?" I asked out loud in my bedroom.

You need some reference letters. I heard her voice in my head. *Get one from a friend of your parents and get another one from someone Catholic. That will go a long way.*

That night I talked to my parents over dinner.

"Martha is Catholic," said Mom. "She was a good friend of Annabelle's."

"That would be great," I said.

"And I'm sure if you asked Joe Conrad, he would give you one as well," said my father. "He's not only Catholic but a professor at the University of Ottawa. He's known you since you were little."

I nodded. "Okay," I said. "I have nothing to lose."

"And everything to gain," said my father, winking at me.

✤ ✤ ✤

I sent in my letters, and within a week, I had an appointment. I dressed like I was going to a job interview at some high-powered company: white blouse, dark brown pantsuit. I walked through the doors with confidence, but then I froze. What was I thinking? I couldn't do this. I didn't have the grades. I had never been good at school.

I had turned around to run out to my car when my ego voice spoke loudly and clearly: *You can't give up that easily.*

I almost laughed out loud. Annabelle had told me this voice could help me with an interview. Land me the job. My ego could make me walk through the door and could give me confidence to go through the interview process.

I turned again and headed right to the reception desk to give my name.

I had nothing to lose and everything to gain.

The girl who interviewed me was young, almost close to my age. I sat across from her. After a little ice-breaking chit-chat, she asked me about my strengths and weaknesses and some other questions that I was able to answer because my father had grilled me. He said they were standard.

After 15 minutes, she stared at me.

"Why do you want to go to St. Paul's?" she asked.

I sat there mute, unable to speak for a few seconds. What was I supposed to say? That I'd heard voices? Yeah, right. The woman would think I was a lunatic.

Finally, I opened my mouth and blurted out, "Because . . . because I'm being guided by something bigger, and I cannot explain it. I guess that's why I'm here."

The woman stared at me for a few seconds and looked down at her notes, then looking up again, smiled and said, "Thank you for your time. We will be in touch."

I walked out of the interview room in a daze.

You sure messed that up.

I heard Annabelle in my head: *Sometimes you have to tell her to be quiet.*

"Don't talk to me like that," I said as I walked out of the school. "Thank you for getting me here to this interview, because I couldn't have done it without you—but I'm not going to listen to you bash me." I held my head high.

Once I was outside, I looked at the blue sky, and as I walked to my car, I said, "And you, Isaiah, and divine team, and *Annabelle*, stop playing games with me, or I'm done with you, too."

❖ ❖ ❖

One week later, a letter arrived in the mail from St. Paul University.

I ran up to my bedroom with the letter and shut my door. My hands shook as I opened it. Two times I tried to look at it, and both times I couldn't. My heart raced like crazy. My throat closed up, and I was sure I was going to pass out from lack of breath.

Finally, on the third try, I read the first line and screamed.

We are pleased to inform you that you have been accepted . . .

I was going to school to study theology (something I still didn't know much about), and I was starting in the fall.

Something bigger than me was pushing me, it was true, and I was moving forward.

Acknowledgments

From Tara

First, I would like to give my deepest gratitude to the readers and all your wonderful comments and support for the series. It is all of you who I am passionate about, and I will continue to share my insight about intuition with you so you can see how amazingly intuitive you already are!

A huge thank you to Hay House Publishing and the Hay House team! You have all worked very hard to launch this book into the world, and your dedication means the world to me. I appreciate each and every one of you. Much love to all of the lovely ladies in the NY office; thank you for making me feel so at home when I visit.

Patty Gift, I just love and adore you to bits, thank you for your love and support. I am deeply grateful to Sally Mason, your talent as our editor helped to really make this series shine, and Laura Gray, you are just amazing!

To my friend and writer Lorna, I am forever grateful for you and all the long hours you have dedicated to our series when you had your plate full with your other projects and books. Words could never express the gratitude I feel for you and your hard work. Thank you for everything, and I love you. We make a great team!

Much love to my family and friends who have supported me throughout this whole journey. My love to Jeff, Buddy, and Roxy always, you all keep me grounded when I need it and pull me away from my computer for much-needed breaks.

My gratitude to Megan Adams for her social media expertise, and many thanks to Judy and the Hasmark team.

Finally, to Cindy (a.k.a. Annabelle), I love you and thank you for giving me the strength to do what I do; this book is dedicated in your memory.

From Lorna

It always takes a team to bring a book to fruition. I would like to thank the many teams at Hay House for creating such a beautiful book: marketing, promotion, creative design, and editorial. In among that group, I would especially like to thank my editor, Sally Mason. Her attention to detail in every edit was amazing and so appreciated. Her work definitely made a better book. I would also like to give a huge thanks to Tara Taylor for allowing me to pick her brain and for sharing segments of her life that I could weave into the novel. Tara's generous spirit also gave me time and space to create, and for a writer that is so necessary and treasured. And, of course, I have to thank my family. They also understand when I'm writing and give me allowance to be absorbed and obsessed. Of course, my pets (my dogs, Molly and Snowball) are another story. They don't care if I'm in the middle of a scene when it's time to be walked!

Questions and Answers

Becoming Indigo, while a work of fiction, is loosely based on the life of intuitive Tara Taylor. To further clarify some of the situations in the book, the writer of the novel has asked Tara to answer questions about the character of Indie.

Lorna. How does Indigo see things?

Tara. There are three ways that Indie can see things:

1) She can physically see with her eyes, and in this book it would be like Green Lady. She can see her in a body, even though she is a lost spirit, and that is because she is in the in between and hasn't gone to the light yet. She also saw Isaiah on the bus.

2) Indie can also see snapshots that come to her, and they are just pictures, like a still camera shot, or sometimes they flash and then they disappear. So it is like a photograph. In the novel, she heard *liver and onions* but she also saw a photo of Juanita with her grandson.

3) The third way that Indie can see is similar to a movie reel. What happens here is that she watches the scene play out, like she is watching a movie. When she was reading for the

girls at Queen's University, she saw the eggs and the hollow egg with nothing in it. And it was moving and bouncing, but there was nothing inside of it. But she did see it moving, and it wasn't just a snapshot.

L. What exactly is a past life?

T. A past life is the life you may have had before you were in this body. So in other words, most of us have had other lifetimes. You could have been male, female, or of a different nationality. Have you ever had that instant connection with someone? Where when you meet with them for the first time, you feel as if you have known them before? You could have been with them in another life. Some of us have had many past lives, some have had a few, and others may be here for the first time. Some people may think of this as reincarnation.

L. What is cord cutting?

T. Cord cutting is when you cut energetic cords between you and another person or spirit. With every person you meet, you exchange energy. Sometimes this energy is balanced, and sometimes it isn't. Indie's energy with John was not balanced. She often felt drained of energy when she was with him. There are energy givers and energy takers. One is not right or wrong. So in essence, cord cutting means that you cut yourself off from someone's energy so your energy isn't being drained from the situation. This doesn't mean you can't be in the person's presence, because you can. You are just learning not to take on their energy. There are different theories of how to cut cords. Indie prefers an old Japanese method, which is where she mimics cutting cords with her hands at the same time as she takes deep breaths.

L. Why did Annabelle teach Indie to use oracle cards instead of tarot cards?

T. Annabelle taught Indie to use oracle cards because it made her use more of her own natural abilities, such as seeing and hearing. The tarot cards, which are also great, are more black and white, and tend to have predetermined answers. Annabelle didn't want Indie to rely on the cards.

L. What are lower-level beings?

T. The example in *Becoming Indigo* of a lower-level being is Green Lady. She hasn't gone to the light yet and is in limbo because she had a traumatic experience. Other lower-level beings could also be in limbo because they are hanging on to something physical from their lives as humans. Eventually they will all go to the light, but some need assistance like Green Lady did in the novel.

L. What exactly is manifestation?

T. In the novel, Indie manifested her trip to Scotland by writing it down over and over. The repetition helped her to stay focused on what she wanted and to create this dream. It could have also brought the fruition of her dream to her more quickly. So instead of going to Scotland when she was 25, she went when she was 18. Your thoughts can become reality. And you can create your own destiny, so keep your thoughts aligned with what you want and with your goals and dreams. To practice this, get a notebook, and every day write out three to seven times: "I am so happy and grateful that I am now . . ." You fill in the blank, and even if you haven't reached the goal, you must write it as if you had. This way you can attract your goal and make it come true.

L. Can you really cleanse a house of lower-level beings like Indie, Sarah, and Natalie did with Green Lady?

T. Absolutely! The lower-level spirits don't realize that they have passed over, and they still think they are human, so they try to get attention. Annabelle taught Indie some tools to try and get rid of Green Lady to encourage her to cross over. The tools they used, sage and crystals, helped to tell Green Lady that they knew she was there. This was good because she got some of the attention she needed. Sage is an ancient native tradition, and crystals absorb the energy of the being. Please do not attempt this on your own. Get help first, like Indie did, before ever trying any of this.

L. What is the purpose behind crystals?

T. Crystals are energy, and they have been used for centuries for healing rituals in all sorts of faiths and traditions. Before electricity, we used stones for heat and power. They act as absorbers for us, and as much as they are pretty and look nice, they also have energetic healing qualities.

Here are three examples of crystal energy:

1) A clear quartz crystal is good for sleeping and grounding.

2) Rose quartz is great for cleaning any emotional issues and is a great love protector.

3) Amethyst is good for intuition and spiritual connection. It helps you listen to your own spirits, your guides.

There are many, many more crystals, and if you want information on them, there are some really wonderful books you can read.

L. What is the difference between the light and the dark?

T. The book was set up in three parts so we could raise this topic. There are angels and good spirits on the other side who want to help you. You have a divine team that wants to look out for your best interest. But there are also spirits that are lower energies that you can connect with through things like the Ouija board. These are self-serving and want only to help themselves. They will do anything to make their pain go away, and they could work through you for their own personal fulfillment. Indie opened herself up in the novel by not protecting herself, and some lower-level spirits latched on to her energy, which is why she was experiencing mixed emotions.

L. What is the mean voice/ego voice that Indie has in the book?

T. I don't want you to think that this voice is all bad. It does serve its purpose and can bolster a drive in you that will help you succeed in life. But you have to be careful, because if you let it control your thoughts completely, it can overpower your intuitive voice. You have two voices. Your ego voice often thinks in problems and not in solutions. It can have words like *how* (how are you going to do that?), and also *should, would, could*. For example: You get invited to a party, and you know it's in your best interest to stay home, but your ego voice may say, "You should go!" If you really listen, your intuitive voice will speak first and the ego voice will speak second. The intuitive voice works on your deepest truth and the ego on assumption. In the novel, Indie allowed her ego voice to control her. She knew it wasn't in her best interest to go with John, but she felt she "should" go to be a good friend. The situation did not work for the best.

About the Authors

Tara Taylor is an internationally known intuitive counselor, spiritual teacher, and motivational speaker. She has been featured in newspapers and on radio and television and has helped many people through her workshops, seminars, and public speaking. Tara counsels people of all ages and guides professional intuitives and children with clairvoyant gifts, as well as friends and family who need help understanding these special children. She is president and CEO of WhiteLight Wellness, as well as Sacred Space, a wellness center located in western Canada, and co-founder of the Just Say Yes seminars. Tara attended St. Paul University, studying world religions, theology, and pastoral counseling. She is also an Integrated Energy Therapy® Master/Instructor, and a Usui/Tibetan Reiki master. Tara is one of the contributing authors to the Amazon bestseller *Manifest Success: The Ultimate Guide to Creating the Life of Your Dreams.*

Visit www.tarataylor.ca and www.throughindigoseyes.com.

Lorna Schultz Nicholson has been a television co-host and reporter, radio host and reporter, community theater actor, fitness coordinator, and rowing coach. Now she is a full-time writer who has published both fiction and nonfiction. Her list includes children's picture books, middle-grade readers, young-adult fiction, and nonfiction sports books for all ages. She has written more than 20 award-winning books, including *Roughing* (Lorimer, 2004) and *Northern Star* (Lorimer, 2006). Her books have been nominated for the Red Cedar Award, the Golden Eagle Award, and the Diamond Willow Award. Her nonfiction 2010 Olympic book, *Home Ice* (Fenn, 2009), was on the *Globe and Mail* bestseller list for many months and was a top-selling sports book during the 2010 Olympics in Vancouver. Lorna divides her time between Calgary and Penticton, where she and her husband share their homes with their crazy golden retriever, Snowball, and whiny bichon–shih tzu, Molly.

Visit www.lornaschultznicholson.com and www.through indigoseyes.com.

We hope you enjoyed this Hay House Visions book. If you'd like to receive our online catalog featuring additional information on Hay House books and products, or if you'd like to find out more about the Hay Foundation, please contact:

VISIONS

Hay House, Inc., P.O. Box 5100, Carlsbad, CA 92018-5100
(760) 431-7695 or (800) 654-5126
(760) 431-6948 (fax) or (800) 650-5115 (fax)
www.hayhouse.com® • **www.hayfoundation.org**

✤ ✤ ✤

Published and distributed in Australia by:
Hay House Australia Pty. Ltd., 18/36 Ralph St., Alexandria NSW 2015 •
Phone: 612-9669-4299 • *Fax:* 612-9669-4144 • www.hayhouse.com.au

Published and distributed in the United Kingdom by:
Hay House UK, Ltd., Astley House, 33 Notting Hill Gate, London, W11 3JQ
• *Phone:* 44-20-3675-2450 • *Fax:* 44-20-3675-2451 • www.hayhouse.co.uk

Published and distributed in the Republic of South Africa by:
Hay House SA (Pty), Ltd., P.O. Box 990, Witkoppen 2068 •
Phone/Fax: 27-11-467-8904 • www.hayhouse.co.za

Published in India by: Hay House Publishers India,
Muskaan Complex, Plot No. 3, B-2, Vasant Kunj, New Delhi 110 070 •
Phone: 91-11-4176-1620 • *Fax:* 91-11-4176-1630 • www.hayhouse.co.in

Distributed in Canada by:
Raincoast, 9050 Shaughnessy St., Vancouver, B.C. V6P 6E5 •
Phone: (604) 323-7100 • *Fax:* (604) 323-2600 • www.raincoast.com

✤ ✤ ✤

Take Your Soul on a Vacation

Visit **www.HealYourLife.com®** to regroup, recharge,
and reconnect with your own magnificence.
Featuring blogs, mind-body-spirit news, and life-changing
wisdom from Louise Hay and friends.

Visit **www.HealYourLife.com** today!

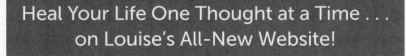
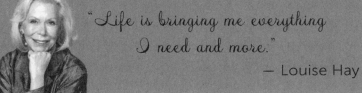